Black Ink Publications Presents
Reverend Cash
Let Us Prey
A Novel by
Sa'id Salaam

Reverend Cash
Let Us Prey

Acknowledgements

Bismillah

As always, First and Foremost All praise and worship is for Almighty God, alone, with no partners. I bear witness that there is nothing worthy of worship except Him.

3

Dedications

I dedicate this book to my blood brothers as recompense for their support.

Oh, and I can't forget one of my favorite readers and supporter, Byron Mathis. He bugged me for three years to write this book so here we go... Enjoy!

Chapter 1

"Go on, William. Let 'em see it!" Mary urged when her younger brother entered her room. She made the request sound like it was for the benefit of her small group of large friends, but she didn't mind getting a peek herself.

"Yeah, let us see!" Bernice dared. The three hundred pound girl cocked her head and twisted her lips dubiously. She just knew that her friend was exaggerating. There was no way that her scrawny little fourteen-year-old brother was packing meat like she claimed.

"Yeah!" Shawna and Shonda co-signed. The two rounded out the well-rounded group of friends.

The whole crew weighed at least three hundred pounds each and because of it they were dubbed The Buffalo Gals in their South Memphis hood. The nineteen and twenty-year-olds were all pretty and kept jobs, that kept their wigs flipped and bellies filled. Memphis was known for its BBQ joints, and the girls were well known in all of them.

"Y'all gotta pay me a dollar each," young Billy demanded. The young boy was already quite the hustler. He knew that anytime anyone asked for anything it had value to it. Knowing this, he did a variety of small jobs/task and made runs to earn a buck or two. That's how he, William Cash, became known as Dollar Bill.

"Here!" the three girls shouted and produced a dollar each. Mary crossed her big arms over her big chest, which translated to she wasn't paying.

Billy snatched up the money with one hand and opened his pants with the other. The dirty jeans he wore fell to his ankles causing his dick to swing free. It was a flaccid eight inches of ashy dick that had them all drooling.

At his age, Billy was too dusty to be considered cute. However, he did have smooth dark skin and a crop of thick curls atop his head. Although he only weighed one hundred fifty pounds he already stood six feet of his eventual six feet three inch height.

"Dayum!" the girls exclaimed in unison. They'd all managed to see a dick or two before but nothing like this.

"Un uh!" Billy protested when Shawna reached out to touch it. The girl was almost hypnotized by the swinging pendulum of penis.

"Hunh," she said, thrusting another dollar at him. That shut up his protest and allowed her a feel. She wrapped her chubby fingers around the shaft and gave it a good squeeze.

"Shawna! What you finna do?" Mary demanded when the other girl opened her mouth and leaned in.

"Nothing!" she lied as she stopped herself from putting it in her mouth.

Billy had never been given head, or had sex for that matter, but he would have let her put it in her mouth for another dollar.

"Let me touch it too!" Bernice demanded, pulling out another dollar of her own. Shonda retrieved another bill as well so that she too could get a feel.

All of the petting and tugging began to get a rise out of the boy. Billy felt his dick stiffen and took off running out the room.

"Hey! Come back! We wasn't finished yet!" the Buffalo Gals called out after him. They wasted their breaths being that he'd torn out of the raggedy screen door and hopped the rickety porch to where his friend awaited him.

"Sup Billy?" Byron asked as he ran to catch up.

"Nothing. I got us some money, so let's go play pool," Billy said when he finally slowed down. At their ages all the two did was drink pop and shoot pool. They were still at an age of innocence, but that was quickly coming to a close.

"I'm finna go!" Shawna announced back at Mary's house. She planned on taking the mental picture of Billy's dick home with her and masturbate. Hers wouldn't be the only fat fingers inside of a lonely vagina either because her friends all had the same idea.

"Me too!" Shonda agreed and stood. It sounded like a stampede as the three big girls rushed from the room and out of the house. As soon as they were gone Mary wasted no time before she dug into her own hot box.

Chapter 2

Billy and Mary's mother's name was Eleece, but around town she was known as Lady. It was one of those contradictory nicknames, like calling a big dude Tiny, because Lady was a tramp. She used what she had to get what she needed. Lady was a beautiful jet black Indian woman from Trinidad. She had jet black silky hair that naturally extended down to her round ass.

Her exotic looks suggested that she had some exotic pussy as well. The only thing men loved more than new pussy was exotic pussy, and they had no problem paying for it. They were rewarded with their money's worth when they slid up into Lady's slippery Patchouli smelling pussy as she whispered Patois in their ears.

This all happened back in the glory days, before HIV, so no one even thought about wearing condoms. Back then the worse that could come from a bad shot of ass was having to get a shot in the ass. Lady's well used hot water bottle was used not only to keep her box clean, but it was used as birth control as well. At the end of each day she would use it to hose out the different semen samples left behind.

That meant that quite a few men ended up eating cum left behind from quite a few other men. The funny thing about it all was that she would tell them that they were drinking semen, but none of them understood Patois well enough to take heed.

Although, the daily douche worked well to prevent her vagina from becoming a petri dish it sucked as birth control. The first time Lady ended up pregnant, the question of her child's paternity was answered at her birth. The baby was born with the yellow hue of a mulatto which meant that white Mr. Jenkins was the father. Mr. Jenkins owned the corner store that played background to the corner whores.

The white man loved black pussy, but refused to pay for it. He and Lady had a bartering system going. Once a week he'd trade her a sack of groceries for a romp in the sack. It was bumped up to two sacks when one day she came in with a baby girl with the same hump on her nose as he had.

Her second pregnancy began with a guessing game, since more men had taken a turn at her box than they had at solving a Rubik cube, and was just as impossible to solve as the colorful cube.

When the child was pulled free from her womb she leaned forward to check it out.

"It's a boy!" the doctor exclaimed.

"A boy? That's a damn man!" one of the attending nurses proclaimed frowning at the appendage that hung between his little legs.

"Either that or he got three legs!" the second nurse proclaimed.

"Leroy," Lady said shaking her head. Billy's big dick had solved the mystery of who his daddy was. All hopes of the man being someone worthwhile were tossed into the pail right along with the placenta.

Leroy Johnson was one of the local pimps and part-time pushers who procured pussy and pills on South Memphis' notorious streets. He was a tall handsome fellow with a mean talk game. One night he'd sweet talked Lady out of the bar and into her bed. At the exact same moment that he had busted a nut in her vagina he'd also tried spittin' some pimpin' in her ear. Lady took offense at it and spit saliva into his face. She was hoe, not a whore and didn't take kindly to the proposition.

Leroy didn't take kindly to being spit on and therefore he kindly whipped her ass to prove it. He beat her with both his hands and his feet. Next came the slaps with his notoriously large dick. It was ten inches soft, but the beating had aroused him and expanded it another two inches. After the beating he raped her in every hole. Lady saw his dick in her dreams for weeks after the incident. Now she saw it's junior between her son's baby thighs.

"I mean William," she said quickly changing both her mind and her baby's daddy identity at the same time. –Leroy would one day get to know his son, but he wouldn't know it. No worries though, since he had plenty other children running around town.-

William, the salesman, wasn't much of an upgrade considering that he barely took care of his real kids. However, he did donate leftover meat from his route a couple times a week until his death a couple years later.

****

Lady was a tramp, but she still loved going to church. She loved the singing and the clapping. She loved the dresses and the hats the ladies wore, and like most of the women in the congregation she loved Pastor Paul.

Pastor Paul was a pretty boy with thick lips who wore his hair slicked to the side. Not only was Pastor handsome but the man could also preach. He spit the gospel with the flair and cadence of a rapper. He would prance and preach until he was drenched in sweat.

His assistant pastor would oscillate behind while co-signing his words like a hype-man. He was to Pastor what Flava-Flav was to Chuck D. The choir would rise and fall like back-up singers. The local juke joint ain't have shit on Calvary Baptist Holiness Church of the Rock.

Pastor Paul could have had his pick of any of the women in his flock, but his wife made sure that he didn't. The First Lady stuck by her husband's side like a secret service agent entrusted with the detail of guarding the president. Dead presidents actually because she would be damned if anyone else got her cut of the collection plate.

First Lady Dawn Paul liked big hats, big cars, and fancy dresses that kept her big titties on display. First Lady made sure to keep the women away from her man by personally teaching the women's classes while leaving the men to her husband.

****

"Y'all hurr' up and get ready!" The sound travelled with ease through the tiny shot gun house as Lady called out from behind her closed bedroom door.

"Man!" Billy huffed at the notion of going to church. The place was just as hot as the place that Pastor Paul warned about. The only upside to going to church was the buffet they ate after the four hour service let out.

"Okay!" Mary yelled back through the wall. Unlike her brother, she didn't mind going to church at all. A lot of church men liked big girls so she went faithfully every week, as did the other Buffalo Gals.

"You hurr' up back there too," Lady said to the man inside of her. He was taking long leisurely strokes, like a child playing in a puddle.

"Yes Ma'am," Tommy said and increased the speed of his strokes. Lady helped out by laying her head on the bed and putting an arch in her back. He in turn hunched his back over hers and threw it into overdrive.

"And don't you cu-...shit!" Lady fussed as Tommy went stiff and came inside of her. "Damn you! Now I'm going to be leaking all on the pews."

"My bad," he said taking a few more thrust. He pulled out and jumped to his feet so he could go home and get ready for church himself. On his way out of the room he paused and put some money on the dresser before continuing on to the front door.

An hour later, the family finally left the house headed to church. The walk over to the church is quite pleasant when made in the fall and spring, but it was downright brutal in both the summer and winter.

It was a normal summer day and the sun was beating down above their heads. Billy's thick crop of curly hair acted like a wool cap atop his head causing sweat to stream down his face and soak his shirt. Both Lady and Mary were protected from the sun's harsh rays by their hats, but not its heat. Both their panties and bras were soaked full of sweat by the time they reached Calvary Baptist Holiness Church of the Rock.

Tommy was pulling into the parking lot as they arrived. He only offer a slight nod as a greeting being that his wife and children were in the car with him.

Mary and Billy shot each other a glance and twisted their lips like 'this nigga here!' Their house was so small that a fart could be heard from room to room, so they'd definitely heard their mama's pussy farting and slurping while Tommy hit it from the back. Now here he was offering a simple head nod.

"Y'all don' made me late," Lady fussed as they walked into the packed church already in full swing.

The kids shot another glance towards one another and smirked. Those last minute back shots were what made them late. Their mama knew it too, but wouldn't admit that she'd needed to squeeze a few more coins out of the man to put into the collection plate and to pay for their buffet plates.

They hadn't missed much because Pastor Paul was still at the front pew putting on. His hype-man trailed behind him wiping the sweat from his forehead and eyes as he preached.

"Can I get an Amen?" he asked and got several. He then asked for a hallelujah and got several of those too. That's when he sent the collection plate around for the second time. "Yes Lawd!"

"Yes Lawd!" Billy repeated with a snicker and got pinched.

"I done tol' you 'bout playing in here," his mother scowled through clenched teeth.

Billy pouted about the pinch as he set and painfully endured three hours of song and dance followed by testimonials and talking in tongues. He had to literally bite his tongue to keep from laughing out loud.

"Thank you, Lawd," he mumbled when the collection plate made its final round accompanied by the final song.

Pastor Paul shook hands with all the husbands while his wife watched the wives. She made sure not one of them got too close to her man. Once the last person left the two went into the office to count up the money.

"Lawd, whatever You want You keep," the pastor announced before tossing the cash in the air. Their Lawd obviously didn't want any of it because it all fluttered down to the floor.

"Thank you, Lawd!" Mrs. Paul shouted and dug in.

Chapter 3

"Hey Billy, come her'," Shawna called when she saw him walking by her house. It had been a few days since she saw his dick and she was ready to see it again.

"If you want Mary I'll go get her....for a dollar," he said as he approached.

"I ain't looking for yo' sister, but I got a dollar for you," she said in a guttural growl. She stared intently at the lump in his pants, the look saying what she didn't.

"One dollar," he said and reached for his zipper. He would have whipped his guy out right there on her porch had she not stopped him.

"Not out here!" she shouted and looked around for any nosey neighbors. "Come on in."

Billy shrugged and followed her inside. He stifled a giggle when he peeked under her skirt as she led the way up the stairs. He found the dimples on her large yellow ass amusing.

"Come on in," she said closing the door behind them once they entered her room.

"One dollar," Billy repeated and held out his palm. The other hand again went to his zipper to produce the goods.

"All I got is a five," Shawna said, her voice quivering with lust. This was the closest she'd gotten to getting laid in years, and she could hardly contain herself.

"You need change?" Billy naively asked. She shook her head no slowly as she handed him the bill.

"You can keep it all. I j-j-j-just need a little m-m-more," she said stuttering at the sight of his dick. She then reached out and fondled it until it was erect in her hand.

Billy's eyes opened as wide as Shawna's mouth did when she leaned in to take him into her mouth. Mary wasn't there to stop her from getting that meat in her mouth this time. Both she and Billy moaned as she took him inside her face. As she sucked him in she reached between her thick thighs to play in her drenched pussy.

Shawna hadn't had much sex, but she'd sucked plenty of dicks. She'd had classmates, cousins, and her mama's boyfriends sticking their dicks in her face since she was sixteen. In no time Billy had grown an additional two more inches in both length and girth in the girl's mouth. Shawna took it out of her mouth to marvel at its size.

"Touch it!" she demanded, opening her legs even wider. Billy was so open from his first sexual experience that he eagerly complied.

"Dang!" Billy cheered when he saw how wet she was. Shawna came instantly from the feel of a touch other than her own. They were both now past the point of no return.

"Fuck me!" Shawna shouted as she pulled him on top of her by his extremely hard dick. She spread her legs even wider and guided him inside of her.

Billy felt his life change as he entered her hot, wet, tight, almost virginal vagina. Once inside he instantly started humping for dear life, like he thought he was supposed to.

"Ouch! Wait! Hol' up!" Shawna protested as she put her hands on his chest to stop the pounding. "You cain't be jumping up an' down in a bitch's guts like that! You gotta take it nice and easy, slow and gentle."

"Like...this?" Billy asked, now taking long slow strokes. Shawna was too busy with an orgasm to verbally reply, but that was an answer in itself. The feeling got even better as she got wetter and tighter from her convulsions. "I-I-I f-f-feel...s-s-something."

"Take it out! Take it out!" Shawna shouted and shoved him up and out of her. It was just in the nick of time too because Billy began skeeting all over her stomach rolls. She graciously grabbed his shaft and worked her hand up and down to milk him dry. "You cain't be cumming in no bitches!"

"Okay," he replied still in awe over what had just happened. He'd been so preoccupied with being a kid that he hadn't been concerned with sex. Now, it would become a big part of his life. He almost asked if they could do it again, as if it was a ride at an amusement park. Luckily for him she beat him to it. Again anytime anyone asked for anything that thing has value.

"I got another five dollar bill," Shawna offered. He was still hard so she sat up and cleaned all the semen off with her mouth and tongue. When she felt it throbbing in her mouth she laid back on her fat back and once again spread her fat legs wide.

"Like this?" Billy asked more confidently as he practiced his stroke. He even had the nerve to get a little fancy with it by rolling his hips.

"Mmm hmmm, just like that," Shawna purred as she came again and again.

Billy left Shawna's house several hours after he entered it.

His balls were lighter, but his pockets were twenty dollars heavier. Five of those dollars were a tip for a haircut. Shawna planned on grooming the kid as her personal gigolo. It was all good because again anytime anyone wants anything it has value.

Chapter 4

"Dollar Bill!" Byron cheered when his right hand man entered the pool hall. His quick smile morphed into a curious frown seeing a new look on his old friend. The fresh haircut and clean shirt totally confused him. "Is it finna be Easter?"

"No, I don't think so," Billy replied, now just as confused. It was proof that both boys needed to spend more time in school instead of the pool hall. "Anyway, call me Five Dollar Bill now!"

"Where you get all that money from, mane?" Byron shouted, as if the wad he'd produced from his pocket was ten grand instead of ten dollars.

"You asking too many questions, mane!" Billy shot back smugly.

"Let's go get us a couple sticks of reefer and a bottle of wine," Byron urged once again. He'd been trying to get his partner to step up and hang out like the older boys did for a while now. "We might can pull us a couple of gals..."

"I'on know mane," Billy said contemplating. His hesitation had nothing to do with the lessons and warnings about drugs that his mom preached. He just didn't like spending his money. He wanted to keep his money in his pocket where it belonged. The debate to get high or not to get high was solved with the next swing of the pool hall's creaky door.

Pimpin' Leroy entered the establishment the only way he could; like a pimp. His large afro looked like it was sculpted from black marble. It had a shine from the Afro Sheen he'd used that morning and an afro pick with a fist sticking out of it. His tight pimp pants were pulled up into his crotch showing off a large ball of pimp dick. The platform shoes on his feet added an additional four inches to the already tall man. If it wasn't for the colorful whores flanking him he may have been mistaken for a basketball player.

"That's Pimpin' Leroy!" Byron shouted in a whisper, of star struck awe, as if the pimp was one of The Beatles.

"I know!" Billy shot back defensively since only a lame wouldn't have known who the man was. His mama kept him in the church so much that he fought that much harder to be a part of the streets.

The pimp had a thick stick of smoldering reefer stuck between his thick lips. It stayed put even when he spoke, how cool was that? He scanned the premises as pimps do and did a double take when he saw Billy staring his way.

"He coming over here!" Byron said excitedly, once again proving his ability to state the obvious. Billy locked eyes on the thighs of the young whore to his left. He remembered her being a few grades ahead of him when they went to school. Mandy was only sixteen, she'd skipped high school for the pros.

"What's yo' mama's name?" Leroy asked seeing how much the boy favored him.

"L-L-Lady," he stuttered. He too realized that the man looked familiar but couldn't place the face.

"Never heard of her," the pimp lied. He retrieved a stick of reefer from a pocket of his pimp pants and passed it to Billy. Now if he really was one of his many children at least he couldn't say he'd never given him anything.

"All y'all youngins get y'all young asses up out of here," Sammy, the pool hall bouncer, announced. The teens were allowed to shoot pool and buy pops until the pimps and hustlers arrived.

"Come on, let's go down by the river," Billy directed as if they hadn't been given the boot. Byron was a year older but accepted the taller teen as his leader.

"Y'all little niggas come check me out tomorrow. I got some work for y'all," Leroy advised as they left. Billy nodded his head in response despite his apprehension.

****

"We finna be skraight if'n Leroy put us on," Byron cheered. The poor kid lived in a rundown shack with no water or electricity, so he was eager to make some money.

"I ain't messin' with no pimp! My mama would lose her mind if'n she found out," Billy surmised correctly. Lady threw fits and dragged him to see Pastor Paul for counseling at his every infraction. Doing so was a win/win situation for the woman, who wanted a chance to talk to the sexy preacher without his wife being present, it gave her time with him and plus the clergy man always seemed to have an impact on her fatherless son.

"You don't want to cuzn' you already getting bread. Where you get that money from anyway?" Byron asked again.

"Look..." Billy paused and let out a deep sigh. He knew the only way to keep a secret was to keep it a secret, but Byron was his best friend. "I'll tell you, but you cain't tell nobody! Promise!"

"Promise, on my mama!" the boy shot back quickly. Billy was too young and far too naïve to know how many rumors and how much gossip was proceeded by that very same vow.

"You know Shawna? Shawna, that be with my sister."

"You talkin' about that big red gal? One of The Buffalo Gals... sorry," Byron said after repeating the offensive nickname of his sister's crew. "What, you stole her purse?"

"Nope! I had sex with her and she gave me ten dollars!" Billy said proudly.

"You fucked that fat bitch?" Byron shouted and cracked up. He laughed so hard that Billy actually started to feel ashamed. The feeling only lasted a few seconds before he remembered how good, wet, and tight she was. Not to mention it had earned him ten bucks to his friend's none.

"Shole did, and I'ma fuck her again first chance I get!"

"Shit, I'll fuck her!" Byron said, having a change of heart. Billy had seen his friend naked before so he knew that he didn't have what it took, but he held his tongue and lit the reefer.

The friends sat on the dock of the mighty Mississippi River and got mighty high. It was yet another new sensation that the young boy couldn't handle. By the time they left young Billy now had two vices in his life at a young age. Pussy and weed.

Chapter 5

"Get in here!" Shawna demanded and snatched Billy inside her house. She'd just gotten paid and was ready to get laid. But first she had a bone to pick with the boy. "I thought I told you don't tell nobody 'bout what we did!"

"I didn't," Billy frowned feeling slightly indignant. The only person he had said anything to was partner Byron. Surely he'd kept his secret.

"So why lil nappy headed Byron came over her' the other day tryna fuck? Talkin' 'bout you tol' him I pay fo' dick! Huh? Huh?" she demanded. She'd left out the part about asking to see his dick before she said no.

"Huh? I mean we...I..." he stammered trying to come up with an excuse. He hoped he hadn't blown his hustle by running his mouth. It would be an expensive lesson not to learn; especially considering he was looking forward to the sex. He was hard as a rock the whole walk over there.

"Come on in her' ol' big mouth boy," she said pulling him into her bedroom. "You like poppin' yo' lips so much so you need to come make 'em pop on this coochie!"

Shawna lay back and spread her big thighs. Billy watched in amazement as her plump vagina swelled and glistened from excitement. His mind flashed back to the time he'd peeked through the crack along his mother's door once while she was getting ate out. One of her men friends had her face down ass up eating her black box from the back. Lady was hooping and hollering about how good it was, so Billy didn't mind doing it at all. Except...

"That's gone be extra," he announced his head down between her legs. She felt his breath on her box and almost came.

"Okay, five bucks more!" she said deciding to skip the dinner her and the rest of The Buffalo Gals usually ate on Friday nights.

Billy agreed to the tip by diving face first between her legs. Luckily for him, she was clean and fresh so her vagina tasted wonderful. The fruity concoction she applied after her bath filled his nostrils as he licked and lapped at her lips.

"Grrrr!" Shawna growled as a vicious orgasm shook the whole room. He had her speaking in tongues when he twirled his tongue around her pearl tongue. "Fuck me!"

Actions speak louder than words so Billy shoved himself inside of her frothy quivering box. The big girl pulled her big legs as wide as she could so he could get it all. He did too, with long firm strokes just like she'd taught him. She began growling and shaking once again as she came once more. Billy had to snatch himself out halfway through her convulsions to bust a nut of his own.

"Shit!" he grunted as he skeeted on her large stomach. She'd left his dick coated with her slippery fluid that he used to stroke himself dry. "I gotta go."

"I got five mo' dollars!" Shawna cried. She flipped over and grabbed some more money from her purse. As soon as she passed the money over to him he pushed back inside of her. A half hour later he emerged from the girl's house fifteen dollars richer. It was time to go find Byron and smoke a couple of sticks.

****

"Who?" Shawna called from her bed when she heard the tapping on the front door. She was still propped up doggy style just like Billy had left her. A tingle spread through her body at the thought that it maybe Billy coming back for a third helping of pie. "Come in!"

"Gurl, what in the world!" Shonda shrieked at the sight of her friend ass up on the bed. She frowned as she sniffed and smelled the sweet scent of sex that wafted in the air. "Gurrrrl!"

"What?" Shawna giggled further telling on herself.

"Who was here?" her big buddy demanded to know as she looked around in case he was still present. Shawna was too naïve and inexperienced with men to know better than to tell. She would have to find out the hard way what happens when you brag about a man. Especially when it's a friendship as tentative as the one The Buffalo Gals shared.

The girl's friendship was one of default since they were the biggest girls in school. They didn't have boyfriends nor did they get invited to dances so they all got jobs and paid for the things that the thin girls fucked for. It was a conditional allegiance based on the condition that none of them could get a man.

"I'ma tell you, but you cain't tell no-o-o-obody!" Shawna said. "'Specially not Mary. Chile, she'd lose her mind!"

"Mary? What she got to...un uh! Gurrrl!" Shonda exclaimed as she put two and two together and it added up to Mary's big dick little brother. "Gurl, they gone put you up under the jail."

"So, at least I'll have a big smile on my face!" Shawna cracked.

"Was it good? Can he work it?" her friend asked, with ulterior motives drooling down her blouse.

"Not at first. Gurl, he was 'bout to puncture a lung with that thang! I had to teach him how to work it niiiiiice and slooooow," she sang feeling herself get wet once more just thinking about it.

"Mmph!" was all Shonda could say back. She certainly couldn't admit that she was planning to fuck him too. "Anyway, you ready to go get us some ribs?"

"Go on 'head. My money a little tight this week. Got some...um...Bills to pay," Shawna lied stifling a smile at her word play. The only Bill she planned on paying was Dollar Bill.

Chapter 6

Byron wasn't home so Billy headed on over to the pool hall to find him. He shouldn't be there since it was after dark but Billy couldn't phantom anywhere else he could or would be without him. He paused and looked at all the pimp's cars lining the block in front of the pool hall. He stood out front for several minutes before building up the nerve to go inside. He braced himself for Sammy's foul mouth as he pushed the door open.

"Sup lil' nigga!" Sammy barked when Billy stepped inside. That much he expected but the man's next words stunned him. "Come on in. They over there."

"Who?" Billy asked staring over in the direction Sammy had pointed in. He got the answer for himself when he saw his friend with Leroy and one of his hookers.

"Come on over!" Byron shouted, waving and smiling, looking totally out of place.

Survival instinct told Billy to turn and leave but curiosity got the best of him. Didn't he know that curiosity got the cat killed, and that there was no way anything good could come of this? With a deep sigh he literally blew caution to the wind and walked over.

When he got closer Billy saw the hooker at Leroy's side was Mandy. His mind flashed to the crush he'd once had on the girl with the long brown pigtails. She'd been turned out on reefer and dick by an older boy before he'd been sent off to reform school. Once word got out that the pretty little young thing liked to get high and fuck it was just a matter of time before one of the city's pimps got to her. Leroy was the one who got to her first. He got her high, fucked her, and put a price on her. The young girl was eye candy, so he kept her by his side. The close proximity allowed him to charge a premium for her.

"This the one they call Dollar Bill?" Leroy asked with a fake enthusiasm designed to make the boy feel important.

"The one and only!" Byron said happily. He was the only person at the table who bought the pimp's charade.

"Mr. Leroy," Billy said with a nod of respect. He turned to say hello to Mandy but her eyes were shut as she swayed back and forth. The girl was off beat to the tune coming from the juke box, because she didn't hear it. The heroin coursing through her body had a melody all its own.

"He got a job fo' us!" Byron said way too loudly. A stern look from Leroy told him so too. He repeated himself but was much quieter the second time. "We work for him now."

"Doing what?" Billy asked his friend but looked at Leroy knowing that he'd answer.

"Odd jobs. Nothing heavy," he replied smoothly. So smoothly one would have actually believed that delivering heroin was legal. "Keep some reefer in you system and cash in yo' pockets."

"No thank you/thank you," Billy and Byron replied at the same time. Leroy heard them both but he only spoke to Billy.

"What, you think you pimpin' cuz you slangin' a lil dick to some fat broad? You a hoe not a pimp!" he spat. The outburst caused Mandy to open her eyes to investigate. A beautiful smile spread on her face followed by stinging laughter.

Billy wasn't sure if he should reach across the table and tackled his big mouth friend or run out the joint in tears. He couldn't decide so he sat there and took more abuse. A spark of hatred developed in his heart, but he was smart enough to know he was in no position to act now. Instead he would let it sit there and fester until he killed one of them.

"I'm tryna put you on, but if you wanna be a hoe I got plenty of old broads that'll pay for dick. Men too! You like ass boy?"

"No!" Billy pouted and swatted away a tear. Mandy's laughter burned a whole in his soul as it cackled in his ear. "We'll do it!"

"That's more like it," Leroy smiled and clapped his diamond laden hands. He'd won, but the love-struck look he aimed at Mandy needed to be addressed. He reached down and pulled his pimp stick from his pimp pants and said, "Huh, Bitch!"

Mandy accepted that he was talking to her being that she was the only bitch at the table and turned to reply. The exposed dick didn't need explaining, so she leaned over and swallowed the tip. Byron giggled as her head went up and down under the table.

"Now, y'all take this to Man-Man over on 4th Street. Don't open it or fuck with it!" Leroy warned as he placed a small envelope on the table. Byron reached for it but Leroy stopped him. "Nuh uh, him!"

Billy looked Leroy in the eye for the first time as he picked up the package. He held his gaze in an attempt to ignore the bobbing head on his lap. The slurping sounds however could not be ignored.

"Come on back and...hol' up," the pimp said frowning up. He made a big show of busting a nut in the girl's mouth. He grabbed the back of her head and tossed his own from side to side. "Damn, it mane!"

"See you in a few," Billy said having seen enough. He stood and turned from the table. Byron had to run to catch him at the door.

"Stop being rude mane! You gon' fuck this up for us!" Byron warned once they were out on the sidewalk.

"If anybody fuck anything up it's gon' be you and your big ass mouth!" Billy spat angrily. Part of that anger came from Byron and his big mouth, but part of it also came from Leroy.

"What you talkin' 'bout? I don't be saying nothin' 'bout nothin'!" Byron vowed. "On my mama!"

"So, you ain't tell Shawna she let me fuck?" he demanded.

"Huh?"

****

"Come on in," Man-Man called from behind his door. The boys looked at each other for a second to decide what to do. Finally Billy shrugged and turned the knob.

"Whoa!" he said into the barrel of a huge revolver. "Leroy sent us!"

"He did? Come on in then!" Man-Man said pulling them both inside. "Where's it at? Give it to me! Have a seat!"

Neither boy wanted to stay but when a man with a gun tells you to have a seat, you have a seat. Man-Man went into a trance as he pulled out his works to fix up a fix. Billy blinked his eyes when he recognized it as the same look that Shawna has on her face before they have sex. He shot a side eye glance at his partner and saw that he was mesmerized by the flame that danced under the spoon. They both could smell the bubbling heroin as it cooked.

"This that shit mane!" Man-Man cheered and pulled the drug into his syringe. He used his teeth and free hand to tie off his arm with a rubber hose.

Billy and Byron had opposite reactions when he ran the dope into his arm. Billy was utterly disgusted and vowed on the spot to never go out like that. Not Byron though, that shit excited him to no end. He could not wait to experience the feeling, which had spread the warm smile on the man's face, for himself. It was the same one that had Mandy swaying and nodding to the beat of a different drummer.

"Let's go, mane," Billy whispered once Man-Man leaned forward into a deep dope fiend nod. He didn't even hear then leave.

Chapter 7

"Yes Lawd!" Lady cheered when she entered the church. Her family was one of the first families inside which meant she was able to get a front row seat. She posted up on the front pew flanked by her children. "Oh, and Pastor Paul wanna have a word with you after the service."

"For what?" Billy shot back in a tone that would've pulled the trigger on Lady's back hand slap had they not been in church. His mother actually flinched from holding it back.

"Cuz yo' teacher tol' me you was being hardheaded!" Lady growled through clenched teeth. "She tol' you to go up to the board and you said no."

"Oh," Billy said twisting his lips ruefully. A few days earlier he'd zoned in on Ms. Water's ass as she wrote on the board. The twenty something year old teacher had a fat ass that had made him rock hard. No way was he going up in front of the class like that.

"Yes Lawdddd!" Pastor Paul's deacon/hype-man co-signed. Had this been the eighties and not the sixties he would be saying *'throw your hands in the air and wave 'em like you just don't care!'*

"Yes Lawd!" Lady too agreed and then swooned as the flamboyant preacher put on. Billy did well in his battle not to laugh. He would save it for later and mock the man to his sister instead. Mary got a kick out of his Pastor Paul impersonation.

Billy felt his neck heating up and turned around to investigate why. He flinched when he saw Shonda staring hungrily at him. She licked her lips lustfully and winked. The naïve boy turned back to the show in the pulpit.

The side of his neck heated up next and when he turned in that direction it was Shawna staring. He whipped his head away only to come face to face with a thirsty Bernice. Billy was in high demand thanks to Shawna running her mouth.

Billy had a few dollars in his pocket but pretended he didn't when the collection plate came through. It came back around two more times before the show came to an end.

"Thank God!" Billy grunted once it was over and stood to leave.

"Oh, no you don't! You gotta stay and talk to Pastor. We'll see you at the house," Lady instructed.

"We ain't goin' to eat?" he asked in horror at the thought.

"We is. You, you gotta stay and talk to Pastor," Lady replied sarcastically. Her tone did a three hundred and sixty degree change when the preacher approached. He was still glistening with sweat and his voice was raspy from his performance.

"Yes Lawd," Pastor Paul greeted. He locked in on Billy as he shook Lady's hand. "Is this the one been back talkin'?"

"Yassir," Lady replied in her mock southern accent. "He need some talkin' to!"

"And he 'bout to get it," Pastor assured her. She took in one last, long, lustful look at the preacher before turning to leave. She made sure to put a little extra in her walk just in case he was watching.

"Come on her' boy," the pastor said before walking off to give Billy a long pep talk. Billy missed most of it because he was busy worrying about the ham and yams he was missing out on at the buffet.

****

"I'll buy my own plate!" Billy lamented as he walked home from church. He hated spending his money but since he had an appointment inside of Shawna he'd make back whatever he spent. He'd already made up in his mind that he was going to eat some pussy to cover his meal. "I'm gon' get me a rib plate, some candy yams, collard gre-..."

"Pst," Billy heard from behind some bushes. He decided it had nothing to do with him and kept on pushing. Until he heard it again followed by his name being called. "Pst, Billy. Over here."

"Shonda?" he asked when his investigation showed the girl concealed behind some shrubs. She still had on the same fancy dress she'd worn to church and she had the same thirsty look in her eyes.

"Yeah, it's me. I need to see you 'fo you go over to Shawna's house," she said which explained why she was hiding in the bushes on her friend's street. Shawna had bragged about getting some wood after church and her friend had set an ambush.

"I gotta go...holla at her cuz..."

'I'll pay you double! Now, come on!' Shonda demanded and led the way. Billy lagged back to look at her ass and saw she had plenty of it.

"We gotta hurr' up cuz my mama will be here after a while," Shonda explained when she got him inside. She produced ten bucks from her purse and proceeded to strip.

Billy watched her undress as he did the same. Whereas Shawna was high yellow Shonda was almost jet black. She had a set of big black titties that were capped by lumpy dark nipples. Her round belly sat atop a dense crop of pubic hair that surrounded her plump vagina.

"Damn!" Shonda said, shaking her head at Billy's large erection. She laid back on her bed and spread both her legs and lips.

"Damn!" Billy repeated as he got a peek at her pink insides. He inched closer and continued to marvel at the glistening black box for a few more seconds before plunging inside. He took a few slow strokes, just the way Shawna had taught him, but Shonda wouldn't hear of it.

"Un uh Boy, you gon' fuck me!" she demanded as she grabbed his hips. The girl then proceeded to slam him in and out of her until he got the picture. Billy planted his feet and commenced to pounding.

"The upper room..." Shonda's mama sang as she entered her house. The forty something year old woman was just as black as her daughter but where her daughter was heavy she had the same tight shape she'd had twenty years ago. She'd only gotten two steps inside before she heard the unmistakable sounds of sex in the air.

"Get...this...pussy!" Shonda demanded as her mother marched down the hall. "I'm finna...cum!"

"You finna get yo' fat ass out my house!" Donna corrected as she bust into her daughter's room. Luckily for Shonda she'd just gotten off before her mother intruded.

"It's not what it looks like, Mama!" she swore and pushed the boy up and out of her.

"Gal, it look li...oh my!" her mama said pausing when she got a glance at Billy's dick. It looked splendid, all hard and wet. The older woman cocked her head to the side and moved in closer for a closer look. "You Miss Lady's boy, ain't you?"

"Yessum Ma'am," he said lowering his head in shame. His mother was going to lose her mind when she found out about this. Just thinking about it caused his erection to begin to deflate.

"Oh, no you don't!" Donna said and grabbed the young boy's dick. She used the slippery fluid left on it by her daughter to stroke it back erect. "Hold my purse, gal!"

"Mama!" Shonda shrieked. "What you doin'?"

"Shit, I'm finna get me some of this here dick! Um hm," the woman vowed.

Billy didn't know what to say. When she put her mouth on him he realized that there was nothing that needed to be said. Shonda pouted and stormed out while her mama sucked the boy off. She vigorously stroked his shaft while working her mouth. The combination did the trick and young Billy exploded on her tonsils.

"Now you won't be cumming all quick," she explained as she came out of her church clothes. She threw them right on top of her daughter's before pushing Billy back on the bed.

"I'm finna ride this thang!" she proclaimed and climbed on top of him. She hadn't had any dick in a decade so it took a minute for her to work him inside. Once she did she was ready to ride. "Ya, gitty up!"

Billy lay there in shock as the woman old enough to be his mama rode him hard and fast. A convulsion overcame the woman as she came, but she fought through it and kept on riding. Donna got her a couple more nuts before she finally slumped over to the side totally spent.

"Let me get some more too, Mama. I paid for it," Shonda protested from the doorway.

"Mama got money too," she said catching her breath for another ride. It was well after dark before Billy finally got out of there. He was thirty dollars richer when he set out to find his partner Byron.

"Where the hell you been?" Byron demanded to know when Billy found him in the pool hall. He sounded angry but was really just lonely. He heard the gruff tone himself and passed the stick he'd been smoking on as a peace offering. Billy looked at the weed for a second before deciding to take it.

"You wouldn't believe me if I tol' you," he swore and took a drag. He would've believed him, but he would've also probably ran over to Shonda's house and tried to fuck her and her mama too.

"Anyway, I'm glad you her'. Leroy got some work for us."

Chapter 8

"I'on know 'bout this?" Billy warned as they ran errands for Leroy. They'd already made three deliveries and still had three more to go. The five bucks per stop beat what he could get out of his Buffalo Gals, but was a lot less fun.

"Don't know 'bout what? We getting' rich! Plus Leroy gon' give us a couple of sticks, plus...he let me fuck Mandy!" Byron bragged.

"He did?" Billy asked wide eyed from surprise and just a tinge of jealousy. The crush he had on the girl was long gon' along with her morals, but it still left a stain on his mind.

"Sho' did! I was like...and..." he shot back demonstrating his stroke in mid-air. An old lady scrunched her face in disgust as she passed by the boy humping the air.

Byron left out the part about her being in a deep nod while he had sex with her. She had moved up from snorting and now mainlined heroin. It was a good thing that he'd enjoyed it so much because she'd missed it.

-In the future, human workers will actually be replaced by robots. Back in the day they used heroin to accomplish the same effect-. Most of Leroy's whores fucked and sucked their day away on full auto pilot. Their minds and bodies were both numb from the powerful opiate. The cold hearted pimp made sure to let them feel a hint of the sickness of withdrawal before he swooped in and saved the day.

Leroy started Byron and Billy off on reefer and wine to ease their way into addiction. Still, he knew the strong willed Dollar Bill wouldn't be so easy to turn out. Unlike Byron, Billy could earn money without him.

"Here we go," Billy said when they arrived at Man-Man's. Once again he greeted them with a pistol and forced them inside. Again they watched him shoot up and go into a deep nod. They took that as their cue to leave and left him with his chin on his chest.

"I'ma get me a line," Byron said confidently. It sounded like a proclamation but he was really seeking permission.

"And you gon' end up like that fool in there!" Billy shouted... We coulda went in that nigga's pockets and took err'thang he had!"

"Sho' coulda!" Byron shouted coming to a stop. He thought about running back and doing just that but knew that Billy wouldn't go for it. He decided to save it for a rainy day and started back to the pool hall instead.

****

"There go yo' lil' boyfriend," Leroy teased when he saw the youngsters walk in.

"Who?" Mandy asked frowning as if it would help her see better. The joke was wasted on her since she didn't remember having sex with Byron. She assumed he meant the handsome boy next to him and nodded her head. "Mm hm."

"All done!" Byron cheered proudly when they reached the booth. If he were a puppy his tail would've been wagging. He wasn't so the bright smile had to suffice.

"Good job lil niggas," Leroy nodded passing each of them a brand new twenty dollar bill. "Here's a lil' somethin' extra fo' being quick about it."

"Thank ya," they both recited, as they'd been taught at home.

"Oh yeah," he remembered and pulled out his cigarette case. He flicked the fancy sterling silver case open and displayed the neatly rolled sticks of reefer inside. He plucked out two and paused before plucking out one more.

"His birthday tomorrow!" Byron blurted in hopes that it would warrant another stick. Apparently it did because the pimp went back in for one more.

"Sho' nuff! How ol' you gon' be boy?" Leroy asked. He guessed he would say seventeen or eighteen judging by his size and the way that he carried himself. And he may have if Byron hadn't answered for him.

"He gon' be fifteen! He just big fo' his age! Most people think he older than me..." he rambled before getting cut off.

"Swing back by tomorrow and I'll let you take a spin in young Mandy here," the pimp pimped. Mandy ran her eyes up and down but kept her mouth closed.

"Ok," Billy agreed even though he had no intentions to do so. In fact he had plans with Lady and Mary just like he'd had for every birthday he could remember.

****

"Get it! Get it! Get it!" Lady demanded as she threw it back. She squeezed her vagina as tightly as it would go hoping to squeeze a few more dollars out of the man behind her.

Billy could hear the sounds of sex clear out on the porch when he came home. He contemplated turning around to leave but had nowhere to go. Besides the weed and wine he'd consumed had him extra tired, so he pushed on inside and headed to bed.

"Oh!" Mary shouted in shock when her younger brother walked in on her. She quickly snatched her hand out of her panties where they'd been busy. The poor girl wasn't getting no dick so she'd resorted to jacking off while listening to her mother getting some.

She was the only one of The Buffalo Gals who wasn't getting any dick. Bernice had also gotten wind of Billy's good wood and gotten in the rotation. More pussy meant more money, but more money often lead to more problems.

"My bad," Billy explained once he processed what he'd walked in on. They shared an awkward silence until screams from the next room broke it.

"I'm...finna...cum!" Lady's vagina's guest announced between last second thrust. Lady scrambled to turn around to offer her mouth since that always got a tip. A real crowd pleaser and favorite.

"Mm hm," Lady hummed, nodded, and swallowed. The trick did the trick for the trick and he pulled out his wallet before he even pulled out of her mouth.

Lady slipped into her worn gown and house coat while her guest put back on his uniform. The cop earned a little extra money in the streets and he used it to buy a little extra pussy. His wife never missed it since she wasn't aware of it. No record of it meant no accountability for it as far as he was concerned.

"See you next week?" Lady asked as she escorted him through her now empty living room. Billy had gone to his room and was now face down in his bed, while Mary was in the tub on her back letting a trickle of water run on her lonely vagina. She covered her mouth with one of her chubby hands when she felt, a hard fought for, nut on the way.

"Sho' nuff!" Officer Rice agreed quickly. He gave her a deep kiss, despite his semen being in her mouth, and departed.

Mary heard her mother marching down the hall and knew she was headed her way. She turned the water up higher hoping to get off before she made it to her, but it wasn't to be.

"Come on up outta there! I need to get to my hot water bottle," Lady demanded while knocking on the door with her open palm.

"Okay!" Mary huffed and climbed out of the tub. She was near tears when she reached her lonely bed. Something had to give and quickly.

Chapter 9

"Hey Lady, Mary. Heeeey Billy!" the server greeted as the family was seated in The Rib Shack. Word was really getting around about the boy's penis prowess, which is why she batted her eyes flirtatiously.

"Hey Carlita. Is err'thang okay?" Lady asked frowning up curiously at her greeting. Mary echoed, her facial expression saying that she wondered the same.

"Just great!" Carlita cheered while poking her chest out towards Billy, who sat staring off out the window.

"O...kay. Anyway, give us three plates of burnt ends with all the fixin'!" Lady ordered in excitement.

"Y'all must be celebrating?" Carlita asked while still trying to catch the boy's eye.

"It's my brother's birthday," Mary tossed in proudly.

"Sho' nuff! I'ma hafta fix him up somethin' special! Somethin' good and hot!' she said finally catching his eye. "Um, Mary, why I ain't seent your gals in her in a bit? They alright?"

The query sounded sincere but Carlita was really just being nosey. Anytime anyone breaks their routine there was a reason for it and she hoped that their reason was juicy. The best and most recent gossip was found at Thelma's beauty parlor, but the waitress's large wig collection kept her from frequenting the joint.

"They fine," Mary replied, although she'd been wondering the same thing. Once the other girls started eating dick they gave up on eating the BBQ tour of Memphis. Shawna was already losing weight from her change in diet.

"That's good!" the waitress said happily even though she wasn't disappointed. She put on a great display of shaking her ass as she departed to fill their order.

Lady twisted her lips as she watched her son watch the waitress's large ass shifting under her tight dress. "Guess you is becomin' a man," Lady admitted. In truth she was the last to notice that her son was filling out and sprouting facial hair to go along with his deepening voice, which he softened whenever he spoke to his mama.

"Yessum Ma'am. Got a job and err'ythang," Billy said lifting his chin proudly. He then reached into his pocket and pulled out a small roll of money. The lone ten atop all the ones made it look like more than it was.

"Where you get all that from?" Mary exclaimed. She planned on checking her stash under the floorboard as soon as they got home.

"From the pool hall. I wash cars, shine shoes, run errands..."

"What kinda errands? And fo' who?" Lady demanded, cutting her son off. Billy may have just discovered the pool hall but Lady was very familiar with it and the type that frequented it.

"Fo' Sammy! I be goin' to The Rib Shack, to fetch soda pops, shine..."

"Oh, okay. I was finna say!" Lady said fanning herself in relief. The last time she was in there some pimp had sweet talked her out of her clothes and into her bed and left a baby behind. "Well, you can pay fo' the meal then big timer. You can start payin' a lil' rent too!"

All banter came to an abrupt end when the food came out. Carlita had let another button loose on her dress so that Billy could see some titty when she served him.

"Ooh! Excuse me," Lady giggled as she ripped one at the end of the meal. Her children joined in on her flatulence. It was a party after all. Besides, a family that smashes together passes gas together.

"Happy Birthday to you...Happy Birthday to you..." the waitress sang as she did the wedding march toward their table. In her hands was a thick slice of red velvet cake with a single candle flaming on top.

Lady and Mary joined in and sang the song until the end. Carlita had now removed her bra and undid yet another button. One of her titties swung free as she leaned over to put the cake in front of Billy.

"Chile, please!" Lady huffed at the thirsty display before she turned to her son. "Go on, William, make a wish."

Billy furrowed his brow as he contemplated on what to wish for. He was quite fond of pussy but was getting plenty so he shook that idea from his thoughts. He also liked money, weed, and wine but pounding pussy paid for those. His mind flashed to Leroy and the power he possessed. Settled on a desire, Billy nodded his head. He then leaned forward and blew out the candle.

Billy paid for his own birthday meal and tipped Carlita. Now he was eager to hit the streets so that he could make a few runs to replenish what he'd spent. The playful tone of his family's conversation changed in an instant once they reach their house.

"Well, I gotta go to work," Billy announced as his mom and sister ascended the stairs to their porch together.

"You finna wash cars all gussied up?" Lady frowned her face into a question mark.

"Huh? I mean...Ma'am?" Billy said scrambling for a lie.

"Go on 'head now fo' you lie to me," Lady said waving her hand. "Don't be out there doing nothin' you ain't got no business doin'!"

"No ma'am!" he vowed truthfully. He was going to see Shonda's mom to lay some pipe and she liked for him to dress up. Laying pipe was his business which made his statement true. He had a smug smile on his face as he headed up the block.

"You wanna play some Tonk?" Mary asked her mother hopefully. The girl was eager to do anything other than her usual nothing.

"Chile, you gon' have to play by yo'self! Mama finna have company," Lady huffed and headed to her room to get ready.

"Okay," Mary mumbled dejectedly. With nothing else to do she went and got on her back in the tub to let the water trickle down and lick her vagina until she came.

Chapter 10

Billy made his rounds around town much like a rooster does in a hen house. After putting the dick to Shonda's mama he went into Shonda's room and broke her off too. He then took a smoke break at the pool hall to smoke a couple of sticks with Byron. They also polished off a bottle of wine before Billy was off to see Bernice and lastly Shawna.

Leroy allowed the boy to run around selling dick even though he had bigger plans for him. Byron was eager but it was clear that Billy was the leader. Dollar Bill was a natural born leader. An absolutely perfect prerequisite for pimpin'.

He made it home shortly before night turned back into day. He was dead tired from sexing so he pulled his clothes off and fell face first on the bed. It was nice and quiet when he went to sleep but the shit hit the fan when he awoke.

"Don't make no damn sense!" Lady huffed as she went around the house gathering clothes so she could do the weekly laundry.

Mary had panties and bras in the front room while Billy had socks and shirts under the sofa. The bathroom hamper was nearly empty since her kid's clothes were everywhere but in it. She went into Billy's room and saw him laid out on his back with his mouth wide open. His morning erection peeked out of the top of his drawers, so she tossed his sheet on him to cover it.

"This can help do the laundry," Lady said when his pants jiggled. She dug her hand in his pocket and pulled out the contents. The bills went on his dresser, the coins went in her pocket, and the sticks of reefer froze her in her place. "William Cash!"

"Huh? What? Wait!" he shouted, trying to fend off the attack from his mother, who'd dove on his bed and got on his ass.

"Boy...I...know...you...ain't...got...no...dope...in...my...house!" she said in between blows.

"Wait! Hol' up, Mama! I can explain!" he tried to explain, while getting whooped with his own belt. He grabbed it but stopped short of snatching it away from his mama.

"Explain then! Cuz I wanna know why you got this shit in my house!" she demanded sticking the sticks in his face. He reached for them too but Lady pulled them away and put them in her bra.

"What's going on, Mama?" Mary asked wiping the sleep from her eyes as she came to see what the commotion was about. She felt her large panties getting wet as her eyes locked on the lump in her brother's drawers.

"This nigga don' brought drugs in my house! Get dressed, you goin' to see Pastor Paul!"

"Wait Mama, I just found it on my way home and picked it up. Just throw it away. We ain't gotta go to Pastor's house!" Billy pleaded as he ran behind his mother. He had to run to keep up with her long angry strides as she marched him across town.

"Mm hm," she huffed and kept right on marching.

"Come on, Mama! I swear fo' God I won't' smoke or drank no mo'! Just don't take me to Pastor Paul's!" Billy pleaded.

"Drank! Oh, so you been drankin' too?" Lady exclaimed and went into the next gear.

Dollar Bill could only shake his head at telling on himself. He decided to keep quiet for the rest of the trek across town. The generous tithes from the poor congregation meant that Pastor and Mrs. Paul didn't live in the hood. Billy frowned in confusion at the big houses with the manicured lawns. Not one, but two shiny Cadillacs sat in front of the preacher's stately house. Lady was still bitching as they walked up the walkway. The front door was pulled open before they reached it.

"How can I help you?" Mrs. Paul asked, indignant by the intrusion. Although Pastor Paul preached that his door was always open that didn't mean to come to his house.

"We need to talk to Pastor! I don' found a stick of reefer in this boy pants!" Lady said producing the evidence.

"What's going on out here?" Pastor asked as he came up the hallway. His wife stepped aside so he could handle the situation.

"I found dope in his pocket!" Lady raised her right hand as if she was testifying.

"Drive Miss Lady home. I got him," Pastor said stepping aside so Billy could enter. Billy lowered his head and did just that.

Pastor led him through the well-appointed house until they reached the den. All Billy saw was plush carpet, wood paneling, and a huge floor model T.V.

"Boys this is William Cash. Y'all say hello," Pastor ordered to the three boys present. They all were slightly older than him and all were slightly feminine.

"Hey William," two of the three quickly greeted before turning back to the western on the T.V. The other batted his long lashes, rolled his eyes, and pursed his thick lips together.

"You too, Earl," Pastor prodded.

"Hey!" the boy uttered real sassy, like sissies do. Billy suddenly remembered him from being a member of the church's choir. None of the congregation knew it but the boy wore nothing but a pair of panties under his choir robe. That's why his mama had taken him to see Pastor Paul. She'd come home one day and found some strange man with his dick way down her son's throat.

"Hey," Billy said stoically and then took a seat on the other side of the room.

"You're now a part of my Junior Pastor Team. I'ma teach you how to preach, pastor, and spread the gospel. You gon' get some new clothes, shoes, keep a haircut, and keep a few dollars in yo' pocket. One day you'll be head of yo' own flock and have a nice house, car, and whatever else it is you want," Pastor Paul explained. Billy was ready to dismiss it until he heard the part about the shiny new Cadillac.

"Oh, but we got rules! Tell 'em rule number one, Earl!"

"Whatever go on in Junior Pastor Team stays in Junior Pastor Team," Earl said, moving his neck like a girl.

"Say it back!" the preacher preached.

"Whatever happens in Junior Pastor Team stays in Junior Pastor Team," Billy repeated.

****

"So...what you gon' do with the um...reefer?" Mrs. Paul finally asked as she drove Lady home. Lady gave her the once over before replying.

"I'ma smoke this shit!" she finally shot back. The First Lady replied with a wide smile and pushed the car lighter in. They were both red eyed and giggly by the time they reached Lady's rundown house. The preacher's wife stared straight ahead so not to be reminded where she'd come from. –People always tell other people not to forget where they came from. Those people need to shut the fuck up. If you came from poverty and hardship who wants to reminisce on that shit!

"See you Sunday," The First Lady said as a goodbye and pulled off.

"Mary!" Lady called out when she walked into the empty front room. A second later Mary came out of the bathroom wet from her date with the faucet. "Chile, you don' bathed again?"

"Mama, it's hot and I'm just tryna stay clean," Mary replied on wobbly knees. "I'm just tryna stay clean."

"Mm hm," Lady murmured skeptically. "Anyway, you wanna play some Tonk?"

Mary did and so they did. Lady was up a few dollars when Billy finally made it home. He was already mourning the loss of his weed and money so a day with Pastor and his crew only made him want a drink.

"Well, what he say?" Lady asked when he walked in.

"Um...I'm on the Junior Pastor Team," he said with all the enthusiasm of someone who'd just received a cancer diagnosis. He stopped and twisted his lips ruefully wondering if he hadn't said too much. He definitely wasn't saying nothing about the T-bone steak and baked potatoes Pastor had fed them.

"My baby gon' be a preacher!" Lady shouted, like she did when in church. She then jumped up and raised her hands in joy, just like she did at church.

"I guess," he shrugged. He didn't know about all that but he was interested in all the perks. Learning to drive, dress, and talk proper were all skills he could use in the streets. Now that's where he really wanted to be.

"Well, mama got company coming so..." Lady said excusing herself.

"I'm finna go holla at Byron," Billy said and made his escape.

"Guess I'll take a bath," Mary said in defeat.

Chapter 11

One thing about black folks is they can't keep a secret to save their lives. Word of Dollar Bill slinging dick all over town had spread all over town. Mary was devastated when she got the news, but at least it explained why her friends no longer had time or money to hang out with her. As a result she had the cleanest vagina in Memphis.

Bernice was so salty about being stood up for Carlita that she'd complained to the wrong person. She was so shook up that she'd spilled the beans. Mary sat in shock as she relayed the whole sordid affair.

"My brother?" Mary asked in disbelief. "Lil' Billy?"

"Gurl, Lil' Billy got a big ol' dick and he know how to work it! And he can go all day!" she bragged as if she wasn't talking to the minor's sister.

"Lil' Billy...wow!" was all his sister could say. She tried to wait up for him to come home but couldn't hang.

****

"Mmm," Billy moaned and smiled in his sleep as felt his dick being removed from his drawers. Even with all the ass he'd been getting he still had wet dreams regularly. They usually starred Mandy with her pretty face and small waist, she was a far cry from his regular customers. The only women he slept with under three hundred pounds was Shonda's mother and most recently Carlita from The Rib Shack. Both were securely in their forties.

He felt his dick grow stiff as it was fondled with an odd curiosity. A warm kiss on its head was followed by a lick on its shaft. Finally he felt himself surrounded by a hot mouth. That's when Billy realized that he was actually awake and not dreaming.

He kept his eyes shut tight and tried to recall the events of the previous night that could possibly result in him getting his dick sucked this morning. He remembered going to the pool hall, making some runs for Leroy, and sharing some sticks and a bottle of wine with Byron. Then he distinctly remembered coming home. Mary had been curled up on the sofa with her thumb in her mouth. He open his eyes and looked down, to his horror there was Mary with his man in her mouth.

"W-w-what are y-y-you doing M-M-Mary?" he whined and stuttered on the verge of tears from the sight of his dick stuffed in his sister's face. Mary reluctantly pulled his penis out so she could speak but kept stroking the shaft now slick from her saliva.

"Mm hm. You done fucked all my friends. Err'ybody don' got some of this but me," she pouted.

"That's cuz you my sister!" he said sitting straight up on the bed. "Plus they pay me!"

"I know. Five dollars," she said, still stroking with one hand while the other hand produced the money. "I want some too!"

"Um...okay," Billy agreed. "But no kissing cuz you my sister and that would be nasty!"

That was all Mary needed to hear. She climbed on top of her brother and threw one of her big legs over each side. She reached back and wiggled the head between her slippery lips and slowly sank down. There was the briefest of pauses when her cherry popped on her way down.

'Mm, mm, mm," Mary moaned as she rocked back and forth on her brother's dick. She closed her eyes and let her head loll as she continue to rock.

Billy closed his eyes too and tried to pretend that she was some-body else. Anybody other than his own blood sister grinding and rocking atop of him. The three hundred pounds of pressure prevent-ed the illusion of Mandy so he thought about Shawna instead. She had the best pussy of all The Buffalo Gals, until now that is.

"Mm hm," Mary moaned as an orgasm crept up on her. This would be the first orgasm she'd had with a man in the same room let alone inside of her. The bed shook as she shivered and came. It took a couple of minutes for her to regain her composure, but once she did she began to rock once again.

"You gotta pay again if'n you tryna go again," Billy said sounding just like a ride operator at the fair. Which in a way he was.

"Okay," Mary eagerly agreed and then went for seconds. "I don't mind, I don't mind at all."

Billy was a professional and always aimed to please his cus-tomers. He would generously allow his partner to get multiple or-gasms before he got off himself. Mary was on the verge of another one when the contractions of the brand new vagina began to over-whelm him.

"Get up! I'm finna cum!" Billy shouted. He tried to lift his sister off him, but her three hundred pound frame was too much for him.

The whole house shook from the mutual incestuous climax. Mary squeezed and rocked as her brother released inside of. Finally, she rolled off of him and collapsed next to him gasping for air. They barely got a chance to recover before they heard sounds of the creaky porch announcing their mother's return. Mary jumped up as quick-ly as a three hundred pound girl could jump up and rushed into the bathroom.

"Mary! Billy!" Lady called out as she walked in.

"Yes!!" they both called back from separate rooms.

"I'm back from the sto'. I'm finna cook somethin' fo' we head to church."

"Okay, Mama!" they replied together just like they'd came together.

****

"What don' got into you, chile?" Lady finally asked her daughter. The girl was giddy over breakfast, clapping and singing loudly at church, and now she was practically skipping as they went to the buffet.

Mary subconsciously shot a quick glance at her brother before replying, "Nobody."

"Oh, I know that," Lady cackled at her dick deprived daughter not knowing that the joke was on her. Mary laughed right along with her since the joke was no longer on her.

Not only was she added into her brother's rotation of dick deliveries she also had first dibs since he was in house. She might even be able to get a line of credit. Get some dick on a Tuesday and pay for it on a Friday.

Chapter 12

"My baby's first sermon!" Lady gushed proudly as she gave her son a once over. He looked mighty fine in his new suit and shoes. –One of the many perks of being on The Junior Pastor Team.

"It's just a revival," Billy said of the Friday night gathering. He would much rather have been in the streets drinking and smoking but had no choice. He had to play the game. "No big deal."

"Hush up, chile! It is a big deal. I always wanted you to preach so gon' on up there and preach!" she demanded. This was to validate herself just as much as him. So what if she slept with married men Monday through Saturday, her son was spreading the gospel on Sunday.

The open air tent set up for the revival was already packed with the flock when Billy and family arrived. Pastor Paul smiled with dollar signs in his eyes. Not only was there an admission fee but the four

Junior Pastors on the bill would allow him to be able to pass the collection plate at least four times. Pastor Paul loved the Lord but he loved the dough a little more.

"You're up first. You ready, boy?" Pastor Paul asked when Billy arrived.

"Y-y-y-yassir," he stuttered unsurely. The preacher raised a brow to remind him to speak proper English, which prompted a confident "Yes sir."

"That's better. Now, go get that money," Pastor coached. Pastor Paul had upped the ante by telling the boys that whoever's basket had the most cash in it could keep it. It was the church version of 'Big Bank takes Little Bank'.

The murmurs of the congregation dimmed as young Reverend Cash took to the podium. It got completely quiet as they all awaited his first words. They would have to wait as he had nearly choked from stage fright. Billy closed his eyes and inhaled deeply through his nostrils. He smelled the scent of money and opened his eyes, his mouth, and then began to speak, preach actually.

"Blessed are the peacemakers, they shall be called the children of God," he boomed in a resounding voice reminiscent of the late great Martin Luther King Jr. All eyes were on him and he loved it. -Without a doubt, fame is the most addictive drug known to man. The young Reverend Cash swayed under a wave of euphoria and clutched the podium.

"Take your time!" a man shouted from the rear.

"Preach baby," his mama pleaded as she also swayed from side to side. And preach he did.

Billy, or Reverend Cash as he'd one day become widely known as, had been mocking Pastor Paul for so long that preaching came easy. He stepped from behind the safety of the podium and went in. His voice rose and fell in a unique timbre. He really turned up when he saw that the collection plate was being passed around.

"Everybody want heaven, but heaven isn't free!" he told them. "What would you pay for heaven? How much is your salvation worth? Huh? Wel-l-l-l-l, put it in the plate!"

"Damn it man!" Pastor heard. He looked around looking to see who had uttered the words and realized he'd said it himself. "This boy is gon' be a star!"

****

"I'm so proud of you!" Lady squealed once she got hold of her son. He scooted his hips back when she embraced him so she wouldn't feel the large lump of cash in his pocket.

The other boys didn't even come close to collecting what Reverend Cash had. Earl poked his lips out and glared at him with a hand on his hip. Billy's take after the church got its share was one hundred dollars. It was the most money he'd ever had in his life and it had him hooked.

"Guess we don't have to worry about this one getting high no more!" Pastor Paul told Lady.

"Why would I get high when I got the Holy Ghost!" Billy shouted. He thought it was a bit much and toned it down a bit. "I'm high on faith!"

"Amen!" Lady cheered and hugged him again. "Come on now, let's go get you a pop."

"Great job! I'll see you tomorrow," Pastor Paul said with a pat on his back as the family departed. A man waved Lady over as they left the tent. He was the same one who'd told Billy to take his time –funny since it didn't take him anytime to proposition the boy's mother.

"You gone have to take a raincheck on that pop. Mr. Jackson wanna go over some scripture," Lady begged off.

"Okay!" Mary and Billy both cheered, for different reasons. Mary wanted to take her brother home and fuck him. She'd been getting some every day for the last month now and was totally addicted to the dick. She spent most of her checks on him and she'd run up a tab that she knew she could never afford to pay.

Billy, however, had other plans. Instead of heading home he headed straight over to the pool hall for a little smoke and drank.

****

"If it ain't Dollar Bill!" Leroy announced with a mock enthusiasm that made the boy hate him even more. "All gussied up too! Where you coming from, church?"

"Yup," he replied smugly and produced his bankroll. "Dranks on me and I'll take a couple of them sticks out yo' pocket too!"

"Okay, okay. I see you getting money, huh?" Leroy said with a deceptive smile. In fact, it bothered him that the boy could make money without him. He already had Byron under his thumb and he wouldn't stop until he had him too.

"A lil' somethin', somethin'. I learned from the best. You the man, Leroy!" Billy said, stroking the man's ego. Leroy nodded thoughtfully as he tried to decipher whether or not the praise was genuine or not. A slow smile spread on his face when he decided that it was.

"Put that money away lil' nigga! All dranks and sticks is on me!' Leroy announced. Billy smiled too at seeing that men could be played just as easy as women –easier actually.

****

Mr. 'Take Yo' Time' took his time making love to Lady. It wasn't until the next day when he finally finished. He'd rocked her world so well she gave him half of his money back.

Both Lady and Mary were sound asleep when Billy got in pissy drunk from drinking free drinks all night. Everything was all good in a bad way, but things were about to get worse, a lot worse.

Chapter 13

"One day you gon' be up there," Lady leaned over and whispered into Billy's ear as Pastor Paul prowled the pulpit. "You got talent."

"Shol' do!" Mary seconded. She, however, was talking about his skills in the bed not the pulpit, and he knew it. Billy twisted his lips and shot her a side eyed glance. Just beyond her he saw Bernice licking her lips lustfully while staring at him. He snapped his head the other way only to find Shawna glaring at him. If he had eyes in the back of his head he'd have seen Shonda and her mama both staring at him as well.

"One day," he replied. Not because he knew the future but because Pastor Paul had told him he would.

Billy noticed that the preacher seemed a lot closer to the other boys in The Junior Pastor Team. He'd share inside jokes, laugh, and spend extra time with them; especially the girly Earl. Billy assumed he did so because he needed the extra attention because he was so extra.

Billy grinned and nodded in appreciation when the collection plate came around once again. It weighed heavily in his hands from being so full of cash. It was that same cash that paid for his clothes and the steaks that Pastor fed him. His mother nodded proudly when he dropped in some more of his own money. Billy knew that he'd get it and more back so it was all good.

"Amen!" Lady shouted once the sermon finally came to an end. It could've ended an hour earlier if her new friend Mr. 'Take Yo' Time' hadn't kept urging Pastor to take his time. Pastor didn't mind because he'd been able to push that plate around one more.

"I'm shol' is hungry! My stomach just a rumbling," Mary grimaced with a hand on her belly.

"I'ma get us a car soon as I turn sixteen," Billy vowed. Again this was no premonition, again he knew because Pastor had told him so.

"That shol' would be nice!" Lady grunted as she led the march to The Rib Shack.

"Hey y'all!" Carlita shouted when the family entered the small diner. She said y'all but only looked at Billy. She fluttered her false lashes at him and smiled brightly.

"Chile, you gone fly away you keep flapping them lashes," Lady teased. It tickled her to no end how much attention her handsome young son got. She noticed it more and more as he grew more and more handsome by the day.

"What's wrong with you, chile?" Lady asked seeing her daughter sitting across the table with a look of distress on her face.

"I'on know," Mary frowned. The strong aromas of fat back, hog maws, chitterlings, bacon, pork chops, ribs, and lard assaulted her all at once. They overwhelmed her to the point that she scrambled to get to the bathroom. Her three hundred pounds slowed her down from getting out of the booth. She only made it three whole steps before her breakfast came gushing out of her mouth.

"Oh Lawd, that chile is pregnant!" Carlita announced with glee. The fact that she hadn't heard it meant she could be the first to spread it.

"Pregnant!" Lady squealed with laughter. "She must be another Virgin Mary then cuz that girl ain't got no man, cain't get no man, and don't want no man!"

Mary's head and shoulders drooped with sorrow as she continued on to the bathroom. Once the last of the grits, sausage, eggs, biscuits, and jelly she'd eaten for breakfast had come back up she washed her mouth out while she counted back. She frowned her face to help her think and obviously it helped because she came up with an answer –not a good answer, but it was the right answer.

"Oh shit! I am pregnant!" she shouted to her reflection. If there was one consolation it was that at least she knew who her baby's daddy was, even if it was her brother.

"You okay?" Billy asked out of breath from holding his breath.

"No, I mean yes!" she said holding her head up proudly to spite her mother's mocking. "I am pregnant! And I'm keeping my baby!"

"Chile, you...you serious? By who? Who?" Lady demanded, making a scene. Mary clamped her lips and crossed her arms over her breast, which meant *'I ain't telling you shit!'*

"Who been in my house!" she turned to Billy and demanded. He was so shocked that he was at a lost for words so he simply shrugged.

"I'on know," he barely got out passed the lump in his throat.

"Oh, so y'all slick, huh? Y'all grown, huh? Well, pay fo' y'all own meals then!" their angry mother said as she slid out of the booth. She then tossed her head back and stormed out of the restaurant.

"She coming back?" Carlita asked when she returned with the three orders and noticed Lady gone. Mary shrugged and then scraped her mother's plate onto her own.

"Prob'ly not. I got it though," Billy announced in dismissal.

"I know you do!" she shot back and made a big show of walking away.

"What you gon' do if you pregnant?" Billy asked once they were alone. It took Mary a full minute to chew and swallow the large mouthful of food in her large mouth.

"Pregnant people have babies," she quipped sarcastically and re-loaded her mouth with ribs and macaroni and cheese.

"Girl, we brother and sister! We cain't have no baby!"

"We got different daddies so it's fine," she suggested and continued eating. She didn't' know if that was true or not, but it didn't matter and she didn't care. She didn't have shit and never had so she was keeping the baby.

The rest of the meal was spent in silence. The only sounds to be heard were Mary's breathing through her nose, since her mouth stayed full, and the clanging of the silverware hitting their plates. The unconcerned girl finished her meal and then sucked down two of her favorite peach sodas. Billy managed to get his meal down and waved for the check.

"We gon' fuck when we get home?" Mary asked, finally breaking the silence.

"Nah, I gotta go holla at Byron 'ndem," he replied. The 'ndem he meant was Leroy. Surely the player/pimp/pusher would know what to do.

****

Billy walked into the pool hall and paused. He blinked rapidly to adjust his eyes to the room darkened by smoke and the black hearts of the patrons inside. Between blinks Leroy came into view. As usual he was posted up in his usual booth. It was known as pimp central since it was where he ran his whores from. For once his main whore, who was usually always be his side, was noticeably absent. Since her head wasn't seen bobbing up and down from under the table Billy assumed she was off with some trick.

"Sup Leroy?' Billy asked making the greeting sound like a question.

"Me! What's up with you?" the pimp asked, volleying the question back over to Billy.

"Um...you ever um...you got any kids?" he asked for starters.

"What yo' mama don' tol' you?" Leroy shot back ready to deny whatever she'd said.

"My mama? Nothing. I ain't asked her," Billy frowned in confusion. "What would you do if you got a gal pregnant?"

"Me?" the pimp laughed, in the way that a pimp does when a woman tells him that she's pregnant. He then quickly regained his composure as he began to understand the boy's dilemma. "Okay, you gotta take a wire hanger, make a lil' hook, and push it up in her. It's gon' stop when it hit the bottom but you gotta keep pushin'. Once it go in some mo' you gotta scrape it all out. Once the blood start skeetin' you..."

"I cain't do that to my...to her!" Billy grimaced at the odious instructions to the barbaric abortion.

"I feel you, must be sweet on the gal. I figured you to be a tender dick nigga. Prob'ly kiss 'em in the mouth and fuck 'em face to face."

Mandy returned in time to catch the lighthearted ribbing. She smile a smile that was devoid of any trace of mirth. Her eyes too had lost the luster of life they once had. She let out a deep loud belch that filled the air with the smell of fresh cum.

"Smells like money!" Leroy laughed while Billy grimaced. On cue Mandy produced a fist full of dollars and handed it over.

That was power too and Billy recognized it. Instead of a collection plate he passed around a whore. Same results because they both came back full of cash.

"Oh, bout yo' lil problem. Slip the broad a lil turpentine in her soda pop and she'll drop that load in the toilet," he explained. "Just a lil though. That shit strong!"

Chapter 14

Lady was a tramp for a fee for most men, but she was always a lady for Mr. Morales. Luckily he only came through town once a year because being a tramp paid the bills. The businessman, from Trinidad, always made sure to coordinate his trip to coincide with her birthday.

Every year he would treat her to a night out on the town for dinner, dancing, and mediocre sex in a five star hotel. Preparation for the big night began a week in advance. Lady would close her legs to all regular traffic from her regulars. Mr. 'Take Yo' Time' got to take his time one last time before the visit.

The day before the visit she would go downtown to Selma's to get a wash and curl. She made sure to dress up for the occasion, knowing that she was a regular topic of conversation at the shop. A number of women had to skip their weekly appointment because their man had spent the money with Lady.

"Mary, I want my kitchen clean 'fo I get back. And when I get back you gon' tell me which one of these niggas put that baby in you!' Lady barked. However, the threat had no bite since she wasn't going to do anything. Not to mention that the truth was worse than whatever she could do anyway.

"See you later, Mama," Billy said and tried to hurry and duck into his room.

"Un uh! You got Junior Pastor Team meeting," Lady reminded him.

"Oh okay," Billy groaned. He had other plans for the day so planned to skip it.

"You wanna fuck?" Mary asked the second their mama stepped out the door and onto the porch.

"When I get in...here..." Billy said and handed her an ice cold pop.

"Thank you!" Mary smiled and turned it up. She frowned from the odd taste but sucked the bottle dry. "I think it was bad. Pick me up another one on yo' way back."

"Okay, Mary," Billy said, saddened at having just poisoned his sister into aborting their baby.

****

A good round of gossip was raging in Selma's Beauty Salon when Lady walked in. The bell above the door tinkled causing all the nosey ladies to look over to see who'd entered. Renise paused and started right back up when she noticed who it was. She was the old school equivalent of a social blogger pre social media.

She had the scoop on everyone and everything. Several of the women present were there to see her instead of getting their hair done. She and Mandy's mother took turns talking about everyone in town that way the focus would stay off their own fucked up daughters. The women present moved their heads back and forth between the two women like they were watching a tennis match.

"Gurl, who dis young boy runnin' round layin' all dis pipe?" Renise threw out. It was a purely rhetorical question since she knew exactly who he was and who his mother was too. "Sellin' it for the low!"

"I'on know, but I hear he a regular meat man! Slangin' dick all over the Southside!" Mandy's mama lied. She hadn't heard anything about it but would not be one upped by her competition. The shop got completely quiet because everyone wanted to know who was selling quality dick for the low.

"I heard they call him Dollar Bill or somethin' like that. They say he a machine! Put a few dollars in him and he go all night!" Renise sang, winding her hips in her chair.

Lady had heard enough to know who they were talking about. It all suddenly made sense, it explained all of the extra female attention, as well as all of the extra cash. She lifted her chin as far as it would go, and still allow her to be able to see, and marched out of the salon.

"What's her problem?" Mandy's mom asked of her hasty departure.

"That big dick lil' boy y'all talkin' 'bout...oh that's her son," Renise cackled.

****

Lady marched all the way across town with her arms swinging like a North Korean soldier. She was so angry that she didn't even register any of the car horns blowing offering her a ride. She was soaking wet from sweat by the time she reached Pastor Paul's house. She began yelling for her son as she walked up the walkway.

"William Cash! You get out her this instant!" Lady demanded.

"Miss Lady! What you out there hollering about?" Mrs. Paul asked with eyes wide from both fright and embarrassment. Her eyes shot up the street and back hoping no one was out.

"I need to see my boy! Send him out right now! Billy!"

"Shush, Miss Lady! He ain't even here. He never showed up," the preacher's wife confessed. Lady did a military about face and started back down the walk. "Hol' up. Let me drive you."

Mrs. Paul ran back inside and grabbed her purse and keys. Lady was half way down the street by the time she caught up with her. She looked at her and kept right on marching. It wasn't until The First Lady produced a stick of reefer that Lady gave in.

"I guess I could use the ride," Lady acquiesced. She hopped into the Caddie and took a toke. "He prob'ly at...that...pool...hall."

"Okay, but um...two tokes and pass, Miss Lady," First Lady said reaching for her weed. "Anyway, what's wrong?"

"Just found out my boy been having sex for money!" Lady huffed. The pastor's wife frowned but held her tongue knowing Lady did the same. "They say he got a big'ne (big one) and he know how to throw it too!"

"Sho' nuff?" Mrs. Paul asked curiously. "So, what he chargin?"

"Ain't chargin' nothin' after I get hol' of 'im!" Lady said. She grumbled and cursed the rest of the way to pool hall. They both had a mellow buzz when Mrs. Paul pulled to a stop out front.

"I better stay out here. Probably wouldn't be good for me to be seen up in there," the First Lady suggested correctly; especially since she'd peddled pussy out of there once upon a time. Pastor Paul knew but she too knew his secrets. Their marriage was more of an understanding and agreement than one of love and honor.

Lady hopped out and stormed inside. It took a second for her eyes to adjust to the dim light and that allowed Leroy to spot her before she spotted him. Seeing her and her son in the same room removed any doubt of paternity. He would never openly admit it but he knew that William Cash was his son. Billy was across the pool hall so he couldn't warn him of his mother's approach from the rear.

"William Cash!" Lady shouted as she popped him upside his head. He spun around ready to fight until he saw his mother standing there.

"What you doin', Mama?" he shouted while he ducked and blocked her blows.

"Don't be asking me no questions boy! Now come on up out of here!" she insisted and dragged him out by his ear. Byron tried not to laugh at his friend's predicament but failed.

"I win then!" he shouted behind him and collected the dollar bets they placed on the table.

"We better take him to see Pastor," First Lady suggested as she got a good look at him through her mirror. "I better drop you off first, Lady, and then..."

"That don't make no sense since you gotta pass your house first! Drop him off with Pastor and me and you can talk one more 'gain while you drop me off," Lady said, unknowingly cock blocking.

Pastor Paul and little Earl had just stepped out of the house when his wife pulled up. He had a one on one session with girly boy a couple times a week. The boy had a pretty bright smile on his face until he saw Billy in the backseat.

"What's going on Mrs. Paul?" Pastor asked of his wife's company.

"I better let her tell you," she replied passing the mic to Lady, who took it and used it to snitch on her son.

"This boy selling himself is what's going on! Tell him!" she shouted and gave him another pop upside the head that got a girlish giggle out of Earl.

"Is that right?" Pastor said shooting a glance to Billy's crotch. He'd never seen any signs of sexual interest in the boy. He'd never heard him speak about girls or a girlfriend.

"Speak up!" Lady shouted as she went upside his head once more.

"Take Earl home while I tend to him," Pastor ordered and led Billy inside. Led him inside to change his life forever.

Chapter 15

"Well, let's have a look," Pastor Paul ordered off handedly when they reached the room. Billy looked confused as he looked around to see if he might be talking to someone else. They were alone so he guessed he meant him.

"Look at what?" he asked hoping he didn't mean the reefer in his pocket. He needed it before his appointment with Carlita later that night.

"At all that dick you s'pose to be slangin' around town," Pastor said with authority.

Billy frowned up like he wanted to cry as he unbuttoned his pants. He looked away as he pulled his limp dick from inside his pants.

"Mm hm. Just as I suspected," Pastor said moving in closer to inspect it. "About a ten inch job, I reckon."

Billy shrugged his shoulders since he had no idea. He'd never saw a need to measure it and The Buffalo Gals didn't seem to mind its size. His eyes were closed so he didn't see the pastor open his mouth and lean in. He'd spent the afternoon freaking off in and on Earl but couldn't pass up the opportunity.

"W-w-what are you d-d-doing?" Billy stammered when he looked down and saw half his dick in the preacher's mouth. He tried to fight off an erection but Pastor Paul sucked a mean dick.

"Mm hm," the preacher hummed and nodded in agreement when he felt the boy growing long and hard in his mouth –so hard and long that he had to pull it out and marvel at it for a second before he put it back in his mouth and went to work.

Billy's mind wandered as pastor sucked his dick. Earl's attitude towards him whenever he came around now made sense. Even though it was usually the other way around the sissy wanted Pastor Paul all to himself. Then he wondered if this meant he was gay too. His answer came a couple minutes later when he did.

"Mph!" Billy grunted from behind the hand he'd used to cover his own mouth with. It stifled his scream but not the explosion. The boy came so hard that some came out of the pastor's nose.

"Mm hm," the preacher said between swallows, with his nasty ass. He refused to let the dick free until it went completely limp. It hit Billy's leg with a thud once he finally spit it out. "I hope I learned you a lesson."

"Yassir," Billy agreed, assuming that the lesson was how to get your dick sucked.

"Now you leave them fast gals alone. You need something you come to me," he offered. It was a set up because nothing in life is free.

"Yassir," Billy repeated with mixed emotions. He didn't mind letting Pastor blow him or take him shopping but he liked pussy too, and wine and reefer, and the danger and excitement of the streets.

"Good, now I guess I'll drive you home since my wife ain't back yet," he said twisting his lips at the clock.

"Yassir," he replied hoping he still had time to make his date with the waitress. The ride was made in total silence –after Pastor sucks your dick what is there to talk about.

"Y'all having a party or something?" the preacher asked seeing quite a bit of activity in front of his house.

"Not that I know of," Billy frowned and craned his neck to see what was going on. The ambulance had just pulled off as they pulled up and took its spot. Billy sprang from the car before it stopped. "Is my mama okay?"

"She's fine," Pastor Paul's wife said stoically. "She just passed out. Your sister dead, she killed herself."

****

The weight of the news pulled Billy to the ground. He plopped onto the porch and broke down. He could not understand why his happy sister would take her own life.

"What done happened?" Pastor Paul leaned in and asked his wife. She scrunched her face up at the smell of semen on his breath and leaned away. She was slightly jealous that he'd beat her to the boy. He always beat her to the boys.

"When I pulled up to drop her off she ran inside to get a...um...then she came running back out screaming 'bout her daughter. I got out and went inside to see what was wrong and found her with her eyes open and foam coming from her mouth. She was already dead."

"Dayum!" Pastor said in reply. No sooner than she finished the coroner attendants came out with Billy's big sister in a body bag. Billy let out a heartfelt moan that sounded more like a wounded animal than a human.

"You go on home. I'll take the boy to the hospital to sit with his mama," Pastor urged. He helped the languid boy to his feet and into the car.

Billy didn't register a single word Pastor said on the way to the hospital. The man rattled off scriptures and song lyrics but the hurt boy didn't catch any of it. He couldn't help but think that if he'd just stayed home and had sex with her that she'd still be alive –and that's a pretty fucked up thought to have.

"Here we go," Pastor said as he led the boy into the hospital. He got his mother's room number and took Billy to see her. "Buck up boy, yo' mama need you!"

"Yassir," Billy finally replied. Lady was seated upright on the bed rocking and wringing her hands in despair. Billy quickly made his way over and gathered her up in his arms. "I'm here mama."

"My baby gurl don' kilt herself cuz of me!" Lady wailed.

"No Mama! Don't blame yo'self. It's not yo fault," Billy said rocking her in his arms. Lady pulled back to make eye contact before she spoke.

"Shol' is. I kept pressing her 'bout who her baby daddy was gone be! She couldn't take it. I lost my baby gurl and my grandbaby!" she moaned and broke down once more.

Pastor fought back a tear as he watched the sorrow before him. Even for a man who only cared about himself this was hard to watch. His mind searched for a way to incorporate it into his next sermon. Misery was always good for the collection plate. Maybe he would send another plate around for the family. He would split it three ways of course.

"Preliminary results are in," the doctor announced as he barged in the room. There wasn't a shred of empathy in his tone as he relayed the bad news. Bad news that made the bad situation even worse. "The girl drunk some turpentine. That's what killed her!"

"Turpentine! Why in the world would she drink turpentine?" Pastor Paul shrieked in horror.

"She was pregnant. Sometimes girls drink it to get rid of the baby," the doctor explained.

Billy's heart died right there on the spot. It turned completely black as his last fuck to give escaped in a solitary tear. He'd killed his sister, it made him a monster in his eyes.

Chapter 16

Billy was already pretty fucked up but his now black heart only made him worse. You can't live a good life with a black heart. Lady's heart, on the other hand, was completely broken and it's hard to live a good life with a broken heart as well. Lady was so distraught that she didn't leave her room for days after Mary's death. A pickle jar served as an outhouse since she wouldn't leave.

It wasn't until the day of the funeral that she picked up a little. The thought of being in church propelled her from her sweaty sheets. She smelled a little pickled herself, but she still slipped on one of her Sunday's best dresses, hat, and shoes.

Mrs. Paul came to give the family a ride to church to say their final goodbyes. She winced from the foul odor that filled the car as Lady climbed in beside her. She almost lit the reefer just to change the fragrance in the air but held out. They would blaze up after she put her daughter in the dirt.

Most of the congregation nodded their condolences to Lady and Billy as he led her to the front pew. However, there were some salty sisters in the church who still turned their noses up at the woman who took money out of their purses by fucking their husbands. Lady's motto was 'if your husband wanted his dick suck you should suck it' and if you didn't she would and she'd get paid for it too. And she did.

Pastor Paul looked dapper in a somber black suit and black glasses. The choir hummed an ol' Negro spiritual, like backup singers, as the preacher began to preach. He paced to and fro with his deacon/hype-man only a step behind ready to co-sign like a good hype-man is supposed to. Every now and again he would run over and wipe the sweat from Pastor's brow.

"Pastor shol' got a mouth on him," Lady admired bringing her word count to ten for the day.

"Yeah, he do," Billy replied. His mother squeezed his hand not knowing he was referring to the pastor's head game. He almost got an erection from watching the man's lips moving.

It didn't matter which chapter or verse Pastor Paul quoted, because it was just some bullshit as far as Billy was concerned. It was all just game to fill up the collection plates that were constantly in motion.

"Take yo' time!" Lady's friend yelled amongst the Amens. It was purely for attention in hopes that Lady would open her legs for business later.

No one really gave a fuck about the girl in the box. Even her friends had ulterior motives for being there. They all stared at Billy hoping to spend a little time and money with him after the ceremony. The preacher eulogized the girl he'd watch grow up but rarely spoke to. You wouldn't know it though by the way he put on. Only about half of the mourners from the church made it out to the cemetery. Lady was in such a daze that she didn't even notice. However, Billy did and it angered him. If he ever got a chance to make them pay, he would.

After more mumbo-jumbo from Pastor Paul the casket was lowered into the hole in the ground. Lady moaned woefully as the grave digger began shoveling dirt back into the hole he'd dug. People passed the grave tossing in flowers and mumbling their final goodbyes.

"I'll take Miss Lady on home," Mrs. Paul offered. She'd gotten hold of some good reefer and couldn't wait to get to it.

"Okay, and I'll take the boy with me," Pastor replied. That meant Lady got high and Billy got head before they made it home.

****

After the funeral Lady retreated back into her room and didn't come out again. She remained closed up in her room where she smoked her reefer and mumbled to herself. Her vagina was in a funk too since she wouldn't bathe.

Billy now had extra expenses and he passed them along to his customers. It now cost ten bucks for him to pay a visit to your cervix. However, his new found aggression made it money well spent. Inflicting pain became his pleasure. He now got a kick out of really beating the pussy up.

"You gotta take it easy this time," Shawna pleaded as they undressed for their latest sexual session. Of all the women in his rotation Shawna was the only one who really couldn't handle it.

"Okay," Billy agreed. He slid into gently and then proceeded to beat it up anyway. Shawna howled for mercy but got none. Luckily for her, he got off quickly from her agony. He decided not to pull out and came inside of her. Whatever came of it would be her problem. Obviously, the apple doesn't fall far from the tree. Like father, like son.

****

Leroy was a criminal so every time the door to the pool hall door opened he shot his eyes over to it. He never knew if it was the police, a rival, or some husband angry about him pimping his wife. Seeing that it was only Billy he nodded and turned back to his drink.

He was far too cool to acknowledge that he was in his feelings over not being able to control Billy like he did Byron. Billy was making his own money from slinging dick and preaching revivals. He liked wine and reefer and not only could he pay for his own, but he could pay for his mama's as well.

"Sup Leroy, Byron," Billy greeted. Mandy was present as usual but as usual she wasn't present so there was no need to greet her. Her mouth hung open as her chin lay on her chest while she was in a deep nod.

"Sup Billy!" Byron cheered while Leroy simply nodded in greeting. "You coming to make these rounds with me?"

"I cain't. Gotta go make sure my mama eat," he said and turned to Leroy. "I need some reefer."

"Boy, I been tryna put you in charge of the reefer. You do and you won't have to pay nar' 'nother day for it," Leroy chided.

"I'm good," Billy declined and pulled out two tens –twenty bucks was a lot of money back then and could buy you a lot of reefer, enough to last both him and his mama for a week.

Byron handled the sale while Leroy glared at Billy. He didn't want his damn money he wanted his soul, and one way or another he vowed to get it. It was fatherly love in a fucked up, sick, twisted, ghetto sense, but it was all the pimp had to offer.

Billy said his goodbyes as he stood and departed. He felt the daggers in his back before he made it halfway to the door. He stopped and turned around to see Leroy staring at him with a snarl. He smiled appreciatively and turned back to the door.

****

"Hey Mama, I'm home!" Billy called as he walked back into the house. His mother's odor greeted him back in return. "You hungry?"

"Shol' is! That sister of yours ain't gone cook nothin'!" she huffed, showing she had slipped another notch into mental illness.

"Don't worry, I'll fix you somethin'. After yo' bath," he replied.

In a rare act of altruism Billy ran his mother a hot bath. He then turned away as he stripped her of her smelly clothes and helped her inside. He lit her a stick of reefer, placed it between her lips, and left her to soak.

Billy left Lady in the tub long enough to clean her room and fix her a plate. He got her situated in her clean bed with a full plate and a thick stick for desert. A peck on her forehead served as a goodbye before he headed out into the night.

Chapter 17

Billy realized that the harder he preached at the revivals the more people gave, so he gave his all to ensure that they would too. It didn't take long before he was the star of the show. People old and young came from near and far to hear young Reverend Cash do his thing.

Earl and Greg pouted when he became the headliner. Dwight, however, was smart and jumped on the Billy bandwagon. He decided to hitch a ride on the other boy's shooting star by becoming his hype-man —technically it's called dick riding, but back then the phrase hadn't been coined yet.

Greg didn't like it but was content with his fade to black. Not Earl, however. The sissy plotted and planned to get rid of Billy; especially once Pastor Paul started to openly cater to him.

The preacher saw that Billy had a stronger will than the others. He was a leader so following didn't come easy. It was obvious to him that Billy enjoyed the oral favors but the boy never initiated them. Earl, on the other hand, threw himself at the pastor, like the woman that he wished he was. The first time he got rebuffed he decided that Billy had to go.

The Junior Pastor Team met at least once a week at the pastor's house. And once a week Earl would steal a small trinket or knick-knack from the pastor's house. Nothing major, just a little something to raise suspicions. He figured since things didn't start to go missing until after the arrival of the new guy that the suspicions would fall his way. It should've but it didn't.

"I gotta pee!" Earl raised his hand and announced as he wiggled in his chair like a young girl

"So, go 'head," Pastor said and frowned up at the unnecessary request for permission. Mrs. Paul made herself scarce most weekends, so the boys had the run of the house. Therefore, they didn't need permission to use the bathroom. Pastor Paul, being Pastor Paul, still took a look at his ass as he left the room.

Earl walked loudly down the hallway then quietly tip-toed into Pastor's room. Once inside he rushed over to the dresser and swiped a pair of the Mrs.' Panties for his personal use and one of Pastor's watches as part of his plan. It might have worked had Pastor not snuck down and saw him. Without a sound he snuck back out and acted as if he hadn't seen the theft.

"Whew! I had to pee bad!" Earl said, still playing it off like he'd gone to the bathroom.

"That's it for the day. Now, let's say we hit the backyard and fire the grill up!" Pastor Paul suggested.

"Yassir!" Billy cheered along with the other boys. They all popped up to rush outside for burgers and hotdogs. Both Pastor and Earl lagged behind the others, but for different reasons. Earl wanted to slip the watch into Billy's bag while Pastor had a call to make.

"What's the matter boy?" Pastor Paul asked when Earl stayed behind. Assuming he wanted the usual he whipped out his dick.

"Pastor, I...oh! Earl paused upon seeing his favorite snack. He rushed over and quickly went down on the man.

"Hurr' up," the preacher said thrusting his hips so he would. Hurry up Earl did and so it was over minutes after it started. Earl wiped his mouth with the back of his hand and stood.

"I'll be right out," he said, hoping for a chance to hide the watch, but it was not to be.

"No, gon' on out. I'll be right out," Pastor corrected so he could make his call.

"I...um...I...um..." Earl stammered in confusion at the changed of plans. He thought quickly and came up with a new one. He then dug in his pocket and produced the watch. "Look!"

"My watch! Where did you get that from boy?" Pastor boomed.

"From Billy! He stole it! He always be stealing. I saw him put it in his bag and I got it out for you. Here."

"You know what...put it in your pocket and hold on to it," Pastor Paul said and shooed him on outside so that he could make his call before joining the party.

Billy frowned curiously at the smug looks the sissy kept shooting his way. Earl just knew that today would be the last day that he had to deal with the intruder and boy was he right. Right after the food was served and they'd all lowered their heads in prayer two police officers entered the yard. Earl giggled, like a little girl, at what he thought was to come.

"Which one of these boys been stealing?" the no nonsense white officer demanded. He hoped in his black heart that the pastor would say all of them so he could lock all of their black asses up.

"Mm hm," Earl chided at Billy. "Bye-Bye."

"I can't say for sure. You better check their pockets," Pastor Paul replied.

"Mm hm," Earl teased once more until the words processed in his head.

The white cop ordered the boys to their feet and then he and his black partner got to work. Billy came up clean, as did Dwight. The two stood to the side and watched as Greg and Earl got frisked.

"What in the world?" the black cop asked when he pulled a pair of Mrs. Paul's panties from Earl's pocket.

"I can explain!" Earl said and looked at Pastor.

"While you at it explain this too!" the cop demanded as he held up Pastor's watch.

"My watch! Boy, what you doing with my watch?" Pastor asked, showing off his acting skills.

"Huh? You...I...I...thought we..." Earl whined as he was cuffed and carted off to jail. Luckily for him he was still a juvenile so he only went to kiddie jail.

"Can I have his burger?" Billy asked once the commotion died down.

"But of course! Y'all dig in," Pastor ordered. The party went on as if the incident never happened. All the boys knew that Pastor had been fucking that boy and they all hoped that they wouldn't be next.

****

"Billy, why don't you wait here while I drop Greg and Dwight off at home," Pastor Paul suggested once the meal was wrapped up. Both the other boys breathed a sigh of relief that they weren't chosen.

"I...uh....I...um...gotta get home. Gotta go take care of my mama!" he begged off and held up Earl's burger as proof.

"Shol' do," the preacher recalled. "You a good boy!"

Dwight raised his brows like 'whew' and pretended to wipe sweat from his face while Billy shook his head in agreement at having dodged a bullet. He would take the money, clothes, driving lessons, he would even take the blow jobs but he wasn't getting fucked.

When Pastor drove to Greg's out of the way house first Billy knew he was being saved for last. He and Dwight shot each other knowing looks and shook their heads. In truth they could only blame themselves for the abuse. They'd traded their dignity in exchange for material things. Pastor Paul was the only one winning.

"See you at the revival," Dwight said when he got out at his house. He waved and went inside.

"I think you 'bout ready to..." Pastor began but got cut off.

"No, I ain't ready! I doubt I'll ever be ready! I..."

"Boy, I'm tryna let you drive and you acting scurred! Don't let me find out you scurred!" Pastor dared.

"Fo' real! I mean, really? I can drive?" Billy asked changing his tone.

"Sure you can!" Pastor replied changing his tone as well. He was about to crack for some booty but saw that the boy wasn't ready. That he wasn't quite ripe yet so he'd slow it down, for now. He figured he might have to buy him a car before he got the ass.

Billy cheesed from ear to ear as he pulled off in the shiny new car. Just like with sex and drugs he had become instantly addicted. He wished he could push past the pool hall so he could be seen. All of the pimps pushed Caddies but none as new as this. Even big shot

Leroy drove last year's model. Proof that there's more money in selling dreams than nuts.

"First Corinthians..." Billy said and began to quote scripture. He had saw Pastor looking him up and down and hoped to take his mind off of whatever it was on.

"Mm hm," he said and reached into Billy's lap. He fiddled with the zipper until he got it down. Once it was open he went inside.

"I'm tryna drive!" he protested in a whiny voice.

"You gotta learn to drive while getting yo' dick sucked too. That shit is an art!" he explained. At least that much was true, it was an art.

The car swerved slightly when Billy felt Pastor's tonsils tickle his dick head. He got it straight and tried to focus as he deep throated him. An orgasm caused him to stomp on the gas, but he eased off before running a light. He'd managed to master the art in only a couple of miles.

Lady was on the porch rocking in the same rocker he'd left her in hours before. The full pickle jar next to her meant she hadn't been inside. She didn't even register the car pulling to a stop. Billy skipped the goodbyes and rushed up to his mother.

"Hey Mama. Did you eat?" he asked softly. The sound of his voice snapped her from her incoherent thoughts that had frozen her in place for hours.

"Chile, I'm starved! Yo' sister still ain't made it in yet!" she announced.

"I know, Mama. Come on. Let's go inside," he urged and helped her up. Pastor stared at his ass as he walked her inside.

"You got some reefer?" Lady asked hopefully.

"Yeah, Mama. I got some reefer."

Chapter 18

"So...what y'all be doing over there at Pastor's house?" Byron asked. It seemed like he snatched the question out of nowhere but really he'd just revived the conversation he and Leroy were having before Billy arrived.

"Huh?" he replied since getting head was the first thing that popped in his head. He certainly wouldn't admit to that so he pretended not to hear the question instead.

"I said, what y'all be doing with Pastor Paul?" he repeated.

"I hear he like boy pussy," Leroy said cutting through to the chase. "You ain't over there fuckin' 'round is you boy?"

"Huh? Nah! Hell nah! I don't know what he be doing with them other boys but not me. No sir! All I do is learn to preach. He's been teaching us how to talk proper, drive cars, uh..." Billy rambled on. As he did it became clear to Leroy that he'd done something. He didn't know what, but he knew it was something and that's why the boy was still explaining. "Teach us how to dress..."

"Oh okay," Leroy cut in. "I hear that lil sissy got sent to reform school for stealing out Pastor's house."

"Who?" Billy asked. He was still shook up about from the first question to remember about Earl.

"That faggot from over on the Westside! The one stay by my grandma 'ndem," Byron reminded.

"Oh yeah. He did?" he asked sincerely since he hadn't heard what the outcome had been.

Earl actually didn't have to go to reform school. The judge had given him the option of two years community service or one year in the reformatory. Once Earl heard about being in a dorm with thirty other boys he chose jail. This is where the adage 'happy as a faggot in jail' began.

"Anyway," Leroy tossed in, indicating a change of subjects, "I may pull that sissy into my stable once he get home. I got a couple of white men who love black boy pussy."

"Leroy say he gone let us get us a stable too!" Byron cheered.

"Sho'nuff," Billy replied with a lack of enthusiasm that pissed Leroy off.

"What, you still slangin' dick boy? You still a hoe?" the pimp taunted.

"You mean am I still having sex with women all over town and getting paid to do it? Yes! Hell yes!" Billy shot back.

"Look boy, I'm tryna get you straight! Gonna start you off with a couple used whores and..."

"I'm good. I just need some reefer fo' me and my mama. I gotta go make my rounds," Billy quipped. It amused him to piss the pimp off. It shouldn't have though because Leroy was a very, very dangerous man.

****

"Woooo-weee!" Bernice shouted as Billy pounded her to yet another orgasm. A glance at the wind up clock on the dresser revealed that she still had six minutes left so she pulled her legs back in search of another one.

"Mm hm," Billy hummed as he gave her the business. He too kept an eye on the clock on the dresser. When her paid half hour eclipsed he stopped abruptly mid-stroke.

"Un uh! Please! I'm right there," she pleaded. She threw her hips up stealing a few more strokes until Billy snatched out of her.

"You wanna 'nother half hour?" he asked getting out of the bed. Bernice quickly scrambled over to get her purse in reply.

Once the ten dollar bill was in hand he pushed back inside. His customer service skills may have been fucked up but he always got the job done. Bernice came so hard the next time that she moved the bed six inches. When the time elapsed again she went back into her purse once more but it was not to be.

"I cain't," Billy said in sorrow as he mourned the money he'd just turned down. "I gotta go get some sleep. I gotta preach in the morning."

****

"You fo' real?" Lady asked for the tenth time as she dressed for church. The news of her child preaching in the church had snapped her out of her funk –literally since she'd even bathed herself that morning. Lady was back!

"Yes, Mama. Sho' nuff. Pastor said I'm ready!" he repeated, even though he'd missed the double entendre of the words. "If I do good, I mean, well, Pastor say he gon' buy us a car!"

"Chile, you cain't get no license yet!" Lady squealed in delight at the good news. She was hoping he would overcome that hurdle and he did.

"My birthday ain't too far off, remember," he reminded.

"Of course, I remember my baby's birthday!" she exclaimed. Her mood darkened as quickly as a southern storm rolling in when she also remembered that her daughter's birthday was just days away.

"Don't start, Mama!" Billy pleaded. It took too much out of them both when the depression set in. Luckily for both of them a horn honked out front signaling it was time to go. "Pastor sent Deacon Hunter to give us a ride."

"Ooh, my son is a big shot!" Lady cheered as she slipped into her church shoes and hat and hit the door.

****

The perfidious preacher viewed the pulpit as a stage, and he knew for a fact that his protégé would put on a good show. And since there was no business like show business he really showed out. Even his hype-man worked up a sweat trying to keep up with him. Every man needs a hype-man –again if you don't have one then you just might be one.

The collection plate stayed in motion the whole four hours that Pastor Paul hooped and hollered. He was trying to get all the twenties, tens, and fives before he passed the mic. After all it was still big bank take little bank. Final-fucking-ly, Pastor announced young Billy.

"Young Reverend Cash, are you ready to send 'em home?" he asked Billy, who sat, next to The First Lady, waiting. Billy nodded that he was and took to his feet. It still took Pastor Paul another twenty minutes to give up the stage. He almost sent the plate around once more but decided to at least let the youngster get some ones.

Billy took to the pulpit and closed his eyes as tightly as he did his mouth. When a full minute had passed people assumed he was praying, but he wasn't. Prayer required faith and the boy had none. No, he was just being dramatic, like Leroy did with his whores. Anytime one of them fucked up the pimp would shut his eyes and not say a word. Then when he finally did speak it would be even more dramatic.

"Take your time," you know who called out. Lady whipped her head around and smiled at her friend. He winked and she winked back and a tacit date was set. Lady was back to being a tramp.

"I'm 'bout to take my time!" Billy shot back sounding almost defiant. "Gon' take my time and tell you about the Glory of God!"

The congregation went wild at the oxymoron. God is far too glorious to be defined in a lifetime, let alone the hour he had. Still, he made a good show quoting scripture to fit his needs. Dwight 'Amened' and 'yes Lawded' behind him as he spoke.

Pastor Paul smiled despite being jealous of his performance. Even the collection plates came back full as people went into their other pocket to spend some of the money they put aside to spend. Lady got caught up in his rapture as well. She threw her hands in the air and waved them side to side like she just didn't care.

"Great job!" the preacher congratulated once they'd finished making small talk with the parishioners on their way out. "Come on to my office so I can take care of bizness."

"Um...I...um...gotta go with my mama. We..." Billy stammered for a way out.

"Go on head." Lady urged. "My friend and I gonna grab a bite."

"Okay Mama," he sighed and followed the pastor into his office. He felt somewhat safe in the office since it was in the church.

Pastor Paul flipped through Billy's collection plate with the dexterity of a cash machine. Billy frowned at the three way split knowing good and well the Lawd wasn't getting his cut. Still, it was a pocket full of cash and that's all that mattered.

Billy let out a sigh when Pastor kneeled before him. He just closed his eyes while he did his business below his belt. Once it was over he went home to change into his street clothes and hit the streets.

Chapter 19

Weak minded people equate money with power. That's why a clownish billionaire would eventually run for president in 2015. That's why Leroy played chess with real people. Moving whores like pawns, sacrificed for the king. That's why Billy started feeling himself at sixteen.

His pockets stayed full of money and his system stayed full of reefer and wine. Between preaching, drug runs, and dick slinging you couldn't tell him nothing. In fact, he got to the point where he thought he could call the shots.

"Not today!" Billy barked and swatted Pastor Paul's hand away from his zipper. The preacher frowned up as if perplexed by a tough question.

"What you mean, not today?" he asked. His money had tricked him into thinking he was powerful as well.

"I mean not today! You cain't suck my meat today! I may...LET you tomorrow, but NOT today," he said smugly.

"Sho' nuff," the preacher nodded as it all came together in his mind. He laughed out loud upon realizing that the boy was feeling himself.

And why wouldn't he when the weekend revivals were now called The Reverend Cash Revivals, and the congregation loved him so much that he now got an entire service to himself once a month. Those were big days for them both since they split the take 50/50. The Lawd didn't get a cut on those days.

"Sho' nuff. Now take me home!" Billy demanded.

"Pride comes before the fall," Pastor quoted.

"What you trying to say?" Billy asked and stepped to the man. Things would've come to blows if Mrs. Paul hadn't stepped in.

"Both of you calm down!" she insisted. The two were about to blow her high with all their bickering.

"Oh, I'll calm down once he gets out my house!" Pastor boomed.

"You brought me here, so you gon' take me back home!" came Billy's reply.

"Shit! I'll take you home. Go on outside and wait for me. Hear?" First Lady said pointing towards the door. Billy and Pastor locked eyes as Billy backed away towards the door.

"I'ma fix that lil' nigga! I'ma learn him today!" Pastor vowed.

"Just calm down Pastor. I'll have a talk with him," his wife offered. However, it fell on deaf ears because Pastor wasn't trying to hear it. Billy had bit the hand that fed him and was now about to get bit back.

****

"Pastor got needs," Mrs. Paul said, finally breaking the silence as they rode. "He's a proud man, give him a couple of days."

"Mm hm," Billy grunted. His hubris convinced him that the man would come around begging him to come back. Have him tell it, Pastor needed him, not the other way around. Mrs. Paul just shook her head. She knew her husband was a punk, but he wasn't a *punk*.

"Where we going?" Billy frowned as he saw his street in passing.

"Pastor's wife got needs too," she replied. Mrs. Paul was high as a kite and horny and had decided that she was not letting this opportunity pass her by.

"So do I and they cost money," he shot back arrogantly and got laughed at.

"Boy, stop!" she cackled and cracked up. "Don't confuse me for one of those broads you sexing for money. Shit, as good as my pussy is, you should be paying me!"

The chastisement put him in his place and shut his mouth. Mrs. Paul drove into the park and parked on the far side away from everyone. She then got out of the front seat and got back in the back. Billy watched her hike her skirt over her hips and pull her panties off. Her bushy vagina was already glistening wet in anticipation.

"Come on back here boy!" she ordered while making little circles on her clit. One leg went over the seat while the other one went near the back window.

Billy finally got out and got in the back. He was already rock hard when he pulled his pants down but still watched the show. She began to shake and buck as her climax drew near.

"Go on and cum for me," he said in a voice that got deeper by the day.

"O-o-o-okay," she shouted as she did just that. "Okay, now boy don't play in it. I want you to fuck the shit outta me!"

"I plan to," he replied and plunged inside of her savagely.

"Grrrr...grrrr" she growled feeling him at the bottom of her box.

"Shit!" Billy shouted seeing she wasn't just talking shit about how good her pussy was. His mind flashed to the cash in his pocket ready to part with a little of it.

The car practically came off the ground as it bounced like an L.A low rider as the two went at it. Billy tried to punish the woman for the sins of her husband, but she kept having multiple orgasms. A few spectators had gathered around and were trying to peek through the fogged up windows. Having an audience only made Billy want to go harder.

"Shit!" he shouted again when he couldn't hold out another second. He quickly snatched himself out of her hot bubbly snatch and scrambled up to her face.

"Aaaaah!" Mrs. Paul moaned opening her mouth and making a target for him to skeet into. Billy milked himself dry, pulled up his pants, and then got out of the car while Mrs. Paul used her panties to clean the semen from her face, pulled her skirt down, and then got out to a bunch of smiling faces. Upon stepping out the car she tossed her panties to the pavement and got back behind the wheel. The ride to Billy's house was made in complete silence, after all, what was left to be said.

****

"What now?" Billy asked aloud when he saw two police cars in front of his house. He hoped nothing was wrong with his mother then saw her come out raising hell.

"Uh oh," Mrs. Paul muttered to herself knowingly. She knew her husband well enough to know this was some of his shit.

"Boy, you told me he gave you all that stuff!" Lady shouted at her son as he approached her. One of the police held up watches, bracelets, and rings to answer the question on Billy's face.

"He did!" Billy swore and turned back to Mrs. Paul for confirmation. Turned just in time to see her pull from the curb and drive down the block. Not only was she not going to contradict her husband, but her purse was full of weed. "I swear fo' G-."

Lady slapped the 'od' back down his throat as another cop came and put handcuffs on him. A third cop came out of the house with all of his new clothes and shoes, since Pastor had claimed that he'd stolen those too.

When you bite the hand that feeds you sometimes it bites you back, and other times it slaps the shit out of you.

Chapter 20

Billy knew he was in trouble when he went to court. It was the first day of his trial and he was just finally meeting his public defender. The five hundred pound white man had his greasy hair pulled into a dirty looking ponytail. His suit had an eclectic design on it from a variety of food and beverage stains going back since the last time it was cleaned. If the man didn't care about himself he certainly couldn't and wouldn't give a fuck about his client.

Both the attorney and the judge read the complaint lodged against Billy by Pastor Paul. The wrinkled old man up on the bench peered over his glasses with a look of displeasure upon his face from what he was reading. Billy's lawyer also set shaking his head in distain. Neither were good signs.

"So you stole from the preacher, huh? The person who was tryna help you," the judge said in disgust. Lady shook her head in shame when the words hit her ears.

"Sir I..." Billy began but was quickly hushed by his so-called lawyer. The man sucked some dried coffee from his mustache before he finally spoke up.

"Yo Honor, my client would like to plead guilty and throw himself on the mercy of the court," he decided all on his own.

"I would?" Billy asked surprised by the decision he didn't make.

"Well, in that case, I sentence you to...forty years in the state penitentiary," the judge said. He had been getting rid of niggers forty years at a time for the last forty years. He added forty more years to the tally etched into his desk.

"Yo Honor, Sir, that's more than fair 'cept it's mo' than the law allows. This boy here is a minor," Billy's lawyer said in his defense.

"A minor! He shol' is a biggin'!" the judged judged as if at a slave auction. "Damn it, I can only send him away until he turns eighteen. I'll get my forty years next time you come in front of me."

"Say thank ya, boy!" his public defender demanded.

"Fo' what?" Billy wanted to know. He was quickly shackled at his ankles and wrists for the shuffle back to the jail.

"My baby," Lady muttered heartbroken. It'd just dawned on her that she would now be alone. Lady could not function alone.

Leroy twisted his lips as if to say 'ain't this some shit'. He was right too because it was some shit; it was some bullshit to be specific. However, he couldn't help but to shoot the boy an 'I told you so' look as he passed. The pimp now had two years to ensure that the boy had nothing and no one else to turn to but him.

****

"Is that her?" Leroy asked when Shawna emerged from her house. With her dick supply cut off she was once again on her way to The Rib Shack to get her eat on.

"Shol' is!" Byron acknowledged from the passenger seat of the pimp's car. He missed his partner already but was delighted to be riding shot gun in the pimp's pimp mobile. It had a diamond in the back, a sunroof top, so he gangsta leaned.

"Watch how a pimp, pimps," the pimp said as he pulled up on the chubby girl. "Hey pretty lady!"

Shawna looked around to see who he was talking to but saw no one. She was actually pretty but had never heard if from a man before. Billy had once blurted that she had some good pussy, but that was as close as it got.

"Yeah you. What yo' name is? Where ya headed?"

"Shawna," Shawna replied and then giggled into her hands. "I was finna go get somethin' to eat."

"Hop in, I'll feed you," Leroy demanded. Shawna climbed into the back of the car and the pimp took her home.

The only thing Leroy gave her to eat was dick, and plenty of it. He put the dick to her every which way but loose. Billy had one stroke, hard and long, but the mature man hit her in a variety of positions, speeds, and angles. She came so many times that she'd lost count. Once she finally stopped shaking and shivering from the last orgasm she reached for her purse.

"This all I have on me," she said apologetically as she attempted to hand him the money. Surely she had gotten more than twenty bucks worth of fucking.

"Baby, keep yo' money! Men 'posed to pay to get some of this sweet ass," the pimp spit.

"Fo' real?" she shot back. The concept of getting paid to feel good intrigued the hell out of the young naïve girl. Hell it beat the hell out of the assembly line she stood at for eight hours a day.

"Hell yeah! Matter of fact..." Leroy said as he hopped out the bed and left the room. Shawna locked her eyes on the pimp's swinging dick and got hypnotized. He came back in with a small tin containing a beige powder. "Here, since I ain't got no cash."

"How I do it?" she asked, instead of saying hell no and running for her life.

Leroy showed her how to use her pinky nail as a scoop and to snort some heroin up into each nostril. Shawna got so high so fast that even she knew that she was hooked. After Leroy put the dick to her once more she was a good girl gone bad. She ended up parting with that twenty anyway. She used it to buy some of the powder that made her feel so good.

"Who next?" Leroy asked after he dropped Shawna back off at home.

"Um...Bernice, Shonda, Shonda's mama, um..." Byron said, naming off all the women that he knew who paid to get laid by Billy.

Leroy put the car back into gear and set out to get them all. Pimp or die.

Chapter 21

"State yo' name, city you from, and the crime that got you sent here!" the reform school guard shouted an inch from Billy's face.

The redneck guard had deep wrinkles in his tanned skin making it look like a piece of leather. He was so close that he spewed tobacco juice along with pieces of the hog maws he'd eaten for lunch. Billy let out a deep sigh trying to keep his composure.

If being sent to reform school for two years for a crime he didn't commit wasn't bad enough the ride up to the mountains pushed it over the top. The small country town only had one stop sign in it and it actually said 'whoa'.

"William Cash. Memphis and I ain't did nothing!" Billy snapped through clenched teeth. The guard gave pause to his attitude before moving on to the other two juveniles that had come in with him from the Memphis jail.

"Name, city, and crime!" the cop demanded down the line. Once all the introductions were made the boys were shown the gun line. "You know why we call it the gun line? Cuz if you cross it we gon' gun yo' black ass down!"

Next came the next stage of degradation. The three guards plopped down in their chairs, cracked cold beers, and ordered the boys to strip. They had no strip clubs, so this would have to do.

"Must be half Chinese," the first cop joked when the first boy dropped his trousers.

"This one is only half black." The next cop joked upon seeing the next boy's dick.

"Dayum!" they all shouted when Billy came out of his clothes.

"Let me see that thing!" one said rushing over for a closer look. Billy flinched when he leaned in and cocked his head sideways. "He had to fuck his mama when he came out her black box!"

"Is that right boy? You fucked yo' mama?" another joked.

"No, but I fucked yo' mama! Right in her fat ass!" Billy snapped. The two other boys took a side step away from his so that they wouldn't catch what he was about to catch.

Not only did the redneck guards at the reform school get a kick out of ribbing the boys they also got a real kick out of kicking the boys in their ribs, asses, and heads. Some of the boys lived, some died. Some even got dragged across the gun line and shot dead.

"What did that nigga just say, Bubba?" the cop standing next to him asked.

"I believe he said he put that thang up in Aunt Betty!" he replied.

"That's what I thought he said," he said raising his stick.

"Just hol' up one second, Jethro! We don't need them folks from the state down here again!" Bubba protested. They had just been investigated for a death barely a week ago. Of course they had gotten cleared, but they didn't need them back so soon.

"You right, you right!" he nodded lowering the stick. "A yellow wicked smile spread across his face as an idea popped into his mind. "This here boy said he was from Nashville didn't he Bubba?"

"No, he said Mem-. Oh yeah, I sure believe he did. Guess we best put him in the Nashville dorm then," the cop laughed. Billy frowned curiously trying to figure out the punch line that cracked the crackers up. He was about to find out real soon.

See, somewhere along the line black people had gotten life fucked up. They'd started believing that black lives only mattered if you wore the same color or are from the same hood –if you weren't or didn't then you were dead. Because of this the dorms had to be segregated and separated by city. Nashville had a dorm as did Chattanooga, Memphis, and every other city. Anytime the guards wanted to punish a boy they tossed him in the wrong dorm.

****

"Y'all boys smoking good, I see!" Bubba barked as he stepped into the Nashville dorm. No one was worried since he was the one who supplied the reefer, wine, and whatever else the boys could afford.

All eyes shot to Billy and looked him up and down as he entered the dorm. Faces frowned when no one could claim him. The boys looked at each trying to see if anyone knew him, but no one did.

"Alright, y'all boys have fun," the cop laughed as he closed the door behind himself. They didn't lock it since they had the gun line.

"Where you from nigga?" Hambone demanded. The super-sized black boy ran the Nashville dorm and called the shots.

"Memphis!" Billy said loud and proud and got his ass whooped. He was punched and kicked until he was lumped up, bloody, bruised, and sound asleep.

"I should fuck him!" Hambone announced. That, of course, woke Billy up and he fought for the life of his butthole.

"It ain't going down like that!" Pickle from Memphis shouted as he and the rest of the Memphis boys stormed in. There was a brief standoff as they debated on going to war or not.

"Man...y'all take this lil' bitch back to Memphis," Hambone said to the relief of most.

A large boy from Memphis picked Billy up and put him over his shoulder. Billy was snoring lightly from the beating when they made it back to the dorm.

"Guess he gotta go in the boom-boom room with Camille," he said, seeing that the other new boys had already taken all the other open rooms.

"Long as he respect the line he'll be a'right," Pickle said.

"Oh my!" Camille shrieked when they barged in on a blow job.

"Un uh, come on," the boy said as he guided Camille's head back into position to finish giving him head. Camille complied, finished him off, and then sent him away for a nap. She then went over and frowned down at the sleeping stranger and realized that she knew him. She was still staring down at him when he awoke. Billy grimaced from the bumps and bruises from getting his ass kicked. He looked up at the girl standing over him and strained to recall where he knew her from. The long hair and lipstick slowed up the identification, but it finally dawned on him.

"Earl! What you doing here?"

Chapter 22

"Who's next?" Leroy asked when he finished with Bernice. He had already ran through Shawna, Shonda, and Shonda's mama. He had them hooked on both the dick and dope, pushing Billy far, far from their minds.

"That's all I know of," Byron shrugged. His not knowing about the waitress and a couple others saved them from the misery that Leroy had to offer.

"Nah, there is one mo' I gotta get!" Leroy nodded in agreement with his sinister plot. When Billy came home he wouldn't have anyone to turn to but him. Not even his closest friend Byron.

Byron watched the pimp carefully as he unfolded a tin of heroin. He scooped a little into his pinky nail and turned to Byron. Byron quickly averted his eyes as he always did which allowed the pimp to dump the powder back into the tin. Byron turned back around in time to see Leroy snort nothing but air up each nostril.

"You wanna hit this boy? You ready to be a man, yet?" the pimp dared. Leroy took the liberty of scooping some more out with his nail, knowing that the impressionable youth wouldn't be able to say no –he would've said no had Billy been around, but he wasn't so...

"No, yes, I mean I..." Byron stuttered. Leroy made up his mind for him by sticking his pinky under one of his nostrils.

"Sniff!" the pimp ordered and the teen sniffed.

"Ugh!" the teen reeled as the bitter powder entered into his life. There wasn't much time to think before Leroy pushed his full pinky nail under his other nostril.

"'Bout to drop you off. I gots some pimpin' to do," Leroy announced and put the Caddie in gear. Byron's chin hit his chest as he went into a deep nod. It was the beginning of the end.

****

Billy found out real quick why his room was designated as the boom-boom room. Shortly after breakfast the boys began stopping by to spend a few minutes inside of Camille's mouth. He was so exhausted from the trip and getting his ass whooped that he just laid in his bunk and tried to ignore the slurping, moans, and eventual grunts of satisfaction coming from the next bunk. He didn't come from under his sheet until chow was called.

"Trays up! Y'all niggas come eat!" the guard yelled when the orderly brought in the noon meal.

Saturday and Sundays offered sandwiches and soup while Monday through Friday were spent in the fields. Lunch on those day was a sandwich of thick peanut butter and water. The boys picked cotton and other crops from sun-up to sundown. Billy arrived on a Friday so he had no idea what was in store for him.

"You better go eat! Them niggas ain't gon' save none," Earl warned.

"Oh, okay. Thanks," Billy said sitting up on his bed. He looked over at the boy he knew and saw a girl that he didn't know. He'd taken a pillowcase and fashioned a short skirt out of it and his already long hair was now even longer and slicked back with pomade. He'd used the dyes from candy to create lip-gloss and eyeliner to complete his transformation.

"You ain't eatin'?" Billy asked as he stood to go eat.

"Un uh, I'm full!" he said rubbing his flat belly.

"I bet!" Billy laughed. The boy had been swallowing cum all morning so it was no wonder that he was full.

Billy's presence at the table in the day area caused a brief pause, then the action resumed. He too paused for a second to figure out the protocol. It was each man for himself so he dug in. After grabbing a sandwich he held his bowl out so the orderly could ladle some soup inside of it. He sat down at the table and dug in.

"I heard you represented Memphis to the fullest," Pickle proclaimed. The other boys became mute when their leader spoke.

The large boy would be turning eighteen in a few weeks but he wouldn't be going home. The manslaughter charge he'd caught at fifteen meant he still owed the state another ten years. Billy peeped how the others deferred to him and realized that he was in charge. He paused for a second to mull his words over before he released them.

"Leroy Johnson told me not to come home if'n I didn't," he replied. The weight of the name he dropped opened most of the boy's eyes wide in amazement.

"Pimpin' Leroy, from the Southside?" a boy cocked his head and dared.

"That's the one!" Billy said lifting his chin proudly. Even Pickle nodded in admiration. The sad fact was that the ghetto kids didn't have many role models. The people who managed to make it out were gone and most didn't come back. All that was left was the ghetto superstars, the pimps, pushers, and robbers.

"You smoke?" Pickle asked. The smile on Billy's face answered for him before his words did.

"Sho'nuff, but...how we gone get some smoke in here?" Billy asked.

"That ain't never a problem!" another boy shouted while the rest of them cracked up.

Once the meal was complete several boys pulled out sacks of reefer while others ripped the pages from a bible and tore them into smaller pieces to be used as rolling papers. The common area soon filled with smoke, music, and laughter as the reefer and homemade wine was passed around.

"Hey now!" a boy cheered as Earl came out shaking his ass. He was helped on top of the table where he proceeded to bump and grind. Billy had absolutely no interest in seeing the sissy put on. He shook his head as he walked into his room.

"He think he too good to watch the show," a boy tattled to Pickle.

Pickle scrunched his face up to process the words and then shook his head no. He hadn't had any interest in the sissies when he'd first came in off the streets either. That was three years ago though and things had changed.

"He'll come around," Pickle decided. Why wouldn't he when Pickle himself had. Pickle turned back around and continued to watch the show with an erection throbbing in his coveralls.

Billy laid on his bed staring up at the ceiling. The wine and weed had put a goofy smile on his face as he lay there thinking that jail wouldn't be so bad with the wine and weed. That thought would change when he hit them fields come Monday morning.

"Shit!" Billy fussed when his solitude was invaded. Pickle came busting in cradling Earl in his arms.

"You can go or stay, but I'm finna get some of this pussy," Pickle announced. He tossed Earl on the bed and dropped his coveralls. Billy was already out the door when the sissy bent over doggy style. He wasn't the only one about to get hit from the back.

****

Lady wasn't expecting any company so she ignored the knock on her door. She figured it was some woman's husband looking to spend a few dollars on stuff that his wife wouldn't do, but she would. That's why her hair stayed laid and theirs didn't.

"Wish I might!" Lady huffed when she heard the knock again. Then it dawned on her that the factories didn't pay until next week and she didn't do credit. What she look like loaning out some pussy. It's not like she could take it back if someone decided not to pay up. Even she knew that pussy had more value before it was fucked. The fifth knock finally got her out of her bed and headed to the door. The small house creaked and complained as she marched to the front of it. She was going to read whoever was disturbing her night.

"Good evening, Lady," the male caller said smoothly as he ironed out his suit coat with his hands.

"What you doing here?" Lady shouted at the last man she'd expected to see at her door.

"Why I came to see you of course," Leroy said with a smoldering stick of reefer in his lips. It moved up and down when he spoke, but it didn't fall. It was some real fly pimp shit.

"See me! Fo' what?" Lady demanded, as she stepped aside so he could enter.

And enter he did. Leroy nodded as he looked around the small front room. He then walked over and copped a squat on the sofa while placing a bottle of wine on the table.

"I'll get us some glasses," Lady said and rushed into her kitchen. Leroy got a glance of all that ass she was toting under her night shirt. When she returned he passed her the weed. "Mm hm."

Leroy smiled at her sitting on the far end of the sofa. It was her way of playing hard to get. He lit another stick when the first one burned to an end. They sipped and smoked in silence for a while before he finally spoke.

"So why you ain't never tol' me or him?" he threw out.

"Would it have mattered?" Lady tossed back. Leroy ducked the question and poured the rest of the wine into the Mason jar glasses.

He waited a while for the weed and wine to really saturate Lady's being before putting some pimpin' in her ear.

"You miss me?" he asked so close in her ear that his lips brushed her ear lobes.

"Ye-, I mean...hell nah!" Lady tried to correct but it was too late. The words came out hoarse and her granny panties were soaked from her desire.

Leroy stood up and took her by the hand. When they reached the hall he fell back and let her lead the rest of the way into her bedroom. She didn't bother closing the door since neither of her children where home, one was in the ground and the other one was in jail. Instead she simply pulled her gown over her head, stepped out of her panties, and got on the bed and assumed the position.

That position was face down ass up, just like the pimp liked it. He dropped his trousers to his ankle and waddled over to her. Lady let out a loud hiss, like a tea kettle, when he slid that pimpin' into her life. He held onto her wide hips, like a school bus driver holding onto a big ass steering wheel, and began to dig her back out.

"Make me damn sick!" Lady moaned and complained when she came the first time. Leroy didn't buy it though.

"Mm hm," the pimp chuckled and kept right on driving that bus. Lady came a couple more times before Leroy finally busted a nut of his own. He decided not to pull out and let go deep inside her for old time's sake.

"Now see, 'member what happen last time you skeeted in me," Lady complained but still squeezed her walls tight around him and rocked her hips to milk him dry. Knowing he was the type to hit and run she decided to beat him to the punch and put him out. "You can go now."

"Not just yet. That was only round one. I'ma rock this thang all night," he said. To prove it he stepped out of his pants and pulled off his shirts. He then pulled out another stick and stuck it between her lips.

"Mm hm," Lady said as a thank you when Leroy lit a match for her to light the reefer. She took two puffs then tried to pass it but he declined."

"I'm cool," he declined shaking his head. He didn't smoke heroin.

Chapter 23

Camille had an open door and open mouth policy that kept Billy up all night long. They still held a grudge from the Pastor Paul days so Billy wouldn't touch him, not that Earl would have let him anyway. Monday morning rolled around as Monday mornings tend to do and it was time to go to work.

"Y'all get y'all black asses out them damn beds and get ready to work!" the guard shouted like an overseer on a plantation. The boys knew that being late out of the bed would cost them to be late in the fields so they rushed to get up and out.

Billy wasn't sure what to do so he did what everyone else did. He put on his coveralls and boots and filed into the day room. Breakfast consisted of grits, biscuits, and jelly and then it was time to hit the fields.

"Hell naw!" Billy protested when he saw cotton for as far as his eyes cold see.

"Don't worry 'bout dat. You coming wit' me," Pickle assured him. If he was connected to a major player like Leroy then Pickle wanted to be next to him.

"Okay," Billy replied in relief at not having to pick cotton like the other boys. Except Earl that is, he was the designated water boy/girl.

Pickle led the way through the fields and through the woods until they reached another field. A greener more pleasant looking field than the one they'd just left.

"That's..." Billy pointed in shock once he'd identified the crop.

"Shol' is!" Pickle exclaimed smiling at the rows and rows of marijuana plants. They were ripe with fat buds that made your fingers sticky from the resin. We 'llowed to carry some back in our pockets."

"Sho' nuff!" Billy replied and snatched a bud off. He quickly stuffed it into his pocket as other elite workers came from the tree line.

"We gotta fill the sacks first!" Pickle laughed. He then instructed Billy on what to do

"See, you got a new gal there Pickle!" Hambone, from Nashville, teased. Billy was ready to go fight but Pickle held him back.

"Prettier than that lil bitch you got with you," Pickle shot back. The two traded barbs until Billy realized that the leaders were cool. It was only the soldiers who fought.

Lunch was a ham and cheese sandwich chased by a soda pop courtesy of the police. They treated the chosen few picked to work their cash crop better than they treated the rest of the boys. It wasn't all good, but it wasn't all bad either.

****

Lady watched with an almost sexual anticipation as Leroy cooked a spoon of dope up. He then pulled the bubbling poison into a syringe and then plucked out the deadly air bubbles. Next he tied off her arm to find a vein.

"Mm hm," Lady said knowingly. She realized that he'd slowly strung her along until she was strung out. He'd eased her into addiction by laying the pipe when he came through. All that was replaced by the needle. He would pop through when she needed a fix and fix her.

"There she go," Leroy cheered when a fat vein popped up as if volunteering. He slid the needle inside and drew up a little blood. That was the old school equivalent to checking the internet connection speed.

"Mm hm," she repeated as she watched the drug disappear into her body. She felt the effects of it coursing through her before the syringe was emptied.

"That's right," he said soothingly as she began to nod. She didn't even notice when he slipped out to go pimpin'. He wasn't the only one pimpin'.

****

The air grew thick with tension as the weeks ticked away. There'd even been a few minor skirmishes as boys jockeyed for the crown that would be vacated when Pickle left. Everyone wanted to be the next HNIC, which ironically was a phrase coined by the racist guards. They didn't want to have to speak to all the niggers, just the Head Nigga In Charge. How that became a good thing is anyone's guess. It was probably the same logic behind turning being called a bad bitch into a compliment.

The position did have its perks though. Being the go to guy of the guards definitely had its rewards. First there was working the cash crop which paid in weed and free world food. Next was exclusive access to the only pussy in the house. Everyone was allowed to use Earl's mouth, but his tail belonged strictly to the HNIC.

The front runners to the position were Billy and Ox, a big high yellow man-child. Ox had whooped everyone's ass except for Pickle's and Billy's, and he was ready to try Billy.

Billy had a lot of support, however, because the boys liked him. Most respected that he didn't touch the sissy even if they did. The boy had the smooth speech of a politician/pimp/preacher that appealed to all.

Billy relieved his sexual pressure by jacking off several times a day. Sometimes at night while Earl slept across the small room, or so he thought. Sometimes Earl was actually sleeping, other times he was watching. The sissy still held a grudge from Pastor Paul's and therefore he never offered his services. He hoped to have the satisfaction of turning Billy down but he never asked. Instead he just lubed up his palm and pulled on his penis.

****

The moment of truth came a few days earlier than expected. While Pickle had a mean fight game, he sucked when it came to numbers. He knew his birthday was in two weeks but two weeks equaled twenty days, have him tell it.

"Pickle!" the guard stuck his head in and called. "Pack it up 'less you just wanna stay here with Earl." Pickle paused for a second to choose before deciding he'd rather leave. The sooner he left the sooner he'd finish his time and go home.

"Yay!" the crowd roared as they did anytime a boy got to go home. Never mind that half of them came back within a year. Half of the other half escaped coming back to reform school by turning eighteen and going to grown man prison, which is where Pickle was headed.

The revelry died down almost instantly once Pickle left the dorm. Ox and Billy were on opposite sides of the dorm, which allowed the other boys to show their allegiance by going to one end or the other. Earl switched his narrow ass over to Ox's side to show him his support. An eerie silence filled the air until Ox stood up and broke it.

"Guess we may as well get to it," the large boy stated as he stood. He made a big display of ripping his shirt off to reveal the ripples of muscles beneath it. Earl swooned, batted his lashes, and fanned himself at the display.

Billy wasn't impressed since he was six feet three inches of lean chocolate muscles himself. He didn't take his shirt off but everyone knew it since they all showered together in one large room He really had no desire to fight the boy or be the HNIC but a challenge was issued and he couldn't back down. Punk out in jail and the other men will be lining up outside your cell to use your mouth like they did Earl.

"Kick his ass Billy!" One of Billy's supporters said as he rose to his feet. The boy made sure to whisper it just in case he lost.

"I'm finna," Billy assured him and stepped forward. The two boys met in the middle of the dayroom where the tables had been pulled out of the way so that they could have room to fight.

Ox was still putting on by popping his knuckles and flexing his muscles, while Billy just threw up his dukes. The larger boy had no way of knowing that Billy had a mean fight game of his own, it had been honed on the rough streets of South Memphis, but he was about to find out quick, fast, hard, and in a hurry.

"Ugh!" Ox grunted as he threw a large looping haymaker. It was so slow that Billy actually laughed at it before ducking under it. He slipped the punch and let a savage body shot go. All the air was evicted from Ox's lungs when the punch connected.

Technically the fight was over at that point. The brutal beating that followed was more to let anyone else who may have had a thought about trying him not to. The body blow had bent Ox in half and a vicious knee to the mouth stood him straight back up. Not only did it stand him up but it also snaggled his tooth and put him directly in the path of a speeding right hook that put him on his ass. Billy proceeded to kick him to sleep and back awake again.

"Anybody don't like what I did?" he asked turning slowly to catch each eye. The eyes don't lie even if the mouth does. No one spoke up so he nodded in acceptance of his new position. "Y'all clean him up, fi' up some of that reefer, and break out the buck!"

The crowd cheered and proceeded to get their party on. Earl had a sour face at now belonging to the boy who had stolen Pastor from him. He sucked his teeth knowing what he'd be sucking next.

****

To Earl's surprise Billy still showed no interest in him. That night he once again pulled out and pulled on his dick until he got off. Then he rolled over and went to sleep. Changes would come with the morning's sun. There wouldn't be many, but they would be drastic.

"Knock, knock," Randy called out before sticking his head in the door. "You mind if I get straight?"

'Getting Straight' was the oxymoron the boys used to refer to having sex with Earl. In actuality it's gay, not straight. Most boys felt like getting oral sex from him didn't make them gay, but they were wrong. Others felt that it wasn't gay since they were locked up, but they were wrong as well. All that shit is gay and so are they.

Billy felt like he had been sexually abused by Pastor Paul. He wasn't gay and that's why he didn't touch the sissy in the room with him. He may not have had a choice then, but he had one now. He chose no.

"I don't mind at all!" Billy said genially as he stood to leave so they could have some privacy. He stopped just short of leaving as if an afterthought and explained the new rules. "'Cept now it cost to get straight."

"Huh?" both Earl and Randy asked as if the meaning of the words weren't clear. They were. Billy was a pimp and this was pimpin'.

"Shit cost now! At least a dollar. I'll take cash, reefer, tobacco, or some buck," Billy explained. He really didn't care for Earl much and would have sold his brown ass for a brown penny.

"I got a dollar in my locker," Randy whined. He wanted to hold on to it, but he wanted to 'get straight' too.

"Well, go get it then!" Billy ordered, sending him rushing out the room.

"So, how much I get?" Earl asked with his hand on his hip.

"Bitch, I'ma pimp! You ain't getting shit but the dick!"

Chapter 24

"Shit!" Billy fussed when another orgasm escaped him. He had a handful of lotion and dick, but all he got from all his stroking was a sore arm. He would get right to the verge of an orgasm just to have it slip away.

Every time he got close memories of his dearly departed sister would invade his mind. He then stroked even harder to prevent his conscious from winning. That's the sign of a true monster. Even a regular fucked up person is held back by scruples, but a monster didn't give a fuck. The devil himself couldn't corrupt this one because he was already corrupt on his own.

"Let me help," Earl finally offered. He'd watched the torment for an hour and felt bad for Billy. All that pulling and no payout was like being a loser at a Las Vegas slot machine.

"Hell naw!" Billy screamed, only in his mind because his mouth remained shut. Earl took his silence as a tacit yes and quickly crossed the room. Billy watched helplessly as the sissy went down on him. His whole body flinched when Earl's hot mouth engulfed him. He closed his eyes to pretend that he was a she, but then opened them back up to watch his head bob in the darkness.

"Mmph," Earl grunted when Billy's explosion caught him off guard. He kept his mouth locked around him as Billy writhed beneath him. He swallowed with a loud gulp and stood. He took one step towards his own bed before Billy stopped him. He took his hand and pulled him back.

"Lay down!" Billy ordered. Earl did and Billy fucked him, with his nasty ass.

****

"Okay, I got two dollars, two sticks, and a pint of buck!" Randy announced when he returned. His dollar had gotten him sent away so he'd gone and collected all he could. He obviously really wanted to 'get straight'.

"It's over with," Billy announced with Earl laying with his head in his lap. "You may as well smoke that reefer and drank that buck cuz shop closed!"

"Closed?" he asked as if it were a new word. He understood the word but didn't understand why Billy was now cuffing the only sissy in the house.

The dorm flipped often as boys came in and out of the revolving correction doors. Sometimes they got lucky and had two or three sissies, and other times drought struck like a famine and they had one or none. The truth of the matter was that Earl was leaving in a couple of weeks so Billy decided to keep him to himself. Randy made a *'will you look at this shit here'* face and walked away shaking his head.

"So you want a party 'fo' you leave?" Billy asked, resuming the conversation while running his fingers through Earl's hair. "I'll tell Vincent to fix up some of his potato liquor."

"I guess," Earl sighed, like women do when they want a man to ask what's wrong.

"What's wrong?" Billy asked proving that it even worked for sissies, "Scared 'bout goin' home? Seeing Pastor Paul?"

"No. I ain't even going back to Memphis. I'm finna go to my Nana's house in Atlanta. Start me a whole new life."

"At-lanta!" Billy demanded as if it were preposterous.

"Un huh! I ain't never going back to Memphis!" Earl huffed.

"Wish I could go to At-lanta," Billy said wistfully. "I cain't tho' my mama need me."

****

"Please Leroy! I needs you!" Lady pleaded into the phone. She held the receiver in both hands, like *Lady Sings the Blues*, as she sang the blues, greens, and reds of a nasty withdrawal.

"I'll be through in a few," Leroy said and hung up. He liked for her to feel the pains of withdrawals before he gave her, her next fix. The lower she got the more she'd appreciate the high.

It was at least another hour before Leroy finally showed up. When he did he found Lady drenched in sweat and curled into a tight ball on her bed. Leroy got right to work and fixed her up a nice dose. He then pulled her arm free and prepped her for her medicine.

"Mmm, you my savior," Lady moaned as she felt the feelings of the drug enter her body.

"Thought you said Jesus was yo' savior?" the piece of shit mocked.

"No, you is!" she said, looking up for the first time and realizing that he wasn't alone. "Oh!"

"Don't fret none. This is my patna' Dave. I tol' him how good that pie was and he wanted to get a lil' slice. You don't mind, do you?"

"No, I don't mind," Lady said and laid back on her back. She spread her legs apart before departing into a dope induced nod. Lady hadn't bothered with panties in months so her bushy box was out in plain view.

"Hell yeah!" Dave clapped and cheered before he passed Leroy the agreed upon ten and dove in. Lady had already left the building so his fondling failed to lube her vagina. Dave shrugged, his indifference, spit on the head of his dick and shoved it inside of her.

"Slow down boy, you..." Leroy began but Dave cut him off.

"Oooooowweeeee!" he shouted and went completely stiff as he busted a nut. He shook and shivered then took a second to recover. Once he did he started stroking again.

"Nuh uh nigga, if you gon' go again you gotta pay again!" Leroy advised ready to snatch him out of the vagina in mid stroke.

"In...my...wallet!" Dave called over his shoulder. The pimp dug into his pocket and retrieved the other man's wallet. There was two more tens inside so he took them both.

This marked the first trick Lady would turn for Leroy. He could and would now mark her off his list of 'The Ones That Got Away'. There weren't many on it being that he had tracked them down and turned them out decades after adding them.

Leroy would have to save up shit to be a piece of shit because he wasn't shit and neither was his son. The old saying was true, the apple doesn't fall far from the tree.

Chapter 25

The last twenty-four hours had been hard on Earl. Billy had kept a hard dick in him for most of them. In fact, he had a mouthful of dick when the guard stuck his head in and yelled for him to pack it up.

"Mgfghpi," Earl mumbled, which translated to 'I gotta go' when you had a mouthful of dick.

"Okay," Billy grunted and threw his hips into overdrive. A minute later he presented him with a going away present. The two shared a hug before emerging from the room.

"Yay!" the boys all cheered at Earl's departure. This one would not be coming back. Mainly because he was eighteen, but also because he had a one way bus ticket to Atlanta, Georgia.

"Bye. Bye-bye!" Earl said as he skipped through the dorm. It wasn't long after he left that the mood turned serious. All the boys scanned each other with the same thing in mind, who could they fuck now.

"Hell naw! Not me!" Cat Eyes shouted when a few eyes locked on him. He wasn't gay or the least bit feminine, but he did have green eyes and that was close enough for the other boys.

"Well, somebody gotta get fucked! We needs us a fuck boy," Ox proclaimed. It was a tense couple of weeks. Tensions flared and fights broke out. It was good thing Carl came when he did.

****

"New meat!" the guard shouted and shoved the new boy inside. Even he knew that the timid child was in trouble.

Carl Clay was also from Memphis, but just barely. He'd grown up in one of the upper, outlying, middle class neighborhoods. As far out as you could be if you were black. He was also black, but once again just barely. Although he had curly hair and his skin was high yellow, courtesy of his white daddy, it wasn't enough to save him.

As a matter of fact, being light skinned with curly hair was enough to turn the boys on and his long lashes and girlish ways only made it worse. He wasn't gay, but he had very feminine mannerisms from being raised in a house full of girls. He'd also been raised with a silver spoon in his mouth which meant he'd never did a hard day's work which in turn left him soft and tender.

"All the way in the back, last room on the right," Billy directed. There were plenty of open bunks but he wanted first dibs on the pretty boy.

"Thank you," Carl replied and walked to the back with all eyes glued to his backside. Billy stuck his tongue out playfully as he followed him to their room.

"That's yours," Billy said and pointed to the bare mattress. "Make sure it's tight come Monday fo' inspection."

"Thank you," Carl said again fluttering his long lashes, making Billy hard.

"Mm hm," Billy said watching him bend to make his bed. "So, what you did? Why you here?"

"Because I was greedy," Carl admitted with a remorseful headshake. "I worked at the department store and stole some clothes."

"You fucking?" Billy blurted from sheer desire.

"Excuse me!" Carl demanded and spun around.

"Nothin'" he said taking his reaction as a no. That only meant he would have to take his time and seduce him. "Got a gal back home?"

"Yes, I certainly do!" he replied exuberantly. His whole face lit up at the very thought of her. He couldn't help but dig her picture out to show her off. He shouldn't have, but he did.

"Pretty," Billy grimaced when he looked at the picture of the gorgeous girl. He couldn't help but notice how much she looked like him. They both had light skin and hazel eyes. Her sandy brown hair looked like a halo over her head.

"Yes, AnJanay is very pretty," he said proudly. "She's going to wait for me for my six months. Then when I get out we're going to get married!"

"That's nice," Billy remarked. He was sincere in his sentiment, but still planned to fuck him. Her too if he could.

****

Carl stayed in the room all weekend and stayed out of trouble. That option was taken away from him when Monday morning rolled around. He was rolled out of the bed to work the fields like everyone else.

Billy debated on whether or not he should put him on the Elite Team to help tend the weed crop. In the end he decided the hard work might make his job a little easier.

"Pick cotton!" Carl shrieked in response to the answer of what they were doing there.

"That's right nigga, pick cotton! Now you can do it with or without my boot in yo' ass!" the guard clarified. The threat was enough to get him started.

"Sup with lil' mama?" Ox asked once he and Billy got to the rows of weed. "You gon' share or what?"

"She ain't shakin' nothin' yet. Give me a second to put this pimpin' on her," Billy replied. The two went back and forth referring to the boy as a girl as they did. That wasn't a good sign.

"After a few days in that sun she gon' be relieved to suck some dick in the shade!' Ox cracked and he was right.

****

"Y'all got ten minutes!" the guard yelled once they reached the dorm. Each dorm was allotted ten minutes in the shower so that supper could be served.

"New gal got a fat ass!" Cat Eyes called out when Carl got naked. He was relieved that he was no longer the object of desire.

"Yeah, he do," Billy agreed. The life of privilege had the boy soft which in turn had Billy hard. He grabbed his erection and began to pull while staring at the boy. He wasn't the only one. Almost everyone was jacking off in the shower and half of them were doing it with their eyes locked on Carl too.

"What the!" Carl screamed when he saw what was happening. The high pitch yell got a couple of the boys off instantly. He looked to Billy for him only to find that he was gunning for him too.

That was the first time Carl saw Billy masturbating but it wouldn't be the last. As a matter of fact, it wouldn't even be the last time he seen him doing it for the day. When Carl went back to the room he found Billy holding AnJanay's picture in one hand and his hard greasy dick in the other.

"Give me that!" Carl demanded while stomping his foot like an eight year old girl.

"Here," Billy said, extending his dick to the boy.

"Not that! Give me my picture," the boy whined with a double foot stomp.

"One...second...mmm...just one...ugh! Shit! Whew!" Billy exclaimed as he got off. Now that he was finished he handed him his picture back.

"Ewwww!" Carl shrieked upon seeing that Billy had skeeted on it a little. He grimaced as he wiped it off before putting it away.

The next day Carl walked in to find Billy reading one of his letters from AnJanay and jacking off. He read it aloud in a girly voice and got himself off again. Things had gotten bad, but they were about to get even worse.

****

"Mane, you still ain't cracked dat egg?" Ox asked again, like he had every day since Carl arrived two weeks ago. "And you say you s'posed to be a pimp!"

"I'm is!" Billy shot back feeling wounded by the other boy's insult. He was doubting his pimpin' and he took that personal. "Bet I hit that tonight!"

"Bet yo' crown!" Ox dared. He only had a few weeks to go on his sentence and he wanted to be king, if only for a minute.

"Huh? Um...yeah. Hell yeah! I bet I hit that tonight. You gon' hear it too!" he nodded confidently. "I'ma set it out too!"

"If you don't, I will! I'll sho' you how it's really done!" he shot back. The rest of the day was spent in silent contemplation of what was to come.

Carl held his head high and ignored the boys masturbating in the shower. His time got shorter by the day and soon he would be able to leave all this behind. He was almost surprised at not seeing Billy pulling on himself none that day. Then night fell and he found out why.

"Good night, my love," Carl said to his girlfriend's picture before giving it a kiss. He then laid it beside him on his pillow and flipped over to go to sleep.

Carl had a bad habit of sleeping on his stomach. Not only was it bad for the heart and lungs, but it was also bad because it gave Billy the opportunity to stare at the curve of his ass and jack off most nights, making him want the boy even more. Not tonight though. Tonight Billy stripped naked and crossed the room.

"W-wh-what are you doing?" Carl gasped when Billy landed on his back. His forearm on his neck held Carl in place while he tore away his underwear.

Carl let out a yell so loud and so shrill that it cleared the sleeping birds from the trees. Even they didn't want to hear a boy get raped. Ox and a few other of the sicker boys smiled with glee upon hearing what was taking place. Others thrust their fingers into their ears to shut out the blood curling screams.

"Hush now!" Billy warned. He then put AnJanay's picture on the back of the boy's head and proceeded to violate him.

The violence of it got Billy off just as much as the feeling of being inside the boy. The combination of the two ended the rape quickly. Not ended in the sense of being over, more like in the sense that it provided a pause. After taking a break to smoke a stick Billy raped him again. Then again. He raped the boy again and again through-out the night. No, the apple sure doesn't fall far from the tree.

Chapter 26

"You got lil' mama walking around her' bow legged! What it hit like?" Ox said when the two came out for breakfast. Carl was wandering around in a state of shock from the rape. He had a blank look in his eye as if he was being maneuvered by remote control.

"Pussy good and tight! I'ma see what that mouth talkin' 'bout tonight," Billy said as if the boy wasn't there.

"Mane, I thought you said you was gon' set it out once you broke it in," Ox whined.

"I'm is. Just give me a minute," Billy vowed. Billy wasn't much on honor, but he did believe in keeping his word when he gave it.

True to his word he raped Carl orally once the lights went out that night. Oddly, the boy didn't even put up a fight this time. He just stared off with a blank look upon his face. The lights were on, but no one was home.

The next day the fields were buzzing with excitement at the up-coming events. Poor Carl picked cotton while all of his peers plotted and planned. As soon as they hit the shower they attacked.

Billy whistled as he washed his muscular body. He was behaving extremely casual while Carl was being gang raped. The other boys ravaged him two at a time. He was fucked from every angle and in every orifice until everyone had had a turn. Billy didn't take part in the rape since he would have him all to himself later. That night Billy had his way with him.

****

"I can't continue to live like this," Carl told the smiling picture of An-Janay. "Just know that I'm always going to love you and that I'm sorry."

Carl took his last night of abuse in stride. He managed to hold his head high while once again being gang raped multiple times and again later that night when he was once again raped orally and anally by Billy when the lights went out. He held his head high because he'd already decided that this would be the last time any of it happened. The next day while out in the fields he took steps to make sure that it never happened again. Those steps were in the direction of the gun line.

"Where you goin', Nigga?" Cat Eyes asked when Carl started his march. Carl tilted his head in pride and kept on moving.

"Where you goin', Nigga?" a guard asked. He got the same answer so he racked his rifle and asked him again. "I said where you goin', Nigga?"

Carl took a deep breath, it would be his last, and took off running. The first shot deliberately struck the ground in front of him as a warning. When that failed to stop him the guard leveled his sights and as Carl stepped one foot over the gun line he gunned him down.

The instant death froze a smile on the boy's face, to be worn later at his funeral.

"What happened?" Billy shouted when he, Ox, and the other Elite boys came rushing to the cotton field. They'd heard the shouts and shots and came running to see who'd been shot.

"Damn fool tried to run off!" a guard explained in disbelief.

"That's cold!" Ox lamented and dropped his head in sorrow.

"Shol' is," Billy agreed with a pained expression on his face as well. "Now who we gon' fuck? Where's Cat Eyes?"

****

I'll be glad when this shit is over, Cat Eyes thought to himself. He certainly couldn't say it aloud with Billy's penis in his mouth. He'd fought the good fight once Carl was killed but Billy was too much for him. He did, at least, give him a choice between head or tail. He'd chosen head to save his tail. In the course of his multiple bids he'd seen multiple boys who lost control of their bowels from anal abuse. They were left dropping turds while they walked, like horses did.

It was almost over since it was both he and Billy's last night in jail. Ironically they shared the same birthday and therefore would be leaving on the same day. Billy had still insisted on one for the road. It too was almost over.

"Mmm baby, yeah AnJanay," Billy moaned to the picture in his hand as Cat Eyes worked him below. Cat Eyes heard the moan and braced himself for what he knew was to come, literally. "Argh!"

"Ptoo!" Cat Eyes spat it out in an act of defiance. Over the last few months that would have been a no-no but Billy decided to let it slide.

"Cain't wait to see my mama," Billy admitted. He'd tried to hold a grudge against Lady since she'd never returned any of his letters. He'd sent one last one asking her to meet him at the bus.

"I cain't wait to see mine either," Cat Eyes sighed.

"Well, you better brush first. Don't wanna kiss yo' mama with nut in yo' mouth!" Billy laughed. He always got a kick out of adding insult to injury. A blow job for the road was already bad enough, so Cat Eyes decided to keep his mouth closed so that he wouldn't get one last ass whooping for the road to go with it. His day was coming, that much he was sure of. He was right too, his day was definitely coming.

****

Going to the same city on the same day meant that Cat Eyes had to share a bus with Billy. Cat Eyes stayed as close to the front of the bus as the law would allow while Billy headed straight for the rear. He turned his nose up as he walked passed Cat Eyes since he didn't need him anymore. Let Billy tell it he was only gay in jail.

The late night sticks of reefer he'd smoked combined with staying up all night in anticipation of going home put him straight to sleep once the bus was in motion. He traveled light, only stuffing his pockets with reefer while leaving everything else behind.

"Hey Nigger! Nigger! It's your stop boy!" the driver yelled. Billy didn't budge so he marched to the back of the bus and nudged him with his foot. "Get up, Nigger! It's yo' stop!"

"Huh? Oh, thank you," Billy said when he realized where he was. He thought the driver was being courteous, but he wasn't. Billy had a ticket to Memphis and the driver was making sure that his black ass wasn't going an inch further than that.

Billy stepped off the bus and inhaled a deep breath of home. He immediately identified what was different about it as well as what had stayed the same. A beat cop walking by reminded him of all the reefer he'd stuffed in his pockets and that it was time to go.

He twisted his lips as he scanned the area looking for his mama. Seeing Cat Eyes hug and kiss his own mama made him chuckle at his own inside joke. When he resumed his search for Lady an old bag lady caught his eye as she nodded on a bench. She wore a red dress just like the one Lady wore for special occasions. The lady was too run down to be Lady so he passed over her with his eyes. An hour later he accepted the fact that his mama wasn't coming and lifted his feet to take the first of many, many steps towards home.

"Damn, err'body on the dope," Billy sighed as he waded through the addicts like a low tide. He tricked himself into thinking that Lady was at home cooking up a big homecoming dinner: candied yams, collard greens, a big ol' ham, hog maws...

"Dollar Bill!" a voice behind him called out accompanied by a car horn. Billy whipped his head around to see Leroy's old Cadillac pulling to a stop. He began to twist his lips up again until he noticed that it was Byron behind the wheel.

"Boy, what you doing driving a pimp car?" he asked as he came over to lean into the open window.

"Cuz, I'm a pimp and dis my car!" his friend shot back. "Now get yo' ass in, 'less you tryna walk way to the pool hall!"

"I need to go see my mama fo' I go anywhere. She probably done cooked me a big dinner," Billy said now that he had thoroughly convinced himself of it.

"Um..." Byron said, looking back at the bag lady on the bench. He didn't want to be the bearer of bad news so he didn't say anything. "Nigga, you needs to get you some pussy! I gots me a lil' stable now and I'll be glad to set you out a lil' bit."

"First things first. I gotta go see my mama. Then I'll fall through when I'm done," Billy insisted.

Byron changed the subject by passing him a thick stick of reefer. Billy debated over showing him his own stash, and shook his head. The two made small talk as they smoked and rode.

"Look-it!" Billy cheered and produced AnJanay's worn picture.

"Damn, she pretty! Who is she?" Byron wondered loudly.

"My gal. She been waiting on me," he replied since he'd convinced himself of that as well.

"Want me to run you over there?" he asked ready to make a detour to delay what was in store for his friend.

"Nah, I'll see her later," Billy replied. He still hadn't worked out the details to that situation. All he knew was that he was determined to make her his own. His desire for the girl had been marinating in his twisted mind for almost a year now. It was simmering in fantasy but would soon come to a full boil of madness.

"Okay," Byron shrugged and continued to the Southside. Their conversation came to an abrupt stop when the Caddie came to a stop in front of Lady's home. He slid Billy a small roll of cash as he got ready to exit the car.

The shot gun shack would have never had made it into Home and Garden magazine at its best, but seeing it at its worse took Billy's breath away. He blinked rapidly hoping that the sight would change, but it didn't. It took several attempts for him to manage to speak.

"I'll...um...later," he said as he stepped from the car. Byron stepped on the gas and pulled away.

The front door swung open allowing a feral cat to enter as a male junky exited. The man looked Billy up and down before scurrying off. The first step creaked loudly when he stepped on it but the second one snapped under his weight. He shook his head and continued on.

"Aaaahhh!" a female junky offered as soon as he stepped into the front room. The thought of sticking his dick into her raggedy mouth caused a frown to spread on his face as he passed.

"Mama! Mama!" Billy called as he marched passed the nasty kitchen. He grew up hearing sounds of sex coming from his mother's room, so he paused when he reached it. Hearing nothing he tapped on her door. "Mama!"

Billy proceeded to open the door only to find a couple having sex. The mattress was now on the floor which did away with the usual squeaking. He was relieved to see that the woman on the receiving end wasn't his mother, but that begged the question, "Where's Lady?"

"She...down...town," the man said not bothering to slow up his stroke as he spoke. "She...had to...pick...up...her...son."

Chapter 27

The long walk back to the bus station was made even longer by the thought of his mama sitting on that bench in a nod. He tried to tell himself that she was just tired from the walk, but the house full of Junkies wouldn't allow him to. He found her in the same spot he'd seen her in hours before when he'd gotten off the bus.

"Mama, I'm home, Mama!" Billy said gently as he stood over Lady. It took three tries but she was finally able to tilt her heavy head back enough to look back. The boy felt his knees buckle when the weather beaten face came up. It lifted to reveal a yellow smile held in place by grey gums.

"Is that my baby?" Lady cheered. She rocked back and forth trying to stand, but couldn't. Billy helped her up and then pulled her into his arms.

"It's me, Mama. I'm here," he said squeezing her tightly. "Come on, let's go home."

"We better wait for Mary. You know that gal still ain't came home!" Lady fussed. If Billy had, had a heart it would surely have broken, but he didn't so it didn't. Instead he got angry and somebody would soon feel it.

"Taxi!" Billy called as he tried to hail a cab. The white drivers looked at the young black boy holding up the black junky and kept right on driving.

An older black driver gave him a *'yeah right, I ain't hardly finna take yo' ass nowhere so you can hit me over the head and rob me'* look. He was about to push on until Billy pulled out some cash.

****

Billy's first order of business when they arrived back at home was to expel all the riff raff. He kicked out all the junkies along with the stray cat with a "Y'all get the fuck out! Now!"

"Will you look at this shit!" he fussed when he looked at the tub. He'd planned on giving his mama a bath but she would get even dirtier if he put here in there. It took some doing but he managed to get it clean.

Billy ignored his mother's nakedness and her stench as he stripped her to put her in the tub. He knew she needed to soak, a good while, so he left her to go clean up her room. The best he could do in her room was to drag the trash out to the curb.

Once Lady was washed he helped her into bed and tucked her in.

"I'll fix us up somethin' to eat," he said and left her to do just that. The gas was shut off so even if there had been some food in the house he still wouldn't be able to cook it. Instead of cooking he walked a block over and got them a couple of BBQ plates.

"Hey Baby! When did you get home?" Lady asked, as if it was the first time she'd seen Billy since his release.

"Just now, Mama. I bought you some dinner," he said softly. He had been back for hours but she'd been sleeping so soundly that he hadn't wanted to wake her.

"Thank yo-," Lady began then paused. Her face turned green and she threw up what little she had in her stomach. Junk food, wine, and cum mainly, all came back up. "I'm sick, baby. I needs me a hit!"

Billy knew enough about dope and dope addicts to know that saying no wasn't an option. He used the works he found in her nightstand and cooked up the small amount of dope. It wouldn't be enough to get her high but it should be enough to get her off sick.

"You a good boy," Lady purred as her son slid the needle into a well-used vein. Lady let out a sigh of relief and farted when the dope began to spread throughout her body. Once she nodded Billy got up and walked out. He could've called Byron but he needed the air so he walked.

****

"Is that Dollar Bill!" Leroy exclaimed when Billy walked in. He knew he was home and was shocked that it had taken so long for him to show up. Billy nodded in reply as he scanned the area for his friend. When he failed to find him he walked over to greet the pimp.

"Sup Leroy?" he said stoically as if he were the only one present. The sound of his voice lifted Mandy out of her nod momentarily. She cracked a smile and then resumed what she was doing.

"Where Byron?" Billy asked, looking around for him once more.

"Byron? You should be getting you some pussy and instead you worrying about Byron! What, you took a liking to that boy pussy while you was away, huh?" the pimp teased.

"Huh? NO! I ain't fuck no boys when I was down there," Billy said launching into a long story that told Leroy that he was lying. "They was fuckin', but not me! No sir! I..."

"Mandy take him to the back and fuck him," Leroy demanded. The prostitute popped up immediately to obey the order. This was actually the precursor to on-demand movies.

Billy was too embarrassed by the talk of boy pussy to say no to some real pussy, so he got up and followed her into one of the back rooms used to turn tricks. She fell back on the narrow bed and pulled her skirt up to her stomach.

Mandy didn't wear panties so her bushy box was in plain sight. Billy fondled it a bit to get it wet but it didn't respond. As a result he was soft and limp when he pulled out.

"What you waiting on?" Mandy wondered. She lifted her head and got the answer seeing he was still soft. She sat up and gulped him into her mouth.

Billy watched with curiosity as she worked her mouth on him. Her dry mouth also failed to get any results. It wasn't until thoughts of Carl popped into his head that he got an erection. Once the wood was good and solid she lay back again and spread her legs.

"Come on," Mandy invited and parted her lips with one hand and pulled him down by his dick with the other. "Go on hump!"

"Hump? It ain't even in yet," Billy replied. He looked down to correct the situation and found he was buried in to the hilt in her worn out box. He took a few pumps but barely felt her walls.

"What you doing?" Mandy protested when he pulled out and roughly flipped her over. She got her answer when he plunged inside of her anus. "I'm telling Leroy!"

"So!" Billy shot back and kept right on going. He didn't even bother pulling out when he came a few minutes later. When the spasms subsided he snatched out and stood. Mandy had fallen into another deep nod so he used her dress to wipe himself clean before leaving the room.

"You good?" Leroy asked with a wide grin. "Where Mandy?"

"Yeah, I'm good. She sleep," he replied and sat down. Leroy pushed a cold beer across to him and he quickly took a sip. Byron finally arrived and spared him from any more uncomfortable small talk with the pimp.

"There go my nigga!" Byron yelled as he slid into the booth. He slid a thick envelope over to Leroy and then hugged his friend.

Billy watched Leroy squeeze the envelope and then put it in his pocket. He wondered why he didn't count the money, not knowing that's what the squeeze was about.

"You ready to get you some money too?" Leroy asked, watching Billy watching him. "Yo' lil partna' got him a lil' stable, a caddy, and a pocket full of bread. Don't you boy?"

"Yassir!" Byron cheered and nodded.

"I guess so," Billy replied unsurely. He'd been the leader when he left so this new role was confusing to him.

"I'm finna take Dollar Bill out! Gon' get him high and get him some pussy!" Byron exclaimed. Billy couldn't help but notice the appeal in his tone. He was stating it, he wasn't asking for permission.

"Yeah, he look a lil' uptight. He done had some pussy, but he still definitely needs some reefer. We'll talk tomorrow," Leroy replied. The boys took their leave and walked out of the pool hall. Byron's car was right outside so they quickly got in.

"What he mean you got some pussy already?" Byron asked once they were seated in the car. He then pulled out a stick of reefer and pushed the car's lighter in.

"If you can call it that! Mandy got the Grand Canyon between her legs. I need to go find Shawna with that good-good, that wet-wet, that tight-tight!"

"There she go," Byron replied pointing towards the corner. Billy looked then squinted his eyes to look again.

"Where? All I see is some skinny junkies!" he gave up.

"That's Shawna, Shonda, and Bernice!" Byron said as he pointed them out. "They all work for me now."

"Damn, err'body on the dope now! Why you ain't tell me my mama was on it too?" Billy asked with pain in his voice.

"Cuz, it wouldn't have changed nothin'. I brang her somethin' err'day to keep her off the streets. That's the best I could do." Byron said solemnly. He then slid Billy a small package to take home.

"That's something," Billy said twisting his lips again at the thought that his mama could've been out on that corner too.

"Look-it!" Byron cheered as he pulled a long pistol from under his seat. "Case one of these niggas try me when I make my pick-ups fo' Leroy."

"Lemme see," Billy said reaching for the pistol. He felt a surge of power when the gun hit his hand. He looked at it lustfully as he studied the pistol in his palm. Byron watched with a curious frown since he'd never had the feeling. Then again he wasn't a killer.

"Here," he finally said trading the reefer for his gun back. He tucked it back under the seat and put the car in gear.

"Drop me by Shonda's house," Billy tossed out as they rode.

"Fo' what? She on the corner!" Byron said ready to turn around.

"Not fo' Shonda, I'm tryna see her mama!"

Chapter 28

"I gotta go," Billy announced when he saw the sun rising outside of the bedroom window. He looked down at Shonda's mama riding him backwards and repeated himself.

"Huh?" she asked looking over her shoulder. The fact that she picked up her pace told him that she'd heard him so he didn't bother repeating himself. Instead he took her hips in his hands and slammed himself upwards inside of her. She came with a grunt and then tipped over to catch her breath.

"I need to hol' yo' car until later, if it's okay?" he asked with great timing. The woman couldn't even catch her breath, let alone say no.

"O-o-o-ok," she huffed and puffed. If he had her car she figured he'd have to come back.

Billy pulled to a stop in front of his house and drifted off into his head. He wondered what he would find once he went inside. If he found Lady dead it would mean a lot less work for him. That thought quickly snapped him out of his head and into the house.

"Lady!" he called out hoping that she didn't answer. "Mama!"

"In here baby," Lady moaned. Billy stepped into her room to find her curled into a tight ball in the middle of her bed. "I needs my medicine. Is Leroy here?"

"Leroy?" Billy asked hotly. "Why you askin' 'bout him?"

"Where Byron at? I needs my shot!" Lady pleaded. She sounded so pitiful he didn't waste any more time fixing up her fix. He'd been so busy pleasing Shonda's mama that he'd left his own to wallow in sweat from the grips of withdrawals.

"That's right, mama," he replied softly to the satisfied smile spreading on her face. He waited until she went into a proper nod before he got up and left.

****

Billy's first stop in Shonda's mama car was to Stein Brother's Clothing. The two old Jews supplied the colorful clothes favored by the flamboyant pimps. He definitely wanted some clown clothes of his own, but today he was looking for something a little more conservative.

The dark grey suit, tie, and shoes he purchased ate up all the money Byron had given him, but it didn't matter. He may have been broke but he looked like a million dollars. He knew the address that he was headed to next like he knew the back of his own hand so he took the back streets to get there.

A scowl grew on Billy's handsome face when he drove by Pastor Paul's street on his way to his destination. It turned back into a smile as he looked at the upscale houses on the good side of town. He found his destination and pulled to a stop. The average person would have had to psyche themselves up to do what he was about to do, but not Dollar Bill. He wasn't the average person, he was psycho.

"Yes?" A very pretty, very light skin black lady asked when she pulled her door open. She couldn't help but to notice how handsome the caller was yet he was far too brown to be calling on her daughter.

"May I speak with AnJanay please?" Billy asked properly and politely, as he'd been taught to do in Junior Pastor Team.

"Why?" AnJanay's mother demanded. They were born and bred to be yellow and she intended to keep it that way. A brown grandchild would be unacceptable amongst her group of high society, high yellow friends.

"Who's there?" AnJanay asked when she heard her name. She looked around her mother to see the boy standing there.

"That's what I would like to know," her mother replied. "Are you selling something?"

"No, Ma'am. My name is Reverend Cash, William Cash and I'm with Pastor Paul at First Calvary Baptist Holiness Church of the Rock and..."

"Well, we attend First Presbyterian," the elder lady said and then began to close the door. The white folks allowed them to worship in their annex so they had no desire to hoop and holler with the niggers.

"Ma'am, I also counseled at the reform school. I knew Carl..." Billy said as the door shut in his face.

"Wait, Mother!" AnJanay insisted and pushed the door back open. Her mother let out a deep sigh and let her by. "You knew Carl?!"

"Yes, Ma'am. I met him along with the other boys at the reform school. I really took a liking to Carl. He was very warm, tender, and tight on the inside," Billy said contritely.

"Tight?" AnJanay's mother frowned.

"Bright, he was very bright. A very smart young man," Billy quickly corrected.

"He sure was! I can't believe that he's gone," AnJanay moaned and broke down into sobs. Her mother shot the intruder a *'look what you did now'* glance from the side. It had taken months to get her daughter to stop crying after Carl's death and just that quickly it had started back up again. To be honest, she was quite relieved that Carl wouldn't be coming back, after embarrassing them all.

"I...don't have..." Billy said as he patted himself down for a hand-kerchief.

"I'll get a tissue," her mother sighed and turned to go get one. Bil-ly wasted no time whipping out a pen and piece of paper.

"Give me your number, so I can call and counsel you," he urged. She got caught up in his sense of urgency and quickly scribbled down her number. He put it in his pocket just in the nick of time.

"Here you are, dear" her mother said when she returned. She frowned suspiciously, feeling like she'd just missed something.

"Well, thank you for stopping by. I'm glad that Carl had nice people in his life in his last days," AnJanay sniffled.

"It was a pleasure to be with him. I really got into Carl," Billy said. He then offered a slight curtsey before turning to leave. Both women watched his butt as he walked away. They didn't close the door until he reached his car.

Chapter 29

"You ready to get this money?" Byron asked when Billy got into his car. He already knew the answer so he didn't bother waiting for a reply. "This shit is easy money!"

"All we gotta do is pick up sacks of money? We ain't gotta count it or nothing?" Billy asked again trying to make sense of it. He saw Leroy pocket the envelopes with never anything more than a squeeze. *'If no one counted it how would they know if any was missing?'* he pondered.

"Nah, we don't even open it. Just take it from here to there," By-ron shrugged. They rode in silence except for James Brown telling the world he felt good.

The first stop was Dynamite's Fried Chicken, a well-known greasy spoon that served up bomb fried chicken and fat nickel sacks of heroin. Billy hopped out and followed Byron inside. He chuckled inwardly at himself now being the follower. It's hard for a leader to be a follower. Sometimes it's impossible.

"Hey Theo, this here's Dollar Bill!" Byron introduced enthusiastically when they entered the back office.

"Mm hm," Theo replied as he handed over Leroy's money. He looked Billy up and down to take a mental picture of him for future reference.

"Hey Theo," Billy greeted and got yet another grunt in exchange. He shrugged his shoulders and followed the new leader back out the door.

The two old friends chatted, laughed, and smoked just like old times as they rode around Memphis. High or not high Billy memorized every stop along with the names and faces along the route. An unofficial moment of silence was declared when they passed by First Calvary Baptist Holiness Church of the Rock. Billy tried not to look, but his head, as if of its own accord, still turned in that direction.

"Say, Dollar Bill..." his friend called getting his attention. "You ain't really steal from the preacher's house did you?"

"Hell naw! I fucked his wife though. That's why he lied on me," Billy said in his classic half-truth style –just like the devil does, tells one truth and adds hundreds of lies.

"Sho' nuff, you fucked the preacher's wife?" Byron laughed.

"Shol' did! And I'ma fuck her again, if I get the chance!"

****

It only took a week or so before Billy realized that his friend was using too. He wasn't just holding boy for his whores or to take to Lady. No, he was putting that shit up his nose too. He wasn't mad about his friend's drug use, instead Billy saw it as his way to take the lead.

"May as well let me run inside and make the pick-up. Save us some time," Billy offered as they neared the first stop on the route. He saw that his friend's nose was running and that he was getting antsy. Those were the same signs Lady exhibited when she was ready for a fix.

"It would, wouldn't it?" Byron agreed. Billy had assumed correctly because he was trying to figure out a way to get a bump without his partner seeing him.

"Hell yeah. Just pull up and I'll run in," Billy assured him.

"Where's Byron?" Theo asked when Billy came in alone. Not that it really mattered, since Leroy had already confirmed the boy's position. He was just nosey.

"He in the car," Billy frowned hoping he didn't fuck up.

"Oh, okay," Theo shrugged and passed him the cash. Billy nodded and turned to leave. He took quick steps to make up for the quick detour he'd planned.

He looked both ways, as if he was crossing the street, then crossed the line instead. Byron was too busy tending to his addiction to see Billy slip into the bathroom. Once inside he broke rule number one by opening the package. He then broke rule number two by pinching off a few bills. Remembering that he'd never seen anyone count the money he pinched off a couple more.

Billy took a few dollars from every stop on the route. He then gave the envelopes to Byron once he got back in the car so that it would be him that presented them to Leroy at the end of the night.

"Dollar Bill and Bye-Bye Byron," the pimp greeted cheerfully when they arrived back at the pool hall. He was chatting it up as Byron handed over the money. He was too busy looking at some young girls at the pool table to notice Leroy's reaction to his squeeze. "Yeah I..."

"Huh?" Byron asked finally turning to face the pimp.

"Nothin'" Leroy said as he began to think. He'd sold the same amount of dope for the same amount of money so the envelope should have the same amount of squeeze, but it didn't. "Err' thang went okay?"

"Yeah," Billy replied as his buddy winked and waved at the girls. Even he had to admit that he looked guilty, even though he knew that he wasn't.

"So, what y'all boys getting into tonight?" Leroy asked them. It too was a test and Byron failed it too.

"Finna spend a lil' bread on that one right there!" he said as the giggling teen waved back.

"I gotta see 'bout my mama," Billy sighed. It was yet another half-truth since he had plans on fucking Shonda's mama and then talking to AnJanay on the phone. The pretty girl would call late at night after her parents were sleep.

Billy was taking things slow and easy with her. They'd made plans for an ice-cream date in a couple of days. She would be spending a night with friends and they planned to steal an hour to talk face to face.

"Okay, y'all boys have a good night," Leroy said dismissing them both. They both stood to leave until he called Billy back. "Let me get a quick word with you Dollar Bill."

"Sup?" Billy asked watching his buddy rush towards the smiling child. He whispered something in her ear and palmed her ass making the young girl giggle even more.

"Y'all made any stops? Did anything different?" Leroy asked and cocked his head to help him hear.

"No, we came straight...wait, we had to stop by Byron's mama's house, but just for a second. He said he had to drop something off."

"Sho' nuff?" Leroy nodded and squinted at Byron across the room. "Sho' nuff."

****

"Billy! Billy!" Lady called out. "Somebody at the door!"

"Huh?" he frowned and looked at his cheap watch. It was just after three in the morning when he'd gotten in and got in his bed. The steady knocking on the door meant that whoever it was wasn't going away.

"Put some clothes on and come on!" Leroy demanded in a tone that sobered Billy up in an instant when he finally answered the door. Instead of asking questions he rushed to his room and got dressed in the same clothes he'd only recently discarded.

"Ready! Where we headed?" he finally asked once they were in the car.

"To a funeral," the pimp replied. Leroy clenched his jaws so tightly that Billy abandoned the rest of his questions. It didn't matter anyway since Leroy had a few of his own. "Byron made all the pick-ups today, right?"

"Uh...yeah. Same as always. 'Cept he told me to wait outside a couple times. Oh and when he stopped by his mama's house," Billy lied again. Leroy knew it was a lie too since he'd already checked his traps. Billy fought the smug smirk that threatened to show up from his friend getting into trouble. Now that Byron had fallen out of favor he'd be the man again.

"Wait here!" Leroy demanded as he pulled to a stop in front of Byron's house. He pet his old Cadillac as he passed it in the driveway. He then began to bang on the front door.

"Who? Huh? Leroy?" Byron stammered when he snatched the door open. He had been ready to kill whoever had been banging on his door until he saw who it was. "Oh hey. What's up?"

"Get dressed and come on!" Leroy growled.

"But I got that lil..."

"Nigga, I said get dressed and brang yo' ass on!" the pimp repeated and then spun on his heels and headed back to his car. Billy giggled with glee at seeing how mad Leroy was.

A minute later Byron came rushing out of the front door. He was half dressed and hopping around on one foot while trying to put his shoes on. He went around to the passenger's side and noticed that it was already occupied so he jumped into the back seat instead.

"Where we going, Leroy?" he asked when the pimp snatched the gear shift down to pull off. Leroy clenched his jaw in reply so Byron turned to his best-friend in the other front seat. "Where we goin', mane? I got lil mama from the pool hole in there giving her the business."

"To a funeral," Billy shrugged since that's all he knew.

"Who died? When?" Byron asked looking back and forth between the two men in the front. Neither had an answer for him so he went on to tell them about the young girl in his bed.

Leroy drove aggressively all the way to the graveyard. Once there he slammed on his brakes causing the car to skid in the loose gravel. Billy and Byron were looking at one another for direction when Leroy jumped out and began marching away. Billy shrugged and got out to follow him causing Byron to do the same. They had to sprint to catch up with him and then jog to keep up with his long angry stride.

"Look!" Leroy demanded when he stopped suddenly at the edge of a freshly dug grave. The boys both inched forward to peer into the empty hole.

"I don't see nothing?" Byron complained as he looked into the hole. At the same time Leroy pulled his pistol and stepped forward. He shot Byron in the back of his head causing him to fall face first into his grave.

Billy got sprayed with both blood and brain matter as his friend fell in slow motion. Leroy had already done an about face and began marching back to his car. Billy was stuck in a state of shock until Leroy called him.

"You may as well jump in there with him if you staying!" Leroy called over his shoulder.

He didn't want to stay or jump in the hole so he ran to catch up. Leroy was putting the car in gear when he got there. He jumped in just as he began to pull off. Billy was boiling hot about the murder but he still didn't accept responsibility.

"Something on ya mind?" Leroy taunted as they rode. He assumed he must be going through it over having gotten his friend killed for nothing. Byron was now on the other side of life wondering what had just happened.

"No," Billy grunted. He frowned at the right hand turn that would lead them back to Byron's house instead of his. He decided to wait and see what was going to happen next so he wouldn't have to talk to him any further.

"Here," Leroy said digging into his pocket. He came out with a spare key and handed it to Billy.

Billy was about to tell him that he didn't want shit from him until he noticed the Cadillac emblem on the key. He looked at the key then turned to Leroy.

"He cain't drive the bitch no mo'!" he laughed, like it was funnier than it was. "Oh, and brang me that lil young bitch up out of there."

Chapter 30

"What's wrong with you boy?" Lady asked seeing that something had her child distracted. It wasn't so much out of compassion but due to him missing her vein as he shot her up.

"Nothing," he replied since it was a lot easier to say than I just got my friend killed with my bullshit. Then I'm finna go on an ice-cream date with the boy I raped girlfriend. Instead he focused on the task at hand and injected his mother. She let out a loud fart to signal that he'd hit the mark.

"I gots me a good son," Lady moaned and swayed to the rhythm of the heroin.

"And I gots me a good mama," he replied as he wrapped up her works.

Billy used the money he'd stolen to hit up Stein Brothers for an outfit. They sold him a casual pair of slacks, a shirt, and a pair of loafers. His next stop was to get his thick hair cropped close to his scalp. The stop after that was to First Presbyterian.

As planned, Billy went to scoop AnJanay up from bible class to take her for ice-cream. Afterwards he would drop her off at her friend's house to spend the night. When he pulled up Billy noticed that all of her friends were clean, pretty, and wore bright smiles. He frowned curiously at the differences between them and the girls from his side of the tracks.

"There's my ride," AnJanay giggled and set off a fit of giggles from her girlfriends. In Billy's twisted mind they were laughing at him, making fun of him because he was poor and his mother was an addict.

AnJanay skipped happily towards the car with Billy's eyes locked on her bouncing breast. The tasteful dress gave up no cleavage or skin, but Billy still felt an erection growing in his pants.

"Hello there, William," AnJanay sang as she slid into the passenger's seat. She saw the scowl on his face and asked, "Are you okay?"

"Me? I'm fine. Ain't nothing wrong with me," he said as he pulled away from the curb. AnJanay was so uncomfortable from his reaction that she wished that she'd gotten out. She now second guessed her decision to sneak off with him. "You asked me that cuz I'm poor, huh?"

"Excuse me? You know what, you can just take me back to the church," she said.

Billy acted as if he hadn't even heard her. In fact he started to drive even faster. He blew through stop signs to make sure she didn't have an opportunity to jump out. AnJanay tried to do just that when he finally pulled into a park and came to an abrupt stop. It was the same park that he and Mrs. Paul had had sex in two years prior. Today like then would be the scene of rough sex. Only today it would not be consensual.

"Hel-," AnJanay screamed when Billy pounced on her. The call for help was cut short by one of his large hands covering her mouth.

His other large hand went under her dress and snatched her panties from her body. Next, Billy fumbled to free his raging erection as he held the girl in place. The girl let out a sorrowful moan when he took up position between her legs.

"You think you betta than me, huh?" he asked as he shoved himself inside of her.

"Mphmmph!" AnJanay scream came out muffled by the hand he still held over her mouth. Tears now streamed down her face and his hand as he tore pass her hymen and robbed her of her virginity.

"You...'bout...as tight...as...Carl was!" Billy relayed as he violently raped her. There was no consolation for it ending quickly since he'd cum inside of her.

All AnJanay could think about was the shame a girl from her church had endured when she'd popped up pregnant as Billy's dick pulsated and pumped his semen inside of her. He grinded on her cervix until he was done and then snatched out just as forcefully as he'd entered her.

"You ain't better than me! Or Lady or Mary!" Billy shouted as he got up and pulled his pants up. He saw the blood on his penis and blamed her for that too. "Done had yo' period!"

AnJanay was wide eyed with shock at being raped. She could only blame herself for sneaking away with him. How could she explain that? She couldn't. She wouldn't. In that moment she decided not to say anything. She wiped the semen from her ravaged vagina, with what was left of her panties before tossing them on the floor board. She then pulled the mirror down and tried to fix herself up as best as she could. The two drove in silence until Billy finally broke it.

"You still want that ice-cream or nah?"

****

"There he go!" Shawna announced when she saw Byron's car pull on-to the block. She led the charge to go break him off with his trap money. "Where Byron at?"

Billy just shook his head as the girl looked into the backseat, as if her pimp was playing hide and see. He knew that it was more serious than that, and that she'd need a shovel to find him now. Leroy paid the same man he'd paid to dig the hole to fill it back up with Byron still in it.

"Byron gone. Y'all work for Dollar Bill now!" he said in a *'Bitch betta have my money'* voice. He already knew the routine so he broke them all off with a small package of dope when they turned their money in.

The lamentation period is short in the wild and even shorter in the hood. Billy shrugged off a lifetime of friendship with Byron and proceeded to assume his position. Billy fired up a stick of reefer and went around town to make his rounds.

The black hearted youngster scoffed at the *'you ain't shit'* looks he got from the distributor. By now they'd all heard the news and knew he was to blame. Every envelope he picked up was taped shut now and the tally called in prior to its pick-up.

Billy arrived at the bar and parked out front behind Leroy's new car. He then walked inside and made his way over to Leroy's booth. Halfway there he saw another girl seated between the pimp and Mandy. Upon closer inspection he noticed that it was the young girl that Byron had pulled. She was in a deep nod due to her brand new drug habit.

"Lil' bitch got the tightest pussy in the world! You gotta take it fo' a spin!" Leroy exclaimed when he saw Dollar Bill locked in on her face. Even covered in colorful whore make-up she still looked like the child that she was.

"I might just have to," Billy nodded in agreement with the sick suggestion. Mandy tried to lift her head to say hello but the heroin in her system made it too heavy. He watched the pimp give the envelopes of money a squeeze before putting them in his pocket.

"Ain't no might! Go on. She's yours," Leroy announced. "She ain't ready for the track yet, so just keep her on yo' arm and rent her out."

"Okay. I guess, I better go on and get home. Gots some stuff to do in the mornin'" he said as he helped his new whore to her feet.

"Where?" he asked surprising him with the question. Billy was so surprised that he didn't even have time to come up with a lie so the truth seeped out.

"I'm goin' to church."

Chapter 31

"How you feeling, Mama? You gon' be okay?" Billy asked Lady once more as he helped her into his car. The last thing he needed was for that monkey on her back to get to squealing in the middle of service. He'd diluted her morning fix because he didn't want to have her nodding in church either.

"Lady gon' be just fine up in the Lawd's house! Yes she is!" she shot back tilting her head proudly. She was right too because the thought of church had breathed new life into the woman. She'd been too embarrassed to go there on her own after her son went to jail, but today she was ready.

Billy felt like a big shot as he pulled into the church's parking lot. He parked next to Tommy's old car just as he got out with his wife and kids. Lady took Billy by the arm and stepped proudly inside. The piano player missed a note when he saw them marching down the aisle.

Pastor Paul was going in so he was the last person to notice their return. It wasn't until the congregation missed an 'Amen' that the preacher realized that something was going on. He had just said some extra fly shit and expected a room full of 'Amens' followed by a couple of 'Hallelujahs' and got none. He looked up just in time to see what had everyone so distracted.

"Well, well, well! The prodigal son has returned!" he announced. The congregation got completely quiet as they watched him approach. Mrs. Paul squeezed her thighs tightly together as she recalled the last time she'd seen him.

There was a tense moment as the two men stood face to face. A sigh of relief was breathed by all when Pastor threw his arms open wide and Billy stepped forward and took him up on the hug.

"Good to see you again," Pastor Paul whispered as he pressed his body against Billy's. Billy flinched when he felt Pastor's erection throb against his leg.

"I see you missed me," Billy whispered back. The perverted preacher totally missed the malice in his tone.

"Sorry it had to go down like that, but I had to learn you a lesson."

"I learned. I learned," he replied.

A slow clap began from the touching reunion. It built hand by hand until it became a thunderous applause.

"Preach, Reverend Cash!" a woman yelled. The request was quickly repeated throughout the church.

"Take yo' time!" Lady's one time friend stood and shouted.

"You ready?" Pastor asked as he passed the mic.

"Blessed are the peacemakers..." Billy shouted in response. He'd had to pause for several minutes for the hooping and hollering to subside. Then he launched into his famous sermon as the collection plates were filled.

Reverend Cash rocked the mic and he rocked the full house for an hour. It then took just as long for him to greet and hug all the parishioners once the service was over. Lady stood by watching her son with a wide smile pasted on her face. Not even heroin could give her the kind of high she got from watching her son preach.

"S'pose you 'pectin' a cut from that last plate, huh? I don't mind long as I get what I like as well," Pastor Paul said discretely through his smile. "Come on out to the house and I-,"

"I ain't never comin' out to yo' house again," Billy replied.

"Okay. Well, meet me out at the Dew Drop Inn on Route 109. Nine o'clock," the preacher offered, licking his lips.

"That way I can have you all to myself," Billy said with a dangerous glint in his eyes. Again the thirsty ass preacher missed the signs.

"Great sermon!" Mrs. Paul clapped as she approached. She too leaned in and got a hug. Just like her husband, she pressed her hot crotch up against him.

"Dear, I got some preaching and pastoring to do tonight," Pastor told his wife. Before she could reply one of the deacons came over and pulled him to the side.

"I guess you the pastoring he got to do tonight?" she quipped sarcastically.

"No, Ma'am. Matter of fact, since he gon' be out I may as well be in, deep in you," Billy said seductively. Now he had two dates since she couldn't say no.

****

"Billy! Is that you?" Carlita shouted when he and Lady entered The Rib Shack. However, before he could answer she'd ran over and slammed into him.

"Ugh, hey," he grunted from the pressure of the violent hug. Lady just laughed and shook her head.

"Ain't no more Billy. That's Reverend Cash!" Lady proclaimed. "That means he out that other business."

"You are?" the waitress asked pouting. She just knew that she was getting some action tonight.

"That's right. I'm just preaching," he replied, leaving out the pimping and dealing that he was also doing. Carlita lowered her head and led them to their table.

"I guess, I better order a to go plate for Kita," Billy mused.

"Boy, what you plan on doin' wit' that chile?" Lady wanted to know.

"She got put out so we gon' have to put her up for a minute," was his reply. What he meant was 'Mama I'm finna pimp that lil' bitch for all she's worth.'

"I guess. I...oh...I," Lady said turning green. A sheen of sweat appeared on her forehead and Billy knew what time it was.

"Guess we better make that three to go plates," Billy said, raising his hand to get Carlita's attention. It was all they could do to wait for the plates to get fixed. The light hit she'd had to start the day meant the withdrawals came with a vengeance. They were mad at her for playing with them.

****

Billy got home and had two addicts to deal with. Kita was soaked in sweat and curled up in a tight ball on the floor. The coolness of the wood floor offered some relief but she needed a hit and bad. She would have to wait because mama always comes first even when it comes to shooting dope.

"Thank you, baby!" Lady cooed and swayed as the drug entered her system. Billy left his mama rocking to the rhythm of the dope and then walked into his room to service Kita.

"I'm sick," the child moaned. She was too naïve to realize she was hooked on dope. All she knew was that a shot would make the pain go away.

"First things first," Billy replied as he came out of his church clothes. Kita stared on curiously wondering what he meant. It became crystal clear when his dick swung free.

Billy sat back on his bed and held his dick out for the girl to suck. She couldn't stand so she crawled over to get it and put it in her mouth. Billy had to help her to her knees before he pushed between her dry lips.

"Argh," Kita gagged as she bit off more than she could chew. Billy got a kick out of watching her gagging and thrust upwards to make her gag again. She did just that and more.

"Damn you!" Billy shouted as she threw up all over him. He felt the clear warm liquid cover both his dick and balls.

"I'm...s-s-sick," the girl repeated pitifully. "I need some of that stuff."

"You need to clean this up first," he shot back. She turned to get a rag but he stopped her. "Un uh. Lick it off!"

All Kita could do as she complied was think about all the warnings her grandma had given her. She'd sworn that the old lady was too strict, but listening to her would've kept her from having to lick vomit off of a man's balls. The young girl had changed hands between three men in just three days. Suddenly everything the old lady had said made sense, but it was too late now. And she still had plenty more degradation to go before she hit rock bottom. All junkies do, some bounce back while others shatter and break.

"Mm, that's right," Billy moaned when Kita finally got back around to the giving him a blow job. The sick youngster multi-tasked by grabbing a rib out of his tray and taking a bite while she serviced him. Kita looked up and added BBQ to the list of things she wanted.

The blow job ended in the way that a lot of blow jobs ended. Kita swallowed while Billy finally fixed her up a shot. She nodded off instantly when the good dope hit her system. Billy still ran up in her to see if it was as good and tight as both Byron and Leroy had said.

"Shit!" Billy grunted a few strokes later because it was just as good and tight as they'd said it was. Greed convinced him that she was worth a million dollars on the track. He was right but Leroy was right too, she wasn't ready.

Chapter 32

"Are you sure?" Shonda shrieked when Billy gave her instructions to school the new girl. Shonda was a vet at selling pussy on the street and she knew that the girl wouldn't last a second out there. Not only were some of the Johns dangerous freaks but there were also predatory pimps out there who preyed on young girls like Kita if they weren't on a leash with a pimp on the other end.

"Bitch!" Dollar Bill shouted like a pimp does, "Who the pimp, me or you? Huh?"

"You is," Shonda said meekly and lowered her head. Kita got out and looked around wide eyed, like a tourist in Time Square. Shonda twisted her lips and just shook her head. Babysitting this chick was going to cost her tricks.

"Good!" Billy told Shonda and drove straight from there over to see her mama. He parked a block away and walked the rest of the way over and rang the bell.

"That was a powerful sermon you gave," Shonda's mama said as she opened the door to let him in.

"Why, thank you," he smiled as they undressed for sex. He knew he had to put on to help his plan so that's exactly what he did. In fact he laid the pipe so good that the woman would've given him a kidney had he asked for one. Luckily for her he only asked to use her car.

"O-o-o-k-kay!" she stuttered from busting a nut so hard her legs were still shaking when he pulled out of her driveway.

Billy had done a lifetime of fuck shit in his short lifetime, but tonight would be a first. His mind was blank as he drove along Route 109. It took a second before the flashing motel sign appeared. He pulled into its parking lot and parked next to Pastor Paul's Caddie. The eager preacher was watching from the window and had seen Billy when he pulled in. He flashed the room's lights to alert him of which room he was in.

The pastor doubled checked himself in the mirror as Billy approached the room. He watched him talking to himself as he walked over. When Billy raised his hand to knock Pastor snatched open the door.

"Surprise!" Pastor Paul shouted. He was right too because Billy was definitely surprised. He was so surprised that he was frozen in place. He knew that Pastor was a freak but this was extra freaky. "You like?"

Billy blinked rapidly trying to make sense out of what he was seeing. However, there was no making sense out of a six foot two inch man in six inch heels, a negligee, wig, full face of make-up with a feather boa around his neck.

"Um..." Billy stammered until he remembered the gun in his hand. He lifted it halfway and fired a round into the man's belly button.

"Nigga, did you just shoot me?" Pastor Paul growled, sounding every bit like the man that he was. That hot lead in his gut had changed his tone real quick. He raised his hands and went after Billy. Billy wasn't expecting it and almost ran. Almost, until he remembered the gun once more.

This time he raised it higher and fired it at his lipstick. Pastor Paul dropped dead and Billy leaned in to get a closer look. It wasn't until he heard a door open that he snapped out of it. He then quickly made it back to the car and pulled back out onto Route 109. He drove swiftly to put distance between him and the murder scene. Besides, he had a hot date.

****

"Right on time!" Mrs. Paul said as she opened her front door. She hurriedly snatched Billy by his lapel and pulled him inside. He tried to say something but she took his open mouth as an invitation and shoved her tongue inside.

The horny woman couldn't wait to get to the room so she scrambled to get his pants off where he stood. Once she did she hopped up into his arms. Billy caught on and got into the act by reaching down and guiding himself inside of her slippery vagina.

"Shit!" he grunted when she began bucking hard against him. She came after just a few strokes then kept cumming after every few strokes.

"That was just the warm up. Let me get you in the bed," she said as he let her down. She wobbled slightly on legs rubbery from having several good orgasms.

"Whoa!" Billy said as he caught her from falling. "What about Pastor?"

"Chile please! That man took a pair of my panties with him so I know he won't be home no time soon!" she huffed indignantly. She then tossed her head back and led the march into Pastor and her bedroom.

Billy was pounding in and out of the Pastor's wife so hard that neither of them heard the knocking on the front door. The knocking sounded pretty much like the headboard did as it banged against the wall. Billy heard it first and slowed his stroke so that she could hear it too.

"Why you...who the fuck?" she said when she heard the knocking as well. "Ignore it! They'll go away."

"You better see who it is," Billy said as he pulled out giving her no choice.

"Ugh!" she shouted and got out of the bed. After snatching her robe around her nakedness she stomped towards the front of the house. She arrived just as the knocking resumed. She snatched open the door to see two police officers standing on her doorstep.

"Mrs. Paul, we...um...we regret to inform you that your husband is dead," the first cop said, lowering his head in sorrow.

"Any reason he would be at the Dew Drop Inn? Out on 109," the second cop asked. He left out the facts about the women's clothes, lipstick, and the extra-large jar of Vaseline.

"Huh?" she asked when she realized he'd spoken. Everything Pastor had was now hers, including the house, cars, and the church.

"I'm sure you must be in shock right now. We'll come back in the morning," the first one added. He'd taken her reaction as shock but in reality she was counting money in her head.

The 'O' was all the cops heard of the okay Mrs. Paul said because she closed the door so fast. She then rushed back to her bedroom pulling her robe off as she ran. To her delight Billy was laying there slow stroking his dick to keep it hard. She leapt from ten feet away and landed on it like a cowboy does a horse.

"Who was that?" Billy asked in confusion. He just knew it had to be the police with the bad news. What better alibi could there be then being up in the wife of the man who was killed.

"Th-th-the p-p-p-police," she stammered out while riding him hard and fast.

"The police! Fo' what?" he asked in mock shock. First Lady just kept right on riding in search of her next nut. He had to grab her hips to stop her in order to get her full attention. "What they want?"

"My husband dead. They found him in a motel," she said and pushed his hands away so she could resume her ride.

"Who killed him?"

"Huh? I don't know. They don't know," she said irritated by all the questions.

That was all he needed to hear. He grabbed her hips again and thrusted upwards into her cervix. A minute later they both howled from mutual release aided by good news. Hers was being rid of her husband and his was getting away with murder.

What he didn't know was that getting away with murder came with strings attached. The main one was that he would definitely kill again.

Chapter 33

"I'm so sorry 'bout yo' loss," Deacon said for the tenth time since Mrs. Paul had arrived at the church. The sentiment was contradicted by the smirk on his face.

"I just bet you are," she shot back. With her husband gone the top spot would go to him along with a bigger piece of the pie. Not to mention he wanted a slice of that pie hanging between her legs. He been knew that Pastor was a punk and wasn't fucking her.

"Don't worry, I'm finna send him off in style." he assured her.

"Oh, about the eulogy...I think it's best that we let Reverend Cash send him home," she said. The man's heart broke so bad that it nearly exploded out his chest.

"I...oh...we..." he sputtered as she walked away. The tight black dress she wore stretched tightly over her round ass giving him a going away present.

"Hey Deacon," Billy greeted as he arrived.

"Don't Deacon me!" he huffed and stormed out. Billy let out a chuckle since he knew what was eating him.

He'd noticed the man sniffing around behind Mrs. Paul. That's why he'd been eating her vagina every morning, noon, and night since Pastor had passed. He planned on moving in with her as soon as enough time had passed. Until then he would keep peddling and pimping while preaching on the side.

****

"Take your time!" Lady's friend called out when Billy took to the pulpit. He looked down at the casket and closed his eyes. It looked like he was saying a silent prayer, but he wasn't.

"Don't worry Pastor. I'ma hold err'thang down for you. I'm fuckin' yo' wife real good fo' you. 'Tween me and you...you give way better head than she do. Oh, more good news, all your suits fit me just right. If there's a heaven I doubt yo' low down ass is going so don't dress too warmly."

"Blessed are the peacemakers..." Reverend Cash began. He had to pause since the church erupted in claps, Amens, and Hallelujahs. He felt a surge of power flow through his whole body. His hair stood on end and his dick got rock hard. Even the gun hadn't made him feel this powerful. He'd hated throwing it out of the window but he knew the fallacy of keeping a murder weapon.

Lady closed her eyes, raised one hand, and swayed to the sounds of her son's voice. Part of it was the dope, but part of it was the fact that he was really spitting. As a matter of fact he sounded quite believable as he sang the praises of the deceased predator in the box below. He couldn't help but wonder if the man had on panties under his clothes. He vowed to find out if he got a second alone with him, plus he also wanted the suit he had on.

Deacon sat back with his arms crossed and lips twisted as the boy put on. He scoffed when he sent the collection plates around every few minutes. Reverend Cash was about that bread and even he had to admire that.

After the church service the congregation moved on to the graveyard. He would have talked for a few more hours and sent the plates around some more if not for Lady. He saw her turning green as the withdrawals began to set in. This congregation was straight from the hood and would know a junkie when they saw one. He had no choice but to wrap it up so he could get her home and give her a fix.

Billy was the first to toss a little dirt on the casket. The congregation followed as Pastor was laid to rest. Mrs. Paul invited him into her vagina later and he eagerly accepted.

"I'll fall through after I check the trap," he assured her as he left to take Lady home.

****

"Bastard," Lady muttered in disgust as her son ran the dope into her vein.

"What I do?" Billy reeled as if she'd slapped him.

"Not you, baby. You ain't no...anyway, I mean that damn Leroy," she sighed. This wasn't the first time she'd brought his name up when she got high. He decided to wait until the rhythm hit her and then pry for information. This was a classic 'be careful what you wish for situation'.

"What about Leroy?" he asked as her head bobbed in a nod.

"First he put the dick on me then he put me on the dope."

"When?" Billy asked soothingly.

"Soon as you went to jail. Then he tried to make me sell my pussy for him! I ain't hardly 'bout to sell my pussy. Lady is a lady!" she huffed indignantly. She'd spent time with men who gave her money but she did not sell pussy. She was a hoe, not a whore.

"See you later mama," he growled and got up to leave. He walked out of her room before she could tell him that Leroy was his father. He got Kita ready for the trap and downed a bottle of wine while smoking on a stick.

He had a simmering rage brewing in him as he drove downtown. The weed and the wine only added fuel to the revelation that Leroy had been the one to put his mama on the dope. The need to cause pain caused him to reach over and jam his fingers inside of the young whore beside him.

"Oww!" Kita whimpered in pain. It was a futile plea since it fell on deaf ears. He didn't stop until he'd reached the block. Shonda rushed over to greet him before he could open his door.

"Hey daddy, don't leave that bitch out here no mo'! I cain't watch her. I had to stop her from getting in Georgia Boy's car last night!"

"Georgia Boy!" Billy grunted upon hearing the name of the notorious ho stealing pimp from Georgia. Even Leroy had lost a whore or two to the flamboyant pimp. Billy had no control over the vicious back hand that flew into Kita's cheek. "Bitch, let me hear 'bout you getting in a pimp's car!"

"Keep that lil' bitch off the track! She ain't ready!" Shonda demanded, which was a mistake. You don't make demands to a pimp.

"Bitch!" Dollar Bill shouted as he sprang from the car. All that could be heard was the 'pap' of the slaps and punches from him beating her down. A crowd filed out of the pool hall to watch the show. Leroy just shook his head at the amateur and went back inside. Georgia Boy watched the scene from his car smiling from ear to ear.

"Okay, okay daddy!" Shonda pleaded once she'd had enough.

"I'll...tell...you when...it's...o...kay!" he replied in between 'paps'. "Now hit that trap and get my money!"

"Okay!" Shonda shouted, but still got a swift foot in the ass that lifted her off her feet.

"Bitches!" Dollar Bill griped as he got back into his car. He lit up another stick and added more fuel to the fire as he set off to make his rounds.

****

"You okay?" he heard at every stop as he went around picking up Leroy's drug money.

"Are you!" he shot back each and every time.

He was already in a foul mood but it was about to get even worse. Billy frowned when he pulled up and didn't see neither Shonda nor Kita on the track. Shawna came running up with bad news pasted on her face.

"They gon'! They gon'!" she said fearfully making sure that she was out of pimp slap range.

"Who? Who gone?" he asked scanning the block. It wasn't unusual not to see a whore or two since they would be off turning a trick.

"Shonda and Kita! Georgia Boy don' stol' them both!"

"I...um...how?" Dollar Bill mumbled, sounding like Lil' Billy. He looked like he wanted to cry as he scanned the block for his whores. They had both been long gone since Georgia Boy swooped in and scooped them both up. It was bad already but it was about to get worse.

All eyes were on Billy as he walked into the pool hall. He wanted to go home and hide but he had to turn in Leroy's money. All eyes averted when he turned in their direction. Leroy had his mouth twisted into a 'yeah right' smirk as Billy approached.

"Here go yo' bread," he said without bothering to sit.

"Sit!" he demanded as Mandy looked at him with disdain as well. Billy wanted to ask her what she was looking at but held his tongue.

"I..."

"You gotta to be the dumbest mothafucka alive! Didn't I tell you not to put that fresh meat on the street?"

"I..."

"You don't listen! Hardheaded just like yo' mama!" Leroy said scraping the scab off the wound. "Now that faggot gon' be braggin' all over town 'bout how he don' bagged one of my bitches. Watch how he gon' put on at the next pimp convention. Mark my words, he gone have that lil' bitch on his arm all dolled up!" Leroy fumed.

"Just stupid," Mandy co-signed shaking her head.

"I need a pistol," Billy announced dryly. The violent request pressed pause on the conversation for a brief second.

"For what? You ain't gon' bus' nothing!" Leroy laughed. When a pimp laughed his whore laughed and that pushed Billy further into the black hole of rage.

"Oh I'ma bus', just get me a pistol," he assured him.

"What happen to that pee shooter Byron had? He don't need it no more," he said setting off another round of laughter at his expense.

"I'on know," he shrugged in reply. Some lies are better than the truth. This was one such lie.

"A'ight lil' nigga! Come on, we finna see," Leroy dared as he stood, and when a pimp stood his whore stood. Billy was the last to stand and follow them outside. He got into his car and followed Leroy out to his house. To his surprise the certified hood nigga didn't live in the hood. His house was way out in the country calm.

Billy pulled into the driveway and got out. It was too dark to appreciate the grounds as he followed them inside. Mandy flopped wide legged on the sofa while Leroy marched deeper into the house. Billy took a seat across from her and ignored the crotch shot she offered. Had he bothered looking he'd have seen clear up to her ovaries.

"We finna see if you gon' bus'!" Leroy repeated when he returned. He sat down next to Mandy and sat a large revolver on the table. Billy stared at it silently until Leroy barked at him, "Pick it up! How you gon' bus' if you scared to touch it?"

"Is it loaded?" Billy asked as he picked it up to inspect it.

"Yeah," Leroy said as his final words. Billy's first shot slammed him back into the sofa. Leroy looked down in disbelief at the gaping hole in his chest. When he opened his mouth to speak Billy pumped another round into his torso.

"Tol' him to stopping juggin' at you," Mandy shrugged as if it were true. It didn't matter if it was or not since Billy shot her too.

"Y'all take care now," Billy said and nodded politely to the dead bodies as he left them. Only they both weren't dead. Mandy lay there taking little sips of air as she held on to life with everything she had.

There were no nosey neighbors to worry about so the coast was clear when he stepped outside. He thought about swapping cars since Leroy wouldn't be driving anymore, but a headshake later he got into his own car and pulled off. The cocky youngster thought nothing about the Oldsmobile that passed him as he rode away.

"Dollar Bill," Smiley muttered as he saw Leroy's old car pass by on his way to pick up the dope to supply to all the distributors.

Smiley knocked on the door harder the second time when the first knock went unanswered. The hole in Mandy's lung prevented her from calling out to him. Smiley knew that the pimp had to be home since his car was in the driveway and he'd just seen Dollar Bill leave. He shrugged his shoulders, opened the door, and ventured inside.

"What in the world?" Smiley exclaimed when he saw the bloody couple laid back on the sofa. He leaned in to take a closer look and asked Leroy if he was dead. A huge smile spread across his face when he didn't get an answer.

"Yassir!" Smiley said and rushed into the room where the dope was kept. After cleaning it all out he then searched for and found Leroy's cash and jewelry. He was taking the watch off the dead pimp's wrist when Mandy finally managed to speak.

"H-h-help m-me-e-e," she moaned. Smiley thought about putting a pillow over her mouth but couldn't do it. He felt a tinge of affection for the girl since he'd spent so much time in her mouth over the years. Leroy often tipped him by allowing him to put the tip of his dick on her tonsils.

"Who did this to y'all?" he asked.

"D-D-Dollar, Billy," she replied. Smiley smiled at having a scapegoat to blame the robbery on. If he suddenly came up with the dope right after the murder the blame would certainly fall on him.

"9-1-1?" he asked when the operator picked up. "I wanna report a killin'..."

Chapter 34

"I put together a nice sermon! A real nice sermon, Pastor would be proud," Deacon Green assured Mrs. Paul. He was still a little salty about not getting to preach at Pastor Paul's funeral, but surely he would get the nod on this first Sunday afterwards.

"Reverend Cash will be speaking today," she said without pause. Her box was still full of the young boy's cum from an early morning sex session. She then took her usual seat behind the pulpit and the Deacon took his.

"Y'all mind if I preach to you?" Billy asked softly as he took the mic. The congregation mumbled a reply but that wasn't good enough for Reverend Cash so he asked again. "I said, do y'all mind...if I...preach to you!"

"Go on preach!" his hype-man Dwight urged along with the congregation.

"Yassir! Preach! Well, take your time!" they shouted.

"I'm finna preach then!" Billy shouted and did just that. He had spent all night and most of the morning inside Mrs. Paul so he hadn't prepared a sermon. It didn't show as he freestyled his sermon, making up stuff as he went along.

Billy noticed a sheriff's deputy walk in and gave a brief pause. Just when he'd convinced himself that he was just there to hear the word another one walked in. The first two were followed by two more who began to spread out and cover the church's exits. There was no longer any doubt in his mind that they were there for him. However, his mouth steady spit his made up gospel while he wracked his brain to figure out which murder they were there about and how they knew that he was the killer. Leroy had taught him to never leave a witness, so he hadn't. He would have to figure it out later, right now he had to figure out a way to get up out of there.

"I want y'all to close your eyes and bow y'all heads in prayer. Squeeze 'em tight!" he ordered a couple of the deputies, along with the congregation, closed their eyes and bowed their heads and Reverend Cash took off.

The stunned congregation watched as he took flight. He hurdled over a railing and through the back of the church. He hit the preacher's office and shot out the backdoor. He shot straight into the arms of Deputy Black Bear. His real name was Lowell but being six foot five inches tall and weighing three hundred and twenty-five pounds the name Black Bear seemed to fit him better.

"Hol' up now Reverend. The Sheriff needs to talk to you," the gentle giant said as he squeezed him tightly in his arms.

"Let me go and I'll..." Billy pleaded but the rest of the deputies arrived and shot him down. They cuffed him up and took him to jail.

****

"Shit!" Billy fussed when he heard his mama raising hell in the police station. He'd been formally charged with the murder of Leroy and assault on Mandy. Smiley had written a highly embellished statement about having been present when Billy robbed and murdered Leroy. Have Smiley tell it he'd jumped through a window and barely escaped with his life.

"Un uh! Hell no! I wanna see my boy and I mean I wanna see him now!" Lady demanded. To hell with their visiting days and times, she wanted to talk to him immediately.

"I'm sorry, Ma'am, we..." Black Bear started to apologize until the sheriff came out to quell the commotion.

"I don't see no harm in letting her see her boy for a few minutes," Sheriff Hartz suggested.

"Thank you kindly, Sheriff," Lady nodded as she regained her composure. She smoothed out her dress, straightened her hat, and followed Black Bear into the back.

"Shit!" Billy repeated when he heard the sheriff give in to his mama. Things were already bad enough without him having to deal with Lady. He expected her to blow up at him but to his surprise she was remarkably calm.

"Hey son," Lady moaned as she walked up to the bars. "Is it true?"

"No, Mama, I ain't kilt nobody!" he assured her but being that he hadn't had enough time to practice his lie and make it believable Lady didn't believe him.

"Yes, you did," his mother said shaking her head. A lone tear rolled down her face, she knocked it away halfway down her check. "I know when you lying, child. Why, baby, why?"

"He kilt Byron," Billy said softly. It was only half the reason since he was half the reason Leroy had killed him. "Plus, Mama, he was a pimp, a dope dealer, a..."

"Yo daddy," Lady added admitting it out loud for the first time. "Boy, you don' kilt yo' daddy!"

****

"Killed his daddy!" the red faced redneck judge boomed at Billy's first hearing. Word had quickly spread far and wide until it had reached him too. "You must've thought I was lying 'bout getting my forty years out of you huh, boy?"

"Sir, this is just a preliminary hearing," Billy's public pretender, not defender because he wasn't there to defend him, offered meekly. He had no qualms about the forty years, but it had to be done by the books.

"Well, if that boy want a trial I reckon I may as well give him the 'lectric chair," the judge announced. If Billy wanted to cost the tax payers money for a trial then he would take it out of his ass.

"Not the 'lectric chair!" Lady wailed and broke down. The deep heart wrenching sobs affected her black hearted son. He couldn't take another second of it and raised his hand.

"Guilty sir! I wanna plead guilty!" Billy announced. The admission of guilt brought yellow smiles to the judge, prosecutor, and public defender's faces. The early day meant they could sip mint juleps over lunch and have a good laugh at his expense.

"In that case I sentence you to..." the judge said and paused as if contemplating. "Forty years!"

"Oh Lawd!" Lady moaned and fell out. Deputy Black Bear came and scooped her up and took her out of the courtroom.

"Get me outta here!" Billy told his lawyer. He had to wait a few minutes longer to get the formalities out of the way before he was then taken back to the jail. A few days later he boarded a bus headed to adult prison.

Usually an eighteen year old going to adult prison is headed for a world of trouble, not Dollar Bill though. In his case it was the other prisoners who were in trouble.

Chapter 35

Dollar Bill reached the Backwater Men's Prison and immediately got on the fuck shit. He hooked up with his old reform school partner Pickle and together they kicked up a bunch of dust. Neither got a coin from home so they had to 'get it how they lived'. They robbed the older weaker inmates as well as the white inmates for everything they had.

Billy had an older vet named Blue, who didn't put up with foolishness, for a bunkmate. The older man was just as dangerous in his own right so the two declared a truce in their cell. Everyone else, however, was fair game.

"Boy, what you gon' do with yo'self?" Blue asked him one day. He was always trying to put something other than fighting and stealing on the youngster's mind. He'd already spent half of his life behind the wall and he hated to see Billy do the same.

"Time!" Billy shot back. "I'm gon' do time and I got an ass of it to do!'

"The state of Tennessee gives two fo' one which means you ain't gotta do but twenty. Plus if you stay out of trouble and get you a work detail you can get even mo' time cut," Blue schooled.

"Guess it'll be twenty, cuz I ain't finna work for these crackers!"

"I guess it is then," the older man said shaking his head in pity. He'd been the same way when he'd come in twenty-five years ago.

"So, what you gon' do when you get out?" Billy asked to make him the subject of the conversation.

"Be free. I'ma be free!" Blue said with his eyes glazed over from the prospect. He had lost both his mama and his daddy since he'd been gone and had no earthly idea where he was going and what he would do. The only thing he knew is that he would be free, and that's really all that mattered.

****

"Looks like you got a new bunkmate," Pickle announced as he saw a new inmate carrying his belongings towards the cell that had just became open.

"New meat," Billy said seeing he was traveling light. Most prisoners accumulated a bunch of meaningless worthless crap during their journey so his lack of baggage told him that he'd just come into the system.

"Don't look like he gon' twerk nothing," his partner said, since the guy looked straight. They were both hoping for a sissy since they were both too low on the totem pole to get one otherwise.

Chain gang sissies were a hot commodity. Only the rich, strong, or powerful could keep one. The boys were wild but couldn't compete with vets of the prison.

"Oh he'll twerk somethin'! He may not know it yet, but he gon' twerk," Billy replied with a twisted snarl. If he could turn his cellie out and keep it quiet then they would have their own sissy. "Let me go holla at him."

Pickle crossed his fingers and hoped that his partner could pull it off. If worse came to worse they could always overpower him and rape him, but that would bring out the vultures. It would make it easy for someone else to come along and offer protection from the two. Most times the victim would choose one dick over being used by two or three. Not to mention being fed and cared for.

"Hey, I'm Billy," Billy said with a rare smile and handshake as he entered their shared cell. He noticed that the man didn't have any calluses on his hands and that was a good sign.

"LeVaughn," his new bunkmate replied, having no idea he was turning Billy on.

"Where you from? You married? You drank? You smoke?" Billy asked trying to feel him out so he could feel him up. LeVaughn gave all the wrong answers and Billy rushed to tell Pickle the good news.

****

"He's twenty-fo', has one kid, and say he in her' for fraud, whatever that is," Billy relayed. "Oh, and he say he drank and smoke reefer!"

"He fuckin'!" Pickle happily announced. "I'ma go holla at Buck fo' some of that shine."

"Un uh, get at Fatman for some of that spud juice!" Billy decided nodding wickedly. Fatman made 190 proof liquor from potatoes, yeast, and sugar. Fatman's liquor was the start of many, many prison romances and rapes.

Nightfall fell, as it always does, and it was time to put their plan into motion. A few other predators had taken notice of the new guy, so the clock was ticking. The goons respected the crimes of rape and murder, but the soft crime of fraud gave an erection to every man who heard it.

"Okay, I'ma go first," Billy announced as he and Pickle went to his cell. He had first dibs since it was his cell.

"A'ight, just don't skeet in him," Pickle pleaded.

"I won't," Billy vowed as he led the way inside the cell. "Sup bunkmate? This my partna' Pickle. He got some smoke and drank."

"Hello, Pickle," LeVaughn greeted extending his hand. Pickle frowned curiously at it before turning to Billy for help.

"Shake the man's hand while I po' us a drank," Billy explained. The handshake gave Pickle a hard on and Billy'a chance to put the fix in. He filled his and Pickle's cups up with 90% water and a dash of moonshine, meanwhile, LeVaughn got a full cup of shine.

"Whew!" LeVaughn grimaced at the first sip of the strong liquor. He saw his new friends gulping theirs down and didn't want to be left out so he manned up and tossed his down as well. Ironic since it was what was going to make him into a her.

"Fiyah them sticks up!" Billy cheered and refilled their cups. Pickle helped LeVaughn light the reefer while he did.

"Put on a lil' music," Pickle said when LeVaughn began to bob his head from the liquor. By the end of the second cup he'd fell over to the side in a drunken stupor.

"Showtime!" Billy cheered. He began to strip the unconscious man while Pickle tore strips from the sheets to tie him up. They had a moment of silence as they looked down at the naked man tied to the bed. Billy then climbed on his back and gave him a sex change.

"Awe man! I tol' you not to skeet in him!"

Chapter 36

"That's right! Take...yo'...time," Lady's friend coaxed as she gave him some nice slow head. Actually she was going in and out of a nod from a recent fix, but head was head.

Billy had been gone a whole year at this point so she had to rely on her orifices to generate enough money to stay high, a task that became more expensive with each passing day. Her son had begun the process of weaning her off the dope but when he left things started going the other way.

Lady used more and more dope everyday as she built up a stronger and stronger tolerance for the drug. As a result more and more men visited her insides to pay for her habit. When she felt her mouth fill with hot salty semen she knew that ride was over.

"Next!" she called out, as she let Mr. 'Take Yo' Time out the front door. Two of the three men, sitting in the living room, looked at each other trying to recall who was there first. One decided he was and hopped to his feet. He followed Lady into her room and then entered her womb.

****

Billy's first year of prison went by in a blur. As the old adage goes time sure flies when you're having fun. Have him tell it, prison wasn't so bad. He was still smoking, drinking, and fucking on a regular basis. It was all good until an enemy from his past showed up to change his future.

"That's that nigga right there!" the newcomer growled when he saw Billy out on the yard. Being in a different cell block meant that they only saw each other in passing, although it was possible to slip into another cell block under the right conditions.

"Who? Which one? Where?" his partners all asked.

"Right there, the one doing pull ups," the newcomer said pointing to Billy working out. He had to be specific, since Pickle was working out doing push-ups and LeVaughn was doing squats to make his booty plump.

"What he did?" someone wanted to know. He was down to go to war but liked to know what it was about.

"Huh? Um...he um...he robbed me on the streets," the victim decided.

"I know that nigga. He in D-block. I can get us in, but you better handle yo' business," the leader of C-block commanded. It was a kill or be killed order and there was no turning back.

****

"Next!" Lady called out to the front when she felt the man behind her shake and shiver from an orgasm. Cum dripped out of her vagina from all the clients she'd serviced. She planned on using her hot water bottle to hose herself out the first chance that she got, but until then men were going to have to splash around in the next man's juice. With her nasty ass.

"Hey Lady, Harold," Melvin greeted as he came into the room. Harold grunted a curt greeting as he got dressed and headed out. Melvin waited for the other man to leave before he made his pitch.

"I...um...I'm a little shawt today..." he began and paused.

"I know yo' thang little already! I don' seent it a million times," Lady shot back. She was a little antsy and irritable since it had been hours since her last fix.

"No, that's not what I meant. I mean on cash," he explained. "I got a little dope I can trade..."

"Let me see!" Lady demanded with her hand out. He pulled out a large bag of pure dope that he was supposed to deliver. Once delivered it would be cut ten times before being put on the street, but he didn't know that. Lady saw the pure dope and passed gas happily.

"I'll take that as a yes!" Melvin said. He'd trafficked enough dime sacks to know the amount and broke her off.

"Mm hm," Lady said as the dope began to boiling and bubbling on her spoon. She then pulled the syrupy liquid into the syringe while Melvin helped her by tying off her arm.

Lady didn't stand a chance against Afghanistan's finest poppy product. The shit could put Superman on his ass so you know Lady was fucked up.

"Uh oh," Lady said when the first drop entered into her system. She wasn't around when the last drop entered it.

"Lady? Lady?" Melvin called out when she tipped over and started foaming at the mouth. He was more disappointed in missing his turn than he was at her overdose. Not to be denied he rolled the deceased Lady onto her stomach and slid into her semen soup. With his nasty ass.

****

"William Cash!" the corrections officer shouted from his booth. It was his job to get up and go get the inmate, but he didn't do his job very well. "One of y'all niggas go get that nigga!"

"I'll get 'em boss!" a step-and-fetch inmate shouted out eager to do something for master. The shameless man shined shoes, kissed ass, and tap danced for pats on the head from the white officers. Every blue moon they would put half a sandwich in the trash for him to eat. Of course, he would have to take it around and show it off before actually eating it.

"Cash! William Cash!" the inmate yelled, as he rushed to his cell. He paused dead in his tracks when he walked in on a gay porn scene. For all his flaws he was still better than them, him kissing ass was figurative while them sucking dick was literal.

"What?" Billy snapped irritably as he continued to guide LeVaughn's head up and down on his cock.

"The police want you!" he said turning his nose up at the homosexuals.

"Okay, give me 'bout two minutes," he said as he began moving LeVaughn's head faster. Three minutes later he was finished and heading up the cell block to answer the summons.

"William Cash?" the guard asked formally, although he knew the troublemaker well.

"Yep," he replied, missing the warning in the guard's tone. Instead he simply fell in step behind him and followed him to the Chaplain's office.

"Chap wanna see you," he explained before tapping on the door.

"Enter!" the chaplain shouted from behind the closed door. He didn't bother looking up from the clutter of his desk when the two men entered. "William Cash?"

"Ye-"

"Yo' mama dead. Close the door on y'all way out," he said still not giving them more than the tanned bald spot in the center of his head to look at.

Billy stood there blinking rapidly as his mind scrambled to process what he'd just heard. He switched the letters of the three words around, like they did on The Soul Train scramble board, but he still couldn't make sense of the news he'd just gotten. Surely a little compassion would accompany a legitimate death notice.

"Standing her' shol' ain't gon' brang her back, so gon' on. Get!" the chaplain said as he finally lifted his weather beaten face.

"Come on, Cash," the guard urged softly. He wanted to dive across the old bastard's desk himself and choke him for his lack of empathy and he knew the volatile inmate well enough to know that he was capable of doing just that.

Billy was like a zombie as he was led back to the cell block. He was so out of it that he missed the hoops and hollers of friends as well as the glare of his foes.

"What's wrong?" LeVaughn asked fawningly when Billy returned. Between Billy and Pickle and all the dick they were feeding him LeVaughn was turning into a girl. Girls know that head makes guys feel better no matter what the problem is, so LeVaughn dropped to his knees again.

"My..." was all he managed to get out before his partner, Pickle, barged in.

"Damn nigga! You stay up in that throat! Today my day so let me get that," Pickle demanded. It's hard for two people to share anything; especially another person.

"Let me go on and keep her tonight. I got some serious thangs to deal with," Billy pleaded. All the while LeVaughn never stopped doing what he was doing as his eyes shifted back and forth between his war daddies as they spoke.

"Hell naw! It's my turn! Come on!" Pickle insisted as he pulled the sissy off of his knees. Billy twisted his lips in anger as he watched him lead him away to his cell.

Chapter 37

"Warden on deck!" a guard shouted, putting the cell block on alert. Accordingly all the inmates rushed to stand at attention outside their cells.

"Y'all niggas smoking real good I see!" the Boss Hog look alike proclaimed as he waddled down the tier. At five feet two inches tall and two hundred and fifty pounds all he could do was waddle. He didn't mind the weed since he got his cut. Plus it kept the savages calm and therefore kept down the violence.

He looked in every face he passed as the men stared straight ahead. The four large guards who flanked him were ready to pounce on the first one who blinked. The warden passed Pickle's cell, stopped and then took a few steps back.

"I hear you got a knife, boy!" he said scrunching his face up.

"Me? No, Sir! Un uh!" Pickle insisted. He looked like he was about to break into a tap dance or shit himself.

"Look under his mat," the warden told a guard, who quickly carried out the command before it was all the way out of the other man's mouth.

"Knife Baws!" he reported holding up a long homemade knife.

"That's not mine!" Pickle squealed in that high pitched voice black folk used when they got in trouble. Not only was it disgusting, but it also showed that they were lying. If they were telling the truth then they wouldn't be whining. Most times that's the case anyway, but this time he was actually telling the truth. Although the knife wasn't his he knew it quite well since it belonged to his partner. But what was it doing under his mat and how did the warden know it was there?

Billy stared straight ahead instead of being nosey like everyone else. Even LeVaughn gawked to see what was going on. Pickle knew then what had occurred and shot a dangerous glare at Billy as he was cuffed.

"Put that nigga in the hole 'til he turn my color," the warden ordered. That wasn't as long as it sounded since he wouldn't get not a single ray of sunlight in that dungeon.

"Guess it's just me and you now," Billy shrugged casually, as if it wasn't him who'd written the kite to the warden. Now the grimy man could add another title to his belt, snitch.

****

"You stink!" LeVaughn gushed and giggled when Billy came in from the yard.

"You know you like it," Billy shot back. They had become quite the couple since Pickle had been carted off to the hole a few weeks ago. Billy put on a little bit as he removed his sweaty clothes to go shower.

"Want me to come?" LeVaughn offered. He had become quite the woman and loved to bathe him.

"I got it," Billy replied and headed out. There was an eerie calm out on the cell block, but Billy paid no attention to it. The showers were a dangerous place. Plenty of rapes, beatings, stabbings, and murders took place in them. Billy was a predator, not prey so he wasn't concerned.

He was relieved to see that the showers were empty and that he could be alone with himself. After rinsing the sweat from his body he began to fondle his heavy penis until it grew hard in his hand. He then closed his eyes and imagined being inside of Mrs. Paul's mouth as he stroked himself. Ironically he didn't consider himself gay since he only fantasied about women.

"Mm, that's it," he told the memory of the preacher's wife. He was on the verge of an orgasm when he was rudely interrupted by a sharp pain in his back. He knew immediately that he had been stabbed but not by who. He had done so much fuck shit since he'd arrived that it could be anyone. Billy quickly moved away and spun around.

"You?" Billy grimaced when he saw Cat Eyes fully dressed and wielding a knife. Two of his partners stood guard ready to pounce as well. He knew he could take one, but three with knives equaled six and that was too many.

"Yeah me, nigga!" Cat Eyes growled and lunged forward again. Billy just managed to dip out of the way and not get stabbed again.

"Why you messing with me man?" Billy asked, as if he had done no wrong.

"Cuz you...you...you robbed me!" Cat Eyes replied and swung again.

"Oh, I know what this is about!" Billy laughed then turned to the other man's friends. "He ain't tell y'all I use to fuck his mouth while we was in reform school, huh?"

"Lies!" Cat Eyes screamed, proving it to be the truth. He went crazy with the knife after that stabbing air and the tile wall while Billy taunted him.

"Y'all ain't fuckin' this pretty nigga? You gotta see the way them green eyes flutter when you put the dick in his mouth," Billy cackled. Cat Eyes' friends had wanted to fuck him but fell for the tough guy role he portrayed.

"Handle yo' bidnezz. We'll see you back on the block," they said and turned and left. Cat Eyes wanted to leave with them but that wasn't an option.

"It's me and you now, boy!" Billy hissed as he circled around to block the exit.

"Ugh!" Cat Eyes grunted as he attacked once more. Billy blocked him with his arm and did a roundhouse with his elbow. The blow removed the other man's front teeth as it sent him back peddling into the shower's wall.

"Gon' stab me, nigga!" Billy demanded and punctuated his words with vicious punches to the body. Cat Eyes dropped the knife and tried to cover up. Billy quickly swept around him and put him into a choke hold. Cat Eyes tapped, clawed, and pulled until he passed out from the pressure around his neck.

"You know you don' fucked up right?" Billy asked as he stripped the unconscious man. The few spectators took the action as their cue to leave, no man wants to see another man get raped.

"Yeeooow!" Cat Eyes squealed when he awoke and felt what was happening to him.

"I bet!" Billy laughed and kept right on going. He used one arm to hold him in a choke hold while he used the other to hold the knife. There was nothing Cat Eyes could do except take it and so he did.

"That was fucked up!" Cat Eyes screamed once the rape came to an end, pun intended.

"No, this..." Billy corrected as he shoved the knife into his neck, "is fucked up!"

He ignored the gargles as Cat Eyes struggled to stay alive. He got back under the water and finished showering. LeVaughn had cooked him a hot meal by the time he returned. The rest of the cell block ignored the dead guy in the shower. It wasn't until the count in Cat Eyes' cell block came up short that he was discovered.

"Uh oh!" LeVaughn warned when all the commotion began.

"Don't worry babe, ain't no one gon' tell on Dollar Bill!" he said arrogantly, which was surprising since he was so well versed in scripture and knew that Proverbs 16:18 read 'Pride goes before destruction.'

Chapter 38

"Warden on deck!" the guards screamed as they stormed the cell block. His red face was even redder from pure rage. All the inmates had begun to scramble to attention by their cells.

"Shit!" Billy fussed at being interrupted from his morning ritual. He liked to start each day with head, a cup of coffee, and the sports section, but the warden had fucked that up.

"I done tol' y'all niggas 'bout all the violence. I let y'all smoke, drank, and fuck all you want but leaving a dead nigga in my shower is unacceptable!" he boomed. All the while his good squad marched straight towards Billy.

"Uh oh," LeVaughn muttered when he saw them coming.

"I was gon' lock this whole cell block down until I got my man. Luckily for y'all I got all these kites!" he said holding up a fistful of letters all bearing Billy's name. Not only would they rid themselves of the bully but they'd free up a sissy as well.

"Cuff up!" a guard demanded pulling out his cuffs. The other guards pulled their billy clubs in case he wanted to do it the hard way. He didn't, he turned around and let them hook him up.

"Your black ass going to the hole until hell freeze over!"

"Can I take him?" Billy asked hoping to take his sissy with him.

"Cain't take nothing to the hole. All you get in there is a bible and paper to write home," the guard assured him.

"Don't worry, I'll be back in a couple of days," Billy called to LeVaughn as he was led away. "Wait for me!"

****

A year had passed before Billy got the hint that he was going to be in the hole for a while. LeVaughn was not waiting for him to return. In fact he hadn't even lasted the day before someone else had claimed him as his own.

Billy spent most of the first year jacking off and doing push-ups. He had no one to write nor any use for the bible. By the second year he'd finally picked it up and read it from cover to cover.

By the fifth year he'd memorized every word of it but didn't believe a word of it. He did, however, learn that he could use the scripture to manipulate people. The natural born hustler began to use it as a hustle and Reverend Cash was reborn.

"What time is service today?" an old timer named Smitty called out from the far end of the tier. Like Billy he was in the hole for killing another inmate. The warden had told him that he'd be there until hell froze solid. That was fifteen years ago.

"Just give me a few minutes. I'm gathering my sermon right now," Reverend Cash called back. The entire cell block stopped what they were reading or writing and prepared to tune in. "In the meanwhile, I'll send the collection plate round."

In this case the collection plate was actually a pillowcase tied to a makeshift wire that stretched from one end of the block to the other. This was how drugs, tobacco, and girly magazines were passed, traded, sold, or borrowed. It was also how Reverend Cash collected his tithes. He made sure to collect his collections before he started to preach. He then based the length, quantity, and quality of the sermon he gave on what he'd been given. If his collection was light then so was his message. If it was hefty then he'd lift all spirits to the heavens.

"There you go Rev.," Peppy in the cell over called when the plate made it back full.

"Yes Lawd! Y'all must want me to preach today, huh?" Reverend Cash asked as he emptied the pillowcase. It had commissary items, sticks of reefer, homemade wine, and a grainy black and white picture of a hairy vagina.

"Preach Rev.!" they cheered and preach he did. Even a few of the guards came in and listened to the word.

It was a full two hours later when he asked the men to bow their heads one last time. He spit some mumbo jumbo that made the men 'Amen', 'Yes Lawd', and 'Hallelujah' and was done.

"Preacher 'bout to take some meditation time now," Reverend Cash announced. What he meant was he was about to smoke some reefer, drink some wine, and bust a nut while looking at whoever's vagina that was.

****

Ten years later Reverend Cash was still in the hole. A few faces had changed but that was about all. Smitty had gone on to the upper room a year ago and hell still hadn't frozen over so he was still stuck. He was still preaching the world and eating off doing so.

"Inmate Cash!" the guard boomed as he made his way down the tier. He sounded official but was actually one of Reverend Cash's flock. He looked both ways to make sure that the coast was clear and then slipped him a rolled up magazine. "Here ya go Rev."

"What's this?" the Reverend asked softly so that he wouldn't be overheard.

"It's a newsletter from Pastor Wesley out in California. I thought you might enjoy it," the guard said in conspiratorial tone and winked. Magazines were still contraband so this was a big deal.

"Thanks," Cash smiled and nodded. He just knew that the inside was full of naked pictures for him to masturbate to. He was wrong. It was full of articles and scripture. As soon as the guard left he flung it into the corner. It was two days later when he finally picked it up and he was glad that he did.

"Damn!" he exclaimed when he saw the huge house behind the smiling preacher. It was no wonder he was smiling with the luxury cars in the driveway and expensive watch on his wrist.

The California preacher was at the helm of a mega-church and T.V ministry that netted him millions. Reverend Cash read the words of the interview but all he saw were the riches. His big titty blonde wife and fancy suits appealed to him way more than the pillowcase full of commissary. The end of the magazine had an order form from Reverend Wesley's bible study.

"Sign me up!" he cheered and did just that. A week later he received the full one year course in the mail. A month later he sent it back completed. A month after that he received a full scholarship to Reverend Wesley's Bible College.

Four years later he was still in the hole but had a degree in Theology. Five years later his name was finally called.

"William Cash! Pack it up," the guard called down the cell block. When he didn't get a reply he went down to the cell. "Pack it up, Cash."

"What hell finally froze over? The warden finally letting me back in population?" he asked sarcastically.

"Population? Boy, you made parole. You going home!"

Chapter 39

Reverend Cash was shocked into complete silence as he was processed out of prison. The notion of parole had never really crossed his mind considering all the fuckery he'd committed. He was especially shocked considering the Cat Eyes situation, but since he'd never been charged with killing him it hadn't been held against him. Being locked in solitary had kept him out of trouble so his record was clean.

He dressed in the state issued going home clothes, which were designed to make you look like you had just been released from prison. Upon release each inmate was given a cheap pair of denim jeans, with an even cheaper button down shirt, along with the cheapest pair of tennis shoes. The state also cut a check for whatever funds an inmate had left in his account. If an inmate's balance was zero then the state would add another zero and put a one in front of the two turning it into a hundred dollars. It could be used to get on one's feet or to re-ignite a drug and/or alcohol problem. Hoping for the latter the state left a light on for those who would return.

"Is this right?" Cash asked blinking rapidly at the numbers on the check. He had earned his G.E.D along with two degrees in theology, but the numbers on the check baffled him. He regretted the words as soon as they were out of his mouth. If the state had fucked up and given him too much money it was his sworn duty to keep it.

"Ten thousand...yup, that's right," the officer confirmed after consulting his computer. "Seems you got a check from when yo' mama house sold a while back."

"Somebody paid ten thousand for my mama's house?" he asked in disbelief. Surely they had gotten over since he knew what she'd paid for it. He didn't consider the fact that that had been well over thirty years ago. In fact it was he who'd got, got. The property had sold for over one hundred thousand and he'd only received a measly ten percent of it.

"Bus ticket," the guard said handing it over. He wondered if inmate Cash could read from the way he frowned down at the ticket.

"Memphis," Cash finally read aloud. He then drifted back inside of his own thoughts and wondered what was there for him. Lady was dead. Byron and Leroy were also dead, along with Shawna, Shonda, and her mama. The Buffalo Gals had shared Aids while sharing needles a decade ago.

Reverend Cash was still wondering as he rode the bus to Memphis. Time flies when you're inside of your head, so the next thing he knew the bus was pulling into Memphis. Or so the driver said because he didn't recognize a thing. He was in awe at the new buildings, street signs, and the huge casino shaped like a pyramid.

The people seemed to have changed as well. Gone were the afros and platform shoes. They were replaced with sagging jeans and dreadlocks. A group of teen girls caught his eye as they giggled their way pass the stopped bus. They were dressed like whores but were actually on their way to middle school.

The exact date was June 1, 2005 when the thirty-eight year old Reverend Cash stepped off the bus as a free man. He closed his eyes and inhaled freedom for the first time in over a decade. He caught a glimpse of the world famous Memphis BBQ as he opened his eyes and it made his empty stomach flutter like a third semester baby in its mother's womb. He recalled an inmate who was constantly in and out of prison telling him he could cash his check at the bank just across the street from the bus station. He exhaled and made his way over.

It took him a minute to build up the courage to cross the busy street. Life now moved a lot faster since he'd been gone, not to mention the crossing sign had also changed dramatically. Cash watched the other pedestrians for a few seconds and then did what they did.

The guard recognized the prison issued clothing and kept an eye on him upon his entrance into the bank. It wasn't too long ago that another man had stepped off of the bus, crossed the street, and robbed the place. He'd wanted to go back to prison, so he'd sat on the curb and waited until the cops came to grant him his wish.

A pretty teller had also taken notice of the man in prison clothes and locked her eyes on him because he was so handsome. Reverend Cash saw the young woman smiling at him and almost ran out. It had been eighteen years since he'd been with a man, but it had been twenty years since he'd been with a woman. Fate caused the line to flow putting him face to face with the pretty woman. He couldn't help but to inhale the sweet smells coming from across the counter. She smelled of hair care products along with a lotion and perfume that smelled wonderful.

"Welcome to First National. How can I help you?" she offered with a bright smile and fluttering lashes.

"I...um..." he replied then frowned in confusion at having lost his train of thought. "Um..."

"You want to cash your check?" she helped. "Let me have it along with the ID card that they gave you."

"Okay," he said gratefully as he followed her instructions. She didn't blink at the large amount on the check, the new age dope boys often came home with large checks. The date of birth on his ID, however, did cause her to blink in shock. Her mental math told her that the man standing before her was thirty-eight, but he didn't look a day over twenty-five, twenty-one if he took his shirt off.

"Is this right?" she inquired.

"Yes, Ma'am. Prison preserves you," he explained. Men who went in young and did long bids often came out looking only slightly aged. Unfortunately, the statement also applied mentally as well. A man who went in at eighteen and did fifteen years usually came home with the mentality of a twenty-one year old.

"Sure does! I wouldn't have guessed it from looking at you, but you almost my mama's age!" she gushed as she counted out his money. She smiled and batted her lashes at him again when she handed it over, just in case he wanted to ask her out.

"Any place I can get some BBQ 'round here?" he asked as he separated his cash into different pockets. It was an old habit he'd learned from the streets. It was done just in case a jack boy got the drop on you. You'd only part with some instead of all of your money that way.

"A few. I don't mess with them fancy places though. Go up the street two blocks and make a right. It's the best in town," she replied. "Oh and there's a clothing store right across the street, just in case you want to change."

"Thank you, Ma'am," Cash said and gave her a polite nod as he turned and walked briskly out of the bank.

"He gay!" the teller mused to herself. She'd seen it before and therefore wasn't surprised. "He gotta be because I know I look good!"

****

Reverend Cash got reacquainted with the taste of Memphis' BBQ before crossing the street to the clothing store the teller had mentioned. His eyes naturally gravitated to the colorful pimp suits he'd worn before he left the street, but luckily for him a sharp salesman saved him from purchasing any.

"Been a minute, huh?" the salesman asked knowingly. Everyone who got locked up twenty or more years ago was drawn to that wall of the shop. He quickly steered Cash away from the wall and over to the more up to date fashions.

"Wow!" Cash uttered as he admired his reflection in the dressing room mirror. The charcoal grey slacks the salesman had picked out for him contrasted perfectly with the black shirt, belt, and shoes he'd paired with them. Cash paid a couple hundred for a couple of new outfits, handpicked by the salesman, and headed back out.

Not having a clue as to where to go ended him right back at the bus station with the aimless. After twenty years of eating prison food the soul food he'd eaten had shocked his system causing him to make a beeline to the station's bathroom. His stomach rumbled and turned flips as he did.

"Shit!" Cash groaned at barely having sat before releasing his bowels. It was so loud that he almost missed the announcements.

"Bus 1080 headed to Atlanta, Georgia now boarding at gate 9. I repeat bus 1080..."

Cash had just enough time to push it all out, wipe his ass, and buy a ticket before boarding the bus. Watch out Atlanta, here comes trouble!

Chapter 40

Usually the thought of moving to a new city with nothing and where you knew no one was a scary prospect, but not for Cash because it meant that he could be whoever he wanted to be. No one knew him so no one could refute whatever he told them. He was Reverend Cash and no one could say otherwise. Besides, he had the degrees to prove it.

Cash settled in a window seat to catch up on what he'd missed. What he'd missed the most was the soft, velvety, slippery feel of pussy and he couldn't wait to get into some. However, he would have to wait and he'd be tested while he did. The first test came just as the bus's backup alarms began to sound.

"Wait! Hol' up!" a lady shouted as she ran along tapping on the bus's door. The driver stopped and let her board. "Ooh honey, thank you so much!"

Cash looked curiously at the tall woman with the obvious wig and ton of make-up applied to her face. She wasn't his type but after twenty years that was negotiable. The woman scanned the bus for an empty seat. There were plenty but she chose the one next to him.

"Hey there honey," the woman sang and extended a large hand. It was then that Cash realized that she was a he. "My name is Akai."

"I'm Reverend Cash," he said, liking how it sounded. He liked it so much that he almost said it again just to hear it again.

"Ooh, I love preachers!" Akai cheered complete with a sissy clap.

Cash had his mind set on a woman, but the effeminate man turned him on. He looked, sounded, and smelled just like a woman and Cash's body responded.

"Mmm, I see that the preacher likes me too!" Akai said, looking at the thick bulge between Cash's legs. It was rock hard and throbbed with every beat of his racing heart.

"You know what..." Cash began as he looked around as they rode. He was checking to see if it would be possible for him to discreetly get some head, just to take the edge off of his desires, but it wasn't meant to be. Not only were all the passengers wide awake but there was also a child sitting directly across from him.

"You wanna hook up when we get to the A?" it offered.

"Hell yeah!" Cash said. He'd convinced himself that it would be his last time with a man, then it would be strictly woman after that. At least that was his theory.

It's a long ride from Memphis to Atlanta and the anticipation of getting his dick sucked upon arrival only served to make it that much longer. Akai had an apartment so that solved the dilemma of where they would be spending the night.

It was just after midnight when the bus pulled into Atlanta. Cash quickly pulled his bag from the overhead compartment and followed his new friend off the bus. Activity at the club across the street immediately caught his eye.

"That's a strip club. Them bitches in there are fierce!" Akai explained. "Let me get my bag and then I'll be right back."

He could be right back all that he wanted but Cash wouldn't be there when he returned. He was pulled across the street like he was being pulled by some type of magnetic force. Pussy had the tendency to do that to a man.

"Twenty," the hostess with the biggest titties he'd ever seen demanded when Cash stepped inside.

"Dollars?" Cash asked slightly confused. When he'd left the streets it had only cost fifty cents to get into a club. The beautiful women he was able to see from the door killed any and all protest from him. Luckily for his pockets it didn't cost two hundred dollars because he would have gladly paid it.

"Oh my!" Cash muttered when he walked fully inside. His knees actually buckled at the sight of all the ass and titties walking around. Stallions of all shapes, colors, and sizes walked by on stilt like high heels causing his dick to grow long and hard against his leg. He knew he had to sit down before he passed out. A couple of guys abandoned a table and he rushed over to commandeer it before someone else did.

"What you drankin'?" a sexy waitress demanded when she arrived at his table. His seated position put him right at eye level with her exposed navel. Right above it set a pair of heavy breast and right below it was a fat crotch put on display by a pair of tiny shorts.

"Huh?" he asked since he didn't understand what the vagina had just said.

"Up here, boo," she said pointing up at her face. "What you drankin'?"

"I'll take a...um..." he paused. He doubted that they sold homemade moonshine and beyond that he was lost since the place didn't look like it sold the cheap whine he'd grown up on either. Another waitress passed by with fluorescent blue liquor in glasses and saved the day. "I'll take one of those."

"One Blue Motherfucker coming right up," she said and gave him an ass cheek show as she went to retrieve his order. However, it was nothing compared to the set of cheeks on display on the stage. A jet black girl was up there bouncing up and down making her ass clap. Cash couldn't take another second of it. He reached for his zipper so he could jack off.

"Table dance?" a very pretty but very young looking girl asked before he could get his dick out which would have gotten him in trouble.

"How old are you?" he couldn't help but to ask. She looked like she was young enough to still get excited when someone waved bye-bye to her.

"Dang! Why people keep asking me that?" she fussed and stomped her foot. Her firm breast shook once and stopped under the crispy white wife beater. She put her hand on her curvy hip and stated, "Old enough. I'm eighteen!"

"That's old enough for me. How much for a dance?" he asked just as the waitress returned with his drink. She placed it in front of him and he handed her a ten dollar bill. There was a brief standoff as they both looked at and waited for the other. He expected some change and she expected a tip.

"Ten bucks. Same as dranks cost," the young stripper tossed in to settle the tacit debate.

"Oh!" they both laughed. He parted with another ten and the waitress left with a smile.

"It's an extra ten for me to come out of my top and ten more for the bottom," she said as she plucked at the elastic of her boy shorts for emphasis. Cash's reply was a twenty for them both.

"Lawd!" he exclaimed as she removed her top and revealed a pair of high yellow breast capped by large brown nipples. She then turned and bent over as she peeled the boy shorts off of her round ass. Her bald plump vagina hung between her legs like a piece of juicy ripe fruit.

"Hey!" she reeled when she felt his hand between her thighs. "They don't let y'all touch! Not unless you in the VIP room."

"How...eh em," he started then paused to clear his throat. "How much for the VIP?"

"It's a hundred dollars to get in, plus I get a hundred and you have to pay every twenty minutes," she explained. She'd gotten a peek at his wad of cash when he paid her so she knew he could stand it.

"I'm going to need more than twenty minutes," Cash said thoughtfully.

"Shoot you can just pay me five hundred for the whole night," she leaned in and offered. The dancers were forbidden from taking customers home, but if the girl wasn't hard headed then she wouldn't be a stripper, now would she?

"Let's go! I'm Cash, and you are...?"

"I'm Meeka," she said pointing her finger at herself the way a toddler does when introducing him/herself. "Let me go change!"

Cash took a sip of the blue drink and frowned. It was super sweet but he could still taste all the alcohol underneath it. He gulped the drink down while watching the women on stage as well as the ones walking by and giving lap dances at the other tables. As he watched he began to rub his bulge through his pants. He would've bust in them had Meeka not returned when she did.

"Ready?" she asked bouncing happily. She looked even younger in her street clothes and that turned him on even more.

"Ready as I've ever been in my life!" he announced.

"I told the manager you was my daddy," she giggled.

"I'm 'bout to be!" Cash returned.

Chapter 41

"This is yours?" Cash frowned when a late model BMW chirped in answer to the remote Meeka pushed. It honked, flashed its lights, and unlocked its doors as the button was pushed.

"Yeah, my granddaddy gave it to me when I got accepted into college," she replied. They climbed in and it started with the press of a button. Cash flinched when thunderous rap music came blaring out of the speakers. That's how she rolled so they were forced to shout to each other for the entire ride.

"I gotta make a quick stop," she yelled while driving as fast as the music was loud.

"Okay," he yelled back and settled comfortably into the leather seat. Soon he was bobbing his head to the beat and by the third repetition of the chorus he was singing along.

Cash couldn't help but to notice the girl seemed to have more pep in her step when she returned to the car after making her stop. She was now dancing in her seat as she dipped in and out of traffic. He also took notice of the way that she sniffled and rubbed her nose a few times. He assumed that she was on dope, but the only dope he knew about made you nod not bob.

Meeka pulled into a gated B rated apartment complex. A quick press of her smart phone lifted the gate and she zipped under it. Cash stared up at her ass as she led the way up the stairs to her unit.

"Nice," Cash admired when he stepped inside. Each room had been purchased as a package straight out of a B rated furniture store. A good night of stripping had paid for each room individually.

"Make yourself at home," she blurted over her shoulder as she sped off into the back of the apartment.

He did too by taking a seat on the sofa and lighting the half joint that was left in the ashtray. Meanwhile, Meeka snorted coke and jumped into the shower. She dried off and slipped on a tiny oriental style robe.

"I'm back," Meeka sang as she breezed back into the room. She sat Indian style on the sofa giving him a peek at her plump vagina.

"I see," he smiled at the vagina then up at her face. She looked even younger without all the war paint on her face. That was enough foreplay for him so he reached over and touched her bald box.

"Mmm," she moaned and reach out to return the favor. He was so hard that it took some doing to get his big dick out of the opening of his pants. "Dang! You got a big ol' dick!"

"Thanks," he shrugged at what he assumed was a compliment. He then looked down and watched her grip his shaft with her tiny hands. She intended to stroke it but only managed one pump.

"Oh, Hell Naw!" Meeka fussed when he promptly erupted into the air.

"My bad. I haven't been with a woman in a very long time."

"I know what you need. I'm tryna fuck all night and you cain't be cumming all quick! Shit, I wanna cum too!" Meeka fussed all the way into her bedroom and back, "...don't make no sense! Got a big ol' dick and..."

"What's that?" he asked curiously as she dumped a pile of white powder onto the table. "Heroin?"

"Boy, don't nobody use that stuff no mo'!" she shot back as she chopped and diced the powder into four lines. She then leaned in and inhaled two and saved the other two for him. "This is some bomb ass coke."

Cash contemplated for all the time it took for her to hand him the rolled up bill. He took it and then repeated what he'd seen her do. The two lines sent him reeling back onto the sofa.

"Damn it man!" Cash exclaimed at the instant euphoria that rushed through his system. Not only was the drug's impact immediate it was also permanent. He now wanted to feel this way all the time.

"Now come on in the back here so that we can fuck!" Meeka demanded. She dropped her robe on the way to her room and he peeled off his shirt. Once they were both naked she pushed him on the bed. A little head had him rock hard even though his dick felt numb. "I'm finna ride this!"

"Careful now, that's a lot of dick," Cash chuckled smugly. He watched as she straddled him backwards and rubbed his swollen head between her slippery lower lips.

To his utter amazement she sank all the way down onto his dick with no hesitation. He just knew it was in her lungs or liver.

"Mm hm," Meeka agreed as she began to ride him in a forward and back motion, instead of the standard up and down one. She moaned, rocked, and came only to start all over again. An hour later she fell over to the side totally spent.

"Nuh uh," Cash laughed. He hadn't gotten his yet so things were far from over.

"You can keep going," she offered and flipped flat onto her stomach. She invited him in by arching her back and spreading her legs.

Cash slid back inside of her until he reached her ovaries. He took a few cursory pumps then proceeded to fuck the daylights out of the young girl. In fact daylight had just broke when he pulled out and bust a nut on her back.

"Finally!' Meeka fussed. "Now let me get a lil sleep. I gotta go to church in a couple hours!"

"Church?" Cash asked in astonishment. That was the last place he figured she'd go. Especially after all the dancing, sucking, fucking, snorting, and smoking they'd just did.

"Yeah, I go to church!" she said almost defensively. "Matter of fact, it's my family's church. My granddaddy was the preacher until he died a few months ago."

"So, so, so w-who the preacher now?" Cash asked eagerly.

"Ain't got one. My Grandma looking for one now since she in charge. Deacon Small be preaching but his old ass is senile as fuck! Now, you mind if I get me some sleep? Please!"

"Sure, no problem. As long as I can go to church with you in the morning."

"That's a first!" Meeka laughed. "Sure, come on."

****

A few hours later a blaring alarm clock absolutely insisted that the two wake up. Meeka was smart enough to put it across the room so she would be forced to get up to turn it off. Once she was up, she was up and didn't go back to bed. Her phone began vibrating on the nightstand as a follow up.

"Hey Grandma...mm hm...of course...love you too," Meeka said and hung up. "Ol' girl always make sure I'm coming to church."

"I see," Cash replied. It took great restraint not to try to fuck her again that morning. Especially when they took a joint shower to save time.

He ran the iron over one of his other outfits while she got into her church clothes. Meeka now looked fifteen in her flowery dress and pigtails with ribbons.

The drive across town landed them in East Atlanta. A neighborhood in transition from hood to chic middle class. Cash was halfway expecting some rundown, juke joint of a church but to his surprise New World Baptist was anything but. The fairly new building was built to hold a congregation that doubled every few years.

"Nice!" Cash nodded at the potential. If he could get his foot in the door here he could make some serious money.

"Believe it or not this use to be a run-down juke joint type church when my granddaddy first got it. Now they own all the land, houses, cars, and a laundry mat..."

Cash had to fight an erection as she ran off a long list of assets. A police officer stood in the middle of the street to direct the flow of traffic. Meeka pulled in and whipped around the back to the VIP parking, that was reserved for family members, Deacons, and it also had a big empty spot that read 'Pastor Parking'.

"First things first," she said as she dug into her purse. She came out with her supply of cocaine. After inhaling a few bumps up each nostril she offered some to her guest. "Have some?"

"Uh..." he debated for a second and gave in. He felt faster than a speeding bullet as they walked inside.

Cash counted heads in the first pew and multiplied it by the number of pews as they made their way to the VIP seating on the front pew. He shook his head at the number he came up with. Deacon Small stood and began to preach or something.

"Uh...welcome to the uh..." the eighty year old stammered. He squinted as he looked around until it came to him, "New World Baptist Church!"

"See why my grandma looking for a new preacher. They holding tryouts soon, then the board gone pick one. She got the final say though," Meeka whispered.

Old Deacon Small caught a groove and starting preaching real good. He misquoted a few scriptures but it sounded good. So did the choir. The mix of old and young, male and females got the joint jumping.

Meeka jumped up and sang and danced. Cash recalled a few of the moves from his table dance last night. The parishioners thought she'd caught the Holy Ghost but he knew it was just that good coke.

"We got anyone who wants to testify?" the Deacon asked as he wrapped up his sermon. Several hands went up in the air as he scanned the sea of pews. He deliberately looked over Sister Johnson because the old lady had no filter and no chill. Somebody would definitely get put on blast and/or cursed out if he let her testify. He zoned in on Cash, being a new face and right up front got him a nod and the microphone.

"Y'all mind, if I testify?" he asked softly and meekly. He asked so softly and meekly that Meeka squinted to make sure that he was the same dude who'd just fucked the daylights out of her.

"Go on and testify! Speak! Well! Take your time!" the congregation advised.

"Okay...I'll testify," he said softly before going in. Reverend Cash knew this was his shot and so he shot for the stars. All eyes and ears were on him as he quoted scripture and made shit up. He ended a half hour after he'd started by introducing himself. "I'm Reverend William Cash and I want to be a part of your family."

"Damn it man!" Deacon Small exclaimed when he got the mic back. "That boy shol' can preach!"

"Come on and meet my Granny," Meeka said once heads lifted from the final prayer.

"Let's," he agreed offering the crook of his arm. She took it and led him over to meet Mother Nancy.

"Grandma, this is my friend Reverend Cash," Meeka announced. The three hundred pound woman was the same light complexion as her granddaughter and was probably just as pretty forty something years ago. She was laced in white lace and diamonds.

"Ma'am," Reverend Cash nodded respectfully. The woman looked him up and down but got stuck on his crotch.

"Grandma!" Meeka called to break the spell.

"Oh!" the old lady giggled and finally looked up, "Nice to meet you. I loved that testimony!"

"I told him y'all looking for a new preacher," Meeka tossed in.

"We is, but we gon' take our time finding one. It's an important job and we gots lots of candidates. We..." she paused to look at his crotch again, "...um, what was I saying?"

"You were talking about taking your time," Cash helped. "I'm sure I'm the right man for the job. Just give me a chance to prove it."

"Well, we'll see," she said. She hugged her darling granddaughter before she shuffled away.

"You wanna get something to eat?" Cash suggested.

"I wanna get high and fuck!" she countered.

"Me too, but let's get something to eat first."

Chapter 42

A month passed and the couple were still getting high and fucking. She reintroduced him to eating pussy and he was hooked. He'd spent half of his money on clothing and coke so something had to give. Luckily auditions were coming up for the preaching position. He made sure to put his bid in every week by testifying. He should have had this fingers crossed since he was lying.

Another young preacher had his eyes on the prize also. Pastor Kenyatta Jones had grown up in this church and considered himself heir to the throne. He was as much street as he was church boy and

he liked weed, pussy, and coke just as much as Cash. Not to be out-
done he got in on the act by testifying each week as well to make sure
he wasn't overshadowed. It could go either way.

"So...who...you...think she...gone...pick?" Cash asked in between
tongue twirls on Meeka's clit.

"Huh? I'on know," she replied irritated. She was on the verge of
an orgasm and he wanted to ask questions. He realized his error and
threw his tongue into overdrive. He licked and sucked a violent nut
out her, causing her to arch her whole body off the bed when she
came. He then gave her a few minutes to recover before getting back
to business.

"Probably me or that light skin nigga with the good hair," Cash
threw out.

"Who Kenyatta? Maybe, he is a good preacher. He can fuck too,"
she said since she knew both to be true first hand. "No telling with
her freaky self."

"Who a freak, Grandma?" he asked curiously. He had a clue she
was since she stared at his dick every chance she got.

"Who? Chile please! Mother Nancy used to get it in. She don'
slowed down now that she old."

"Well, just how old is she?"

"Let me see, I'm finna be nineteen, my mama is forty, so...she gotta be sixty-five or sixty-six, I believe," she guessed correctly.

****

Reverend Cash showed his ass when it came time for him to audi-
tion. He was Martin, Malcolm, and Big Daddy Kane all rolled into
one. Some of the board laughed joyfully while others wept. He almost slammed the mic down once he was done. Instead he gently
placed it back in its cradle and glared over at Kenyatta like top that.

"Mph," Kenyatta scoffed as he walked passed Cash to the stage.
Two contenders walked out knowing that they didn't stand a chance

as the young Reverend Jones took a breath, took the mic, and went in.

Reverend Cash felt smug when he left the stage but by the end of Jones' act he didn't feel as smug anymore. The board, as well as Mother Nancy, gave no indication one way or the other. The two would just have to wait.

"I wanna thank everybody for coming out. Deacon Small will announce the new preacher at Sunday's service," Mother Nancy announced. The two competitors nodded and parted ways.

****

"You better go on and get ready," Cash told Meeka down below him. It had become a habit of hers to give him a good blow job before they hit the club. In theory it was supposed to act as Salt Peter so he wouldn't get turned on by all the ass walking around.

"You don't want me to finish?" she whined. It is just plain rude to leave a dick half sucked and she didn't want that on her conscious.

"Later. I'ma drop you off and then make a few runs," he replied.

They smoked a fat blunt and snorted the rest of the coke before hitting the strip club. Usually he would post up at the bar and drink while she shook her ass for tips. Not tonight though, tonight he had church business to tend to.

****

"Welp, this is either a really good idea or a really dumb one," Cash told himself as he pulled to a stop in front of his destination. The weed, wine, and coke in his system told him that it was a good idea and so he got out and walked to the door. He reached the point of no return when he rang the bell.

"Reverend Cash? What you doing here this time of night? Where's Meeka? Why..." Mother Nancy rambled. She would have kept right on rambling off questions if Cash hadn't stepped in and put his tongue in her mouth.

The old woman went stiff for a split second then softened. She reached down and finally got a hold of that cock she'd been peeping through his pants.

"You tryna fuck something, I see," she said when he got hard in her hand.

"Yes, Ma'am. I want that job!" he explained so there wouldn't be no misunderstanding.

"Let's see what you talkin' 'bout then," she dared and led him into her bedroom. She and the board had already made their choice but she wasn't turning down any dick.

The woman pulled her nightgown over her head and revealed a pair of big bloomers and an old school bra that made her breast look pointy. When she unhooked the clasp her old titties pointed straight down at her feet. Then off came the bloomers and she climbed on the middle of her bed.

'Stay hard dick' Cash pleaded to himself as he came out of his clothes. His dick must have known what was at stake because it remained rock solid. Mother Nancy had a big belly that looked like a beige bean bag chair and directly under it lay a nice plump vagina. It was old school fat like J.J Evans lips. Now that's some Good Times.

"The motor still get nice and hot, but sometimes it needs a little oil," she explained when his fingers failed to get her wet. He let out a deep sigh at the thought of going down on the old lady. He would have, but luckily she had a better solution. "Run to the kitchen and grab the blue can with the white lid."

"Blue can, white lid," he repeated as he set off to retrieve the item. He made sure to keep pulling on his erection as he did so that he wouldn't lose it. With all the coke he'd snorted he had no way of knowing if he'd be able to get it back up or not. He found an item matching the description she'd given but frowned at it in doubt. This couldn't be it. "Ma'am!"

"Blue can, white lid!" she shouted back hoarse from sexual desire. Cash shrugged, picked up the can, and took it to her.

"That's it!" she cheered happily. She took a handful of the creamy shortening and slapped it between her thighs. "Now, come on!"

"Damn it man!" Cash exclaimed as he pushed inside. As he slipped in to the hilt he realized the secret that old men already knew; that old ladies got some good pussy. All those wrinkles and folds that it had were like little fingers massaging his penis. Not to mention it was hot. The heat along with the Crisco Mother Nancy had applied could fry a chicken.

"Mmm...you...slangin'...that...dick!" Mother Nancy admired as Cash pounded in and out of her. He kept on until she came, shaking like Jell-O.

"Mmm," Cash growled when his own orgasm drew near. He wanted to snatch out and put it in her mouth like he did her granddaughter but didn't.

"Ain't no babies coming out of there, so do what you do," she said giving him permission to skeet inside of her. And skeet he did, busting the best nut he'd had since coming home.

"So, I got the job, right?" he asked breathlessly.

"Chile, you been had the job," the old lady cackled. "This part of the job now too since that's how you wanted to play it."

Chapter 43

"He must be waiting for you," Meeka fussed when she pulled into her parking spot and saw Reverend Jones lurking.

"I wonder why," Cash frowned curiously. He hopped out and walked over while Meeka went on in.

"Reverend Cash," Kenyatta said extending his hand. Once they had shook he started his speech. "You seem like a good dude. For you to be hitting Lil' Meeka you must get high and party. I like that. As a matter of fact, I respect your hustle.

"Thanks, but uh, where you going with this?" he asked cautiously.

"Just wanna let you know that I got the position on lock. I'ma fuck with you though, make you my assistant."

"Assistant? Like a hype-man?" Cash laughed. "What makes you think you got the position anyway?"

"Cuz I'm a smart nigga. You fuckin' the grandbaby, but what you should've done was push up on ol' girl. That's what I did!"

"You did?" Cash asked baffled. "When?"

"Last night, 'bout 2:30 in the morning. I went over there and sucked that old pussy inside out! She came so hard gobs of it was running out that box. And I gulped all that shit down!"

"Oh wow!" was all Cash could say. He'd left her just after 2 am. "Well, that's a bet. I like your style too. If I get the position you can be my hype- eh my assistant.

****

Deacon Small preached one last confusing sermon that sounded similar to an Otis Redding song. The congregation was thrilled to hear him announce the new pastor, but not as thrilled as Reverend Cash.

"Thank you!" he exclaimed in mock shock. The congregation called for him to say a few words so he did. He went right up to the pulpit and thanked everybody but God.

The good Reverend took control of the church and immediately got on the fuck shit. His first order of business was to fuck the members of the choir. It took a month for him to run through half of its members. That was only because he didn't fuck the half that was males. That's not to say that he didn't want to fuck some of them too, he just knew better than to open that can of worms.

To his dismay the church had an accountant to account for the cash in the collection plates. His dynamic preaching doubled the take in a matter of weeks, but he didn't have unlimited access to it. However, he still took him thousands every week. The house he took it home to was a newly renovated split level Ranch on the outskirts of East Atlanta. He was also given a two year old Cadillac with all the bells and whistles included, yet he still wasn't satisfied. With some carefully laid pipe he managed to convince Mother Nancy to approve a brand new one. With a closet full of clothes, a fancy house, and a new car under his belt it was now time to party.

****

"Yeah nigga, I like your style," Kenyatta nodded as he rode shotgun in the updated Cadillac. He took a hit of coke up each nostril then pinky fed two to Cash behind the wheel as well.

"Argh! Shit!" he responded as the strong drug tingled his brain. "Likewise my nigga. This club better be all that!"

"Newest in the city! Three levels. Hip hop in the basement, R&B main floor and don't go up to the roof level," he laughed.

"Why? What's up there?" Cash asked curiously. Anything off limits or forbidden appealed to his black heart.

"Fuck niggas and dykes! Straight homo shit! I ain't mad at the owner though for getting' all that money!" Kenyatta said.

"Speaking of money, you heard about that new mega church that they building over on the Eastside?"

"The one in Lithonia? Yeah, I heard about it. Them niggas about to get rich!"

"I know they are!" Cash snarled from jealousy. As well as he was doing and it still wasn't enough. He'd set his sights on Greater First Baptist Church and would do whatever it took to get in there.

"Here we go," Kenyatta said pulling him out of his malicious thoughts. Cash followed his pointed finger and pulled in front of the club. The valet came up and took the car away as they went inside.

"Twenty dollars please," the hostess requested. Cash pulled out a big roll of collection plate money and parted with two twenties.

"Well, I know you an R&B nigga, but I'm straight hip hop! These young bitches fuck quicker than them middle age broads!"

"We'll see about that. I got a band that says I pull us two broads quicker than you do," Cash challenged.

"Bet!" Kenyatta agreed and they shook hands to seal the deal before parting ways. Both men were tall, handsome, and well dressed. And each had enough cash and coke to use as bait. It could have went either way if Reverend Cash hadn't gotten sidetracked.

****

"Cognac," Cash ordered when he reached the bar. He figured that would be a good place to start since it had a good view of the entire floor.

Some of Atlanta's finest thirty and forty something year olds were all dressed to impress and hoping to catch something. Everywhere Cash looked there was a woman looking back. There were plenty of successful middle aged women who had their own homes, businesses, and cars. They had their own everything, everything that is except for their own man. That's why they were in the club.

"Ooh, I think I'm on the wrong floor!" a flamboyant little man gushed as he came up beside him at the bar. Without looking the sound of his voice said that he was gay, but Cash looked anyway.

"What you looking for?" he heard himself ask seductively. A few women sighed and gave up on him when they saw him talking to the sissy.

"Not what, who...and that would be Mr. Right," the little fellow giggled. Cash felt the blood rush below and give him an erection.

He had been trying not to open that door but it seemed to be easing open all on its own.

"Say, Cash!" Kenyatta called from halfway across the club. He called him again, this time raising his hand to be spotted. Cash raised his too and he made a beeline over to him. "Come on my nigga. We out!"

"Already?" Cash exclaimed looking down at his watch. They hadn't even been inside the club a full ten minutes yet.

"Told you how I get down! And they fine!" Kenyatta bragged leading his partner to towards the exit. There two young hoodrats in skimpy clothes stood waiting. "Tosha and Nita, this is Cash."

"Hey Cash!" the girls sang in unison as they were led off to slaughter.

The foursome sat around the den of Cash's home and smoked and drank. The men set out some coke for the girls but didn't indulge themselves since they planned on using their dicks.

"Let me holla at you for a minute, Nita," Cash suggested as he stood. The girl giggled at her friend as she was led out of the room. Kenyatta had his dick in Tosha before they made it up the stairs.

Cash stripped as soon as he got Nita in his room. She knew why she was there and quickly shed her clothes as well. She looked up and saw a semi erect dick in her face and took it in her mouth and sucked it until it was fully erect.

"Un uh, flip over," Cash directed when she laid back on the bed and spread her legs wide.

"Mmm, back shots!" the young girl giggled and complied. She quickly flipped onto her stomach and arched her back. Cash reached into the small jar on his nightstand and retrieved some of its contents. The jar itself was fancy but there was plain old Crisco inside. He smeared a little on her anus and pushed a finger inside.

"Whoa! I don't take it up the ass!" the girl protested. She tried to get up but Cash held her down.

"Shush!" he insisted as he forced his way into her intestines. She let out a brief howl until he clamped his hand over her mouth.

"Mmp...hmp," Nita screamed behind his hand and struggled furiously as he savagely fucked her in her ass. The excitement of forcing her caused him to explode in her bowels.

"Don't holla," he warned and released his hand from her mouth. He quickly handed her a handful of cash when she flipped over.

"That's fucked up!" Nita pouted. She took the money, grabbed her clothes, and ran downstairs. "Come on Tosh, let's go!"

"Hol' up lil' mama," Kenyatta protested. He had to speak for her friend since his dick was on her tonsils.

The preacher and his assistant hit the clubs almost every night. They almost always took at least one woman home with them. All the while they planned and plotted on moving up to the big leagues.

"Boy they better pray we don't get up in Greater First Baptist," Kenyatta said rubbing his hands together greedily.

"No, let them pray. Let us Prey!"

Chapter 44

Reverend Cash had doubled the congregation at New World Baptist in the last five years. His name rang loudly as one of the best preachers in the city. Still the riches and fame didn't satisfy the man. Everything he did at New World Baptist was done bigger and better at Greater First Baptist Church. When he heard that the pastor was looking for a team of assistants he saw it as his way in. The Reverend Darren Sanders was hosting a mega rally at The Convention Center and he had to be in the house.

****

"This shit poppin'!" Kenyatta exclaimed from their booth at The Convention Center. "It got plenty of hoes!"

"It's a'right," Cash said twisting his lips up ruefully. He was in his feelings about not being able to secure a speaking slot at the conference. He just knew if Reverend Sanders heard him he would pick him to be one of his assistants.

To make matters worse the royalty among Southern clergy walked around laced in platinum and ten thousand dollar suits. He may have arrived in a brand new Benz but there were Bentleys and Rolls Royces outside in the parking lot.

"Damn!" Kenyatta cheered as a short, sexy, bow-legged woman walked by. She had a nasty little walk that advertised how good the pussy must be. Church function or not the women attending were sexy. "I'ma have to take one of these hoes into a closet or something!"

"I'll be back. I need to stretch my legs," Cash said and set off behind the woman. He had no intention on speaking but he did enjoy the movement under her dress. He traced the panty lines hugging the curves of her ass.

"There go y'all mama," a short well-dressed man called out when he saw her. The two small children took off towards her as Cash kept going. He would have kept on going if he hadn't heard something that stopped him dead in his tracks.

"Dollar Bill! Is that you?" he heard and seized with fear. Whoever knew that name knew too much. He could lose his present and future because of his past.

"That is you!" the man confirmed as he came around and stared up at him.

"Um..." Cash frowned trying to place the vaguely familiar face.

"Now don't tell me you don't remember me!" he said putting his hand on his hip. He quickly caught himself and straightened up. "Earl, from Memphis. Pastor Paul."

"Is that you? Wow, you look so different!" Cash exclaimed. It was true now that he was twenty years older and slightly heavier with a mustache and goatee combination surrounding his mouth. The last time he's seen him he'd had his dick in that same mouth.

"Yup, it's me! That's my wife Donna, my son Henry, and my daughter LaDonna," he said proudly.

"Hello," Cash said with a smile and a wave at his family. "I see a lot has changed."

"Everything...has changed!" Earl confirmed to include his sexuality. His grandmother didn't play that gay stuff and had forced him straight. Now he was married with kids and doing well for himself. "Oh, and I'm the choir director at Greater First Baptist Church in Lithonia, Georgia.

"You are? That's great!" Cash exclaimed. This was his way in, and once he was in he would claw his way to the top. "I heard you guys are looking for assistant pastors. I'm trying to come on board. Maybe you could put in a good word for me?"

"You?" Earl reeled back scrunching his face up in disgust. "I don't know if it's the right place for you!"

"No?" Cash asked while wearing the same friendly smile, even though internally he'd flown into a rage. Having the same sissy he'd fucked and pimped turn his nose up at him had him thirty-eight hot. Still he was too smooth to show it. "Did you hear about Pastor Paul?"

"Mm hm, got himself killed," Earl said slightly effeminate at the mention of the man he'd once loved.

"Yeah, but that's not all," Cash whispered in a conspiratorial tone. Sissies love secrets so he made it sound like one. It was the same principal as putting a worm on a hook and using it for bait.

"What?" Earl whispered back, taking the bait. He looked around to make sure no one else could hear the secret. What good is a secret if you can't be the first one to spread it?

"Come on," Cash suggested and walked off. Earl rushed behind him just like he'd expected.

Cash led the way haphazardly as he searched for seclusion. He wasn't exactly sure how to play it but knew it had to be private. Kenyatta frowned curiously as he led him past their booth without as much as a side glance. He was on a mission and completely focused.

"Through here," he suggested as they left the main floor and hit the maintenance area. He tried all the door knobs until one opened and he entered the empty closet. "In here."

"So wha- argh!" Earl gasped when Cash snatched him into the air by his throat. He pulled at the large hand wrapped around his neck as he kicked his shiny size seven loafers trying to get free.

Cash suddenly forced him down to his knees and went for his zipper. The violence had him rock hard when he freed himself from his slacks. A squeeze on Earl's throat forced his mouth open and Cash forced his way inside.

"You...don't...think...I'm...good...enough!" Cash growled as he brutally fucked his face. Earl gagged as tears streamed down his face as Cash slammed into his larynx.

The oral rape only lasted a minute or so before it turned consensual. Old habits die hard and soon the old Earl was reborn. He was soon bobbing and slobbing on the pole like back in the day. He batted his eyes up at Cash as he took over.

"Yeah, that's the lil' mama I remember," he coaxed. Earl really went to work when he saw him pull out his phone to record the action. He wanted a copy for himself so he performed his heart out.

The episode ended with loud gulps that made Cash wonder if Earl wouldn't be high from all the coke he'd snorted earlier. There had to be some in all the semen he'd just swallowed.

"Now..." Cash said as he got himself together, "You, gon' get me that position as Assistant Pastor or the whole world gon' see just how well you suck dick!"

"You wouldn't!" Earl reeled like an old southern belle.

"Nigga, try me!" Cash dared. "And you better get a mint or something so your little wife don't smell all that nut in yo' mouth."

"Well, can I at least get a copy?" he pouted.

"Sure. Turn your Bluetooth on."

Chapter 45

Leaving New World Baptist Church behind also meant leaving behind the perks that went along with the job. The transition took a few months which was more than enough time to rape and pillage the church's assets.

Mother Nancy was well over seventy now and Reverend Cash was still putting the dick to her. One because he liked it and two because she'd sign whatever he said sign after she got a good nut.

The old lady had unknowingly mortgaged all of the church's assets. First was the house he lived in then came all the rest of the church's properties. She even took out loans on her own home and then finally the church itself. Having her sign the papers and collect the cash kept Cash out of the picture. He made sure the payments were made until he was officially named as an Assistant Pastor at Greater First Baptist Church. Soon after the banks foreclosed and took what was now theirs.

****

"Shit!" Reverend Cash muttered as he watched Greater First Baptist fill to capacity. The huge dome facility would fill, empty, and fill again.

Having had services of his own to hold this was the first Sunday that he'd got to attend the actual service. The place was impressive empty but seeing it full was surreal. He had to admire Reverend Sanders swag as he came out onto the stage. If he had been wearing a hat he would've tipped it in salute. He was determined to do whatever it took to take his spot.

"I am pleased to introduce to you, the newest members of our Greater First Baptist Church family. Our newest Assistant Pastors, Reverend Jack Wilson, Reverend Victor Wheeler, Reverend William Cash..."

With that, his foot was officially in the door. He knew it would be wise to take it slow because only fools rush in. There was so much ass running around but he did the smart thing and didn't touch any of it. He took his perversions out on Meeka as well as a bevy of strippers and hookers.

His new office was bigger than the old one he'd had at New World Baptist Church, yet he still wasn't content. This was just a start, he wanted it all.

"Reverend Cash," his secretary called via phone intercom. He was quite amused by the short pudgy girl assigned to him. She'd made it perfectly clear that she was available but he had his sights set higher than her. Pastor Sanders' new secretary Anita had a lovely face and a bubble ass that drove him wild.

"Yes, Tammy," he replied via intercom and then giggled. The high tech devices still amazed him after twenty years in a no tech prison cell.

Your two o'clock family therapy session is here," she informed. He told her to send them in, so she did.

"Mr. and Mrs. White," he greeted cordially as the couple in need entered his office. One of his duties was to offer marriage therapy, although he'd never been married himself. He loved hearing their secrets; especially the sexual ones. He could tell at first glance that this was going to be juicy by the embarrassed expression on the wife's face.

"Rev.," he replied with a nod while she looked down wringing her hands.

"How can I help you guys?" the preacher asked sounding so sincere.

"Go on and tell him!" the feisty wife dared. It was her idea to take this intimate matter to the church. "Tell him what you tryna do to me. Tell him!"

"You make it sound like I asked you to cut off an arm, or leg or something!"

Reverend Cash stifled a smile and watched the back and forth volley like it was a tennis match. He could have stepped in to ease things along but what fun would that be. They went a few more rounds before they got to the matter at hand.

"I just think it's unnatural, unsanitary, and...and...I bet it hurts," Mrs. White moaned and pouted.

'Jackpot!' Cash thought to himself. He was both amazed and amused at how many couples came to the church to settle issues of the bedroom. One would be surprised at how many times he'd had to advise to *'suck that dick', 'eat that pussy',* or *'let him hit you in the ass'.*

"It won't hurt. We can use a little lube," Mr. White offered softly.

"Crisco is good," the preacher heard himself say. It was too late to take it back so he went with it. "Or so I've heard. As a matter of fact from what I've heard any water based lubricant works well if you're using condoms. If not any oil based product is fine."

"Reverend Cash, would you have anal sex with your wife?" Mrs. White asked plainly.

"Well, I'm not married, but if I was I most certainly would. I would do absolutely anything to please my spouse and hope that she would do the same for me," he said causing Mr. White's head to nod in agreement. "Does he take care of you? Are the bills paid?"

"Yes, I mean...he's an excellent provider. I just..."

"Just nothing. Let that man get what he wants. Take a deep breath and..."

"Thank you, Pastor, Sir," Mr. White cut in. He'd heard enough and stood to leave. "Crisco?"

"Crisco," he assured them. He watched her wide ass as they left knowing what was in store for it.

"Pastor Cash, choir director needs five minutes with you," Tammy sang into the intercom.

"Send him in," he replied. Knowing five minutes wasn't a lot of time he hurriedly went for his zipper. "You got five minutes."

"All I need is three!" Earl bragged as he came around the desk and got to work. Exactly three minutes later they happily parted.

"Pastor Cash, you have a young lady on the line who says it's urgent. Says her name is Meeka," Tammy announced sounding slightly jealous. Cash didn't reply, he just took the call.

"Hey, it's me, Meeka" she said sadly. So sadly that her next words came as no surprise. "My Granny passed away. The people from the bank sold off the church and she had a heart attack."

"Damn!" Reverend Cash exclaimed. "Sorry to hear that."

"Quite a few people, including myself wanted you to do her funeral. I know y'all were close and that she would want you to also."

"Huh? Um. Well...nah...I'm too busy," he declined. Meeka began to say something else but he'd already hung up.

Chapter 46

Reverend Cash waited and watched for his opening. In the two years that he'd been at Greater First Baptist Church he'd managed to work himself into the middle of the pack. He was making progress but he still had a few rings to climb. He still hadn't figured out a way to get Reverend Sanders off his throne. He figured his wife to be the chink in his armor and began to follow her.

"And just where are you going Mrs. Sanders?" he wondered out loud as they entered the hood of Southwest Atlanta. She was a long way from the gated estate she lived in with her husband and kids. The plot thickened when she pulled into the raggedy parking lot of a run-down liquor store. He became worried when a couple of the goons in the lot approached the truck. If she got robbed or killed her husband would be a hero/victim and harder to get to. To that end he cocked his large pistol and prepared to come to her rescue.

"Sho'nuff!" Cash laughed when he recognized the obvious drug buy. A young brown teen passed something into the window and got cash in return.

Cash debated over whether or not to follow as she pulled out of the lot and into traffic. He decided that he would follow her again tomorrow, right now he needed to find out what her drug of choice was. He pulled across the street and entered the lot. He looked down at his pistol for comfort as the young dealers rushed his car.

"What you tryna cop?" the quickest dealer asked when he reached the car first. This trap sold everything from marijuana to meth, crack, coke, and smack. Plus a variety of pills and synthetics.

"Let me holla at my man with the braids," he said pointing at the kid who'd served Teresa Sanders. "I always shop with him."

"What you need?" the kid asked when he answered the summons.

"Let me get ten sacks of that loud," Cash replied with a crisp hundred in his hand. He would have just copped one dime but he really was out of weed.

"All I got is hard," the boy replied and called for one of the other dealers. "Say Milo, this dude want some green!"

"So, what did you just sell that lady in the SUV?" Cash asked offhandedly.

"Shawty on them yams! She be down here err'day! I heard that she even gave Lil' Red some head once. I think he lying though cuz she spend real good!"

"Crack! She smokes crack?" Cash reeled in disgust even though he snorted cocaine daily. For some reason people try to say there's a difference, but there's not really. It's like tomato vs tomatoe, same shit.

"What you tryna get?" the weed boy asked when he arrived. He threw in an extra sack in exchange for the hundred.

****

The next day proved the young dealer right as Cash followed Teresa back to the liquor store. Again she copped some dope before leading the way to a nearby motel. Cash parked in the lot and watched as she got a room key. He snapped off a few pictures of her entering a room. They would go nice with the ones he'd already gotten of her buying drugs. Reverend Sanders was on his way out.

Reverend Cash was so giddy about his discovery that he laughed and clapped his hands. Things got even better when a souped up hoopty pulled into the parking lot. The driver made a call on his phone and Teresa opened the door. She stood back but he could still see that she was butt naked. He snapped a few pictures of that too.

"It's about to go down!" he cheered and snapped more photos of the two sharing an intimate kiss. The church's First Lady then jumped into the stranger's arms and closed the door behind them. Cash rushed over to the door and heard the sounds of skin slapping and moaning. The curtain covering the room's window had a small gap in it allowing the assistant pastor to get a few shots of the two in the act. When Teresa's head lolled to one side in ecstasy he got that money shot too. The live porn show had him hard as a brick. Luckily the motel was famous for prostitutes.

"Date?" a skinny little crackhead asked. Cash had recently started slanging dick through the congregation so initially he turned his nose up at the offer.

"On second thought, yeah. Sure. Let me just run across the street to the store first," he agreed.

"I got condoms!" she proclaimed and produced one of the free ones that was handed out by the health department in a futile at-

tempt to stem the spread of STD's during drug use. Euthanasia was
more fitting.

"First of all," Reverend Cash said and laughed at the tiny condom, "I'm gonna need an extra-large. Oh and some Crisco."

****

With enough ammo to bury Reverend Sanders, Cash then turned
his attention to his right hand man Assistant Pastor Edwin. It was
obvious that they were very close which meant that more than likely
he'd appoint him as his predecessor after the coup d'etat. To prevent
that he needed to find something on him as well.

Reverend Cash got high, got some head, and got laid in his
church office on a regular basis. He assumed correctly that all the
other assistant pastors did so as well. They did. Everybody was fucking everybody else at Greater First Baptist Church. Tammy had finally given up on Cash and threw the vagina at Reverend Wheeler instead.

Earl had turned into a regular super-head, sneaking in and out
of offices delivering three minute blow jobs. Reverend Sanders' sexy
secretary Anita had delivered two babies in the last two years with no
man in sight. Speculation ran wild as to who was hitting that. Everyone was doing something so Cash knew that Edwin had to be as well.
Now all he had to do was prove it.

"And...that should do it," Reverend Cash nodded as he placed
the last of the many tiny spy cameras in Edwin's office. The web was
spun via web-cam. Now all he had to do was wait. He wouldn't have
to wait very long either.

****

"Thanks for coming everyone," Reverend Sanders greeted in such a
genial tone one would think that the meeting was optional. It wasn't.

He liked to meet with the assistant pastors on a regular basis. All were required to be in attendance along with their secretaries to take notes.

Cash couldn't take his eyes off the gorgeous Anita. He didn't believe in God but still prayed that she would stand up so that he could get a peek at the fat ass on her. It was so round that it tilted her forward as she sat.

"Whoa, what have we here?" Cash asked himself when he caught the lustful looks passed between Reverend Sanders and Anita. He watched how she watched him as he spoke. He caught how he slightly brushed up against her. There was no doubt in his mind that they were fucking. It made sense since his wife was a crackhead.

This was his way in. If he could get inside Anita then he could push Reverend Sanders out of the way. Now he had an excuse to fuck her.

"So, we all need to head over to Calvary Baptist Church for Reverend Butt's retirement party today," Reverend Sanders said in closing.

Cash had been so busy scheming that he hadn't heard anything that was said after 'thanks for coming'. He lagged behind playing on his tablet to give everyone a chance to file out of the conference room. He looked at Anita's bubble butt and claimed it in the name of himself. He then crept down the hall and caught the two bed buddies in a heated, yet subdued argument.

"Well, why not?" Anita demanded.

"You already know good and well why not! You know that my wife and children will be there. You keep forgetting about them," Reverend Sanders whispered back.

"How can I forget about them when you always make sure to put them before me and our children? Sometimes I think you've forgotten about us!"

"Not at all! I told you, as soon as things calm down I'll divorce her, and we can get married," he reassured her.

"Yeah, you've told me. Been telling me for years! As a matter of fact, every time you cum you tell me that!" she said louder than necessary.

"I don't have time for this right now!" he insisted and stormed off.

"Got a second, Rev.?" Cash asked when he rounded the corner.

"Not right now," he said without breaking stride. Cash watched him until he hit a side door and drove away. A smile spread across his face when he heard Anita's soft sobs. She was plenty sad but he needed her mad.

"I hate what he's doing to you," Cash said as he came upon Anita at her desk.

"Who?" she asked in a slightly sassy voice. She had quickly wiped away her tears so he wouldn't think that she was a punk.

"Pastor, that's who. He's always laughing about stringing you along and how good the sex is. He's never going to marry you, you know," Cash informed. He had enough dirt to use on Reverend Sanders just in case this didn't go well.

"I know," she said and started crying once again. "He used me so bad. Treated me like a whore!"

"I'm going to marry you. I need you to just go along with things like normal and when the time is right, I'll make you my wife!" he insisted.

"You for real?" Anita asked excitedly. That's all she wanted.

"I'm for real. Matter of fact, come to my office real quick," Reverend Cash rushed Anita down the hall, around the corner, and into his office. She was so caught up in the momentum that the next thing she knew she was bent over his desk. Cash lifted her dress over her hips and marveled at her fat ass.

"Mmp, mmp, mph!" he said shaking his head. He pulled her lacy panties down and she stepped out of them. He then pulled her big cheeks apart and attacked her vagina with his tongue.

Anita came with a gush of pussy juice which he eagerly swallowed. Next he moved up an inch and licked her anus until she came again. Then out came the wood and he eased it inside of her soaked vagina. Anita laid flat on the desk and got up on her tippy toes to give it up completely. Cash took her up on her offer and took it completely, tapping her cervix with each stroke. There wasn't many strokes before her tight, hot, wet box made him explode.

"Fuck it," he decided as he pushed in instead of pulling out. Anita whimpered softly as he filled her with semen.

"You for real about marrying me?" she asked again. She may have been young and naïve but she knew enough about men to know plans and promises could change once you gave up the pussy.

"Of course I am dear. I'm gonna be the head preacher and you're going to be right by my side as my First Lady," he assured her.

Chapter 47

"What have we here?" Reverend Cash wondered aloud as he watched the live feed form Edwin's office. He hit the record button when the preacher's wife walked in. He also turned the volume up so that he could hear every word spoken.

"Oh, I didn't think anyone else was here," Teresa said apologetically. Both Cash and Edwin twisted their lips up dubiously at the bad acting.

"I'm the only one left, I believe. Everyone else is over at Calvary for Reverend Butt's retirement."

"So it's just you and I, alone. Interesting," she said easing in and closing the door behind her.

"I did not see this coming," Cash giggled. "Things just keep getting better and better!"

"Mrs. Sanders, I am not comfortable being in a room alone with you!" he said sounding down right scared.

"You were comfortable with putting your dick in my mouth while I was unconscious. Oh, I read the police report," she laughed wickedly. "I lied on your ass then and I'll do it again now!"

"W-w-what do you want?" Edwin asked in defeat. "What I gotta do?"

"Everything, that's what! But first I want some dick," she demanded. She came around his desk and pushed his chair back with her foot then sat on his desk and pulled her panties off.

"I wouldn't do that if I was you," Cash warned. He'd followed the man Teresa had fucked in the motel and found out that he was a dope boy turned junky. Definitely not the type that you'd want to fuck behind let alone eat pussy after.

Of course Edwin couldn't hear him so he dove in face first. Teresa's pussy tasted slightly bitter and smelled slightly fishy but he pressed on anyway. He flicked and sucked until she squealed from an orgasm.

"My turn," he said as he stood and whipped out an impressive erection. He practically jumped inside her still quivering box and pounded away savagely.

"Well, fuck her then!" Reverend Cash laughed. He couldn't believe that he was getting this all on tape. It was practically too good to be true.

Teresa tossed her legs onto his shoulders giving up another inch of pussy. The sound of skin slapping almost drowned out her moans. She came once, then came again. Edwin pulled his handkerchief out and bust a nut inside of it.

"I read the police report too," he explained breathlessly. It was his semen inside of her that prevented him from fighting the bogus rape charge she'd put on him in college. "So what now?"

"Look, my husband is on his way out. He's not going to be around much longer. You can either go with him or take over his position. Either way I'll always be First Lady of this church!"

Teresa furthered her cause by kneeling in front of him and taking him deep into her mouth. Edwin loved the preacher dearly but not as much as he loved himself. Plus she had some dynamite head.

"I'm with you," he assured her. Neither he nor Reverend Cash knew exactly what she meant by her husband not being around much longer so they both decided to wait and see. It didn't take long.

****

"Okay," Anita shrugged when Reverend Sanders told her that he wouldn't be over that night. She was tired of being used and was also getting use to riding Reverend Cash backwards. She especially liked the part when he used a little Crisco on his finger to finger fuck her in the ass while she rode him.

"Well, okay then," he said relieved at how well that had went. His wife had invited him to dinner to discuss some urgent matter. Things had finally settle down enough for him to ask for a divorce. He would then wait a few months before he married the beloved church secretary. Once he did he would be viewed as a hero for taking care of her and her two kids born out of wedlock. A true redemption song. He had no way of knowing that Reverend Cash was coming to knock her boots all the way to Beijing as soon as he left.

****

"Cornish hen stuffed with wild rice and mushrooms," Teresa sang as she placed his plate in front of him.

"Where are the kids?" he asked as he leaned in to smell the food. He didn't pick up on the smell of any Arsenic or Cyanide but was still skeptical. "Why are you being so nice to me?"

"Because I love you. You are my husband," she said externally while internally she said, 'because it's your last meal, you sorry son of a bitch'.

Her words really caught him off guard. He'd stopped loving her years ago and had assumed that she had stopped loving him as well. If he was honest with himself he would admit he only asked her to marry him to impress her well connected father. And because they were at her hospital bedside in college after Edwin had allegedly raped her.

"Well, the only way to say this is to just come out and say it. Teresa, I want a divorce," he announced.

"Okay, that's fine. I'm sure Anita is running out of patience. You guys have some beautiful children," she said without a hint of anger, sarcasm, or malice even though her heart was filled with all three.

"You knew? Well, I know about your...indiscretions as well. Got pictures and everything," he warned.

"No need for threats, dear. I want this to be civil. I have only one request and I will not take no for an answer!"

"What?" he asked, cocking his head defiantly. He was prepared to give her the house and cars since he was leaving his children too. He knew that the divorce would cost him a few grand in monthly child support and alimony, but he didn't plan on giving her any more than that.

"Make love to me one last time," she said softly, sounding quite pitiful.

"Why not?" he replied mainly to himself. Anita had become stingy with the pussy lately and he was backed up. If he didn't know any better he would swear that she was seeing someone else.

They stood from the table and made their way up to the master bedroom. As soon as they got undressed she took him deep into her mouth. Once he was good and hard she climbed onto the edge of the bed on her hands and knees.

"Wow, was it always this hot?" Reverend Sanders exclaimed as he pushed inside of her. The heat was actually courtesy of the combustion of several infections fighting for dominance.

"Mm hm," she moaned. Meanwhile her crackhead fuck buddy eased in the backdoor. He then crept upstairs just like rehearsed. Teresa had made sure to position him with his back to the door so that he wouldn't see what was coming. "You miss this good pussy?"

The preacher opened his mouth to say 'hell yes' but M.J fired two rounds into the back of his head silencing him. He dropped dead right on the spot.

"Shit, you could've given me another minute! I almost got a nut out of his sorry ass," she fussed.

"I got you," he said and dropped his dingy jeans He stepped right over her dead husband's body and slid inside of her. M.J pounded out a nut for her and one for himself as the preacher lay dead in a puddle of blood.

"I know you brung some dope!" she said hopefully.

"Yeah, I got a couple sacks," he replied. He sat the murder weapon down on the bed and pulled up his pants. He then dug into a pocket and produced two of the three tiny bags of crack.

The couple chit-chatted and smoked hits of crack over the dead preacher. Once they were done it was time for part two of her plan.

"Babe, get them sacks out of my purse please," she said sweetly.

"Okay!" he said excitedly and sprang into action. He quickly kneeled down and fished around in her purse in search of more dope. "In here?"

"Keep looking," she smiled as he put his well-known fingerprints on everything. He was so focused on getting his next hit that he didn't see her pick the gun up and approach him.

Teresa took aim and fired the four remaining bullets into his back. None were instantly fatal which meant it would be a slow and painful death. It would be made even slower and more painful by having to watch her get high without him.

"My bad. It's in my drawer," she giggled and retrieved the dope. She couldn't call the cops until he was dead so she smoked while she waited. M.J batted his eyes lovingly as she exhaled plumes of the noxious crack smoke. "Are you serious? Okay."

Teresa wasn't all bad so she took a deep pull of the pipe and blew the smoke into his mouth. Some of it came out of the holes in his back while the rest of it went straight to hell with him. A peaceful smile spread across his face as he left this existence.

"9-1-1, what's your emergency?" the operator asked calmly.

"Um...a man broke into my house. He shot my husband and raped me," Teresa replied so calmly that the dispatcher wondered if she'd heard her correctly.

"Ma'am, did you say someone shot your husband? Is the intruder still there?" she asked.

"Yeah, and he's dead. I shot him."

"Police and Rescue are on the way! Please stay on the line."

The plan to make the hit look like a robbery gone wrong worked like a charm. M.J used a screw driver to pry open the backdoor, he'd been too dumb to wonder why she hadn't just left it unlocked since she'd left the security alarm off. A rape kit confirmed her story of rape since he'd left semen inside of her. Case closed, for now.

Chapter 48

The news of the violent murder of the beloved preacher rocked the city to its core. Not too long before an accountant from the church had been shot dead in his Atlanta home too. Scores of child porn had been found in his home and on his computer.

"Get...the fuck...out!" Reverend Cash exclaimed when the mugshot of the deceased intruder flashed on the screen. He quickly checked his surveillance pictures and sure enough it was the same man he'd seen Teresa having sex with at the seedy motel. He wasted no time in calling the police.

There was no time to waste since an emergency pastor's meeting had been called. A new head pastor had to be named immediately. A flock with no shepherd is easily led astray. Cash knew that it was between him and Reverend Sanders close friend Edwin in line for the position. So it was time to make him bow out gracefully or be disgraced.

"Excuse me Reverend, can I get a quick second before the meeting starts?" Cash asked humbly via the phone intercom.

"I don't have time," Edwin said dismissively. He was eager to get crowned king of the kingdom and the riches that came along with it.

"Eddie, I assure you that it's of extreme importance and it affects you directly," he said. "Besides, you have to pass my office anyway."

"Eddie!" Edwin growled as he marched down the hall. He didn't like the flamboyant preacher to begin with but calling him Eddie like they were cool really pissed him off. "I should fire his ass!"

"Make this quick!" he said as he barged into Cash's office without knocking as a sign of disrespect. Reverend Cash found it amusing and laughed out loud. He then lifted his remote and pressed play.

"I did the editing myself. Not too bad for a novice, huh?" Cash asked the stunned man. He had combined several of Edwin's sessions with Teresa into one steamy presentation.

"We don't have much time. My husband just started preaching!" the Teresa on the screen announced as she rushed into his office.

"I'm ready!" the TV Edwin replied with his erection in hand.

"You sir, lay some serious pipe!" he laughed as the sound of sex filled the office. Cash flipped through several of their tryst to make him understand how deep the river ran. There was no explaining this away. "I'm going to need you to decline the position of head Pastor and recommend me."

"Well, what's to stop me from taking that disk and telling you to go fuck yourself?" Edwin growled and puffed up like a puffer fish. Cash found it amusing and let out a little chuckle. He clearly had no idea who he was fucking with.

"Take it. That's your copy," he said putting emphasize on the word copy. "Oh, and if you ever try me I will kill you!"

"Well, my co-star there has a tremendous amount of say so in the matter. After all she is the grieving First Lady," Edwin pleaded.

"Her?" Cash laughed pointing at the woman on the screen with a mouthful of dick. "She's on the tape too! Besides..."

"What's this?" he asked when Cash handed him a yellow envelope.

"Open it and see for yourself," came the reply.

"Oh my!" he exclaimed seeing Teresa having sex with yet another man. He blinked and squinted at the vaguely familiar face and asked, "Is that the guy? The one on the news!"

"Same one! This just gets better and better!"

"I know about what you been up to as well! Fucking half the staff, including a certain choir director..." Edwin threw out desperately. "If I go down, you go down!"

"Which one, him?" Cash asked fast forwarding to a scene with Earl on his knees blowing him too. It's over with, let it go. The police will pick Teresa up and the insurance will go to the church. Don't worry, I'll break you off!"

****

"Yay! Now we can get married!" Anita cheered and clapped once Reverend Cash got moved into his new office. He'd waited until after the funeral which had given him time to have it gutted and completely redecorated.

"Huh?" Cash asked as if it was the first time he'd heard anything about it.

"Fuck you mean by huh?" Anita growled. She was far from ratchet, but she was tired of being used by men; especially preachers. "You've been fucking me for months, talking 'bout marrying me, and now you saying huh, like you don't know what the fuck I'm talking about!"

"Baby, I..."

"Baby my ass! It wasn't huh when you wanted to fuck me in my ass! It wasn't huh when your dick was in my mouth! It wasn't huh..."

"Okay, okay chill! We getting married," he said trying to calm her down before anyone else heard her. "We getting married, just like I promised."

"When?" she demanded to know, softening a little.

"Next weekend. Tell you what, I'll come by tonight and we can talk about it, set a date, and arrange to make an announcement."

"Okay baby!" she gushed happily. "I'm finna go home and cook you a big dinner!"

"That's great. Oh yeah, I need you to do me a favor. Take my laptop home with you. I got some work to do later."

"Okay babe!" she agreed. They shared a passionate kiss and off she went. Reverend Cash watched out the window as she drove away. As soon as she cleared the huge parking lot he picked up the phone.

"Hello police, I need to report a theft..."

Chapter 49

"I just heard from her! She called me and told me to bring her some money to the motel!" Edwin shouted when Cash took the call.

"Call the police and tell them where she is. She's quite the wanted woman, you know."

"Okay, okay!" he agreed. He had become quite the flunky since Reverend Cash took over.

Teresa saw the police pull-up and went on the run again. They both would breathe easier once she was dead or in jail. It would be the former if Cash had his say so.

He was nice enough to drop theft charges on Anita in exchange for a restraining order. She was forbidden to come anywhere near him or the church. That gave him freedom to fuck as he pleased. He slung the dick around like a cowboy does a lasso. It was eventually going to get his ass in trouble.

Reverend Cash's name began to ring in paternity questions but they were kept quiet because the church couldn't stand another scandal. He wrecked vaginas, anuses, and homes at will. Despite all that he was doing to families his favorite pastoral duty was the family counseling.

"Reverend Cash, your one o'clock is here," Tammy announced.

"Send them in please," he said sweetly since he knew they could hear him. A few seconds later the attractive family sheepishly entered. "The Hudson family."

"Yes, sir, Pastor, sir. I'm Ralph, this is my wife Janice, my son Kenneth, and my daughter Shante," the father said humbly. Cash had analyzed the whole family by the time they sat down in front of his desk.

Dad was a wimp, wife was sexually frustrated, daughter was a little hoe, and the son was gay or about to be he summed up.

"And how can I help you guys?" he asked softly.

"Well, my wife and I are very distant and grow more so by the day. My daughter wants to be a video vixen or..." he said causing the teen to pop her gum even louder and cross her arms over her breast. She then crossed her legs, opening them widely giving the freaky pastor a flash of her white panties. "And I don't know where to begin with him! My son is..."

"*Gay,*" the pastor thought to himself. The boy pursed his lips together, folded his arms, and crossed his legs just like his sister had. He could tell that his dad didn't spend a lot of time with him and so he'd picked up feminine habits and traits from his mother and sister.

"He works all the time. Overtime, double time, triple time, any-time!" Mrs. Hudson sighed desperately. "When he is home he's too tired to...to...to do anything but sleep!"

"I have to work! You guys want nice things and they cost money! Our big house, money! The cars in the driveway, more money!" Mr. Hudson defended.

"I think I'll have to spend some time with each of you individual-ly to figure you out first and then as a family. Next Saturday I'll meet with her and him and then the following week..." Reverend Cash said plotting to divide and conquer the family.

"Well okay, if you think it'll help," the husband and father sighed. He would do anything to provide for and protect his family.

****

"You watching the news?" Edwin cheered into his phone.

"I am!" Cash replied just as ecstatic. The troubled preacher's wife had been found murdered in a rundown motel. "Stay put, I'm on my way to scoop you up. This calls for a celebration!"

"Um, okay," he wearily agreed. The preacher unnerved him for some reason yet he still agreed. A few hours later they were in Cash's new Bentley floating towards downtown Atlanta.

"Yeah Eddie, now that that bitch is dead I can breathe easy. I hate loose strings. You gotta cut them off," Cash said as he drove.

"I was the one worried, she ain't have nothing on you."

"True, but if you go down, I go down. Ain't that what you said?" he reminded.

"B-b-but I..." Edwin stammered. He now regretted making the threat to the dangerous man.

"Nah, it's cool. We're good. No more worries after tonight."

"Where we going?" Edwin asked when Cash pulled the car onto the exit to Martin Luther King Blvd. They were right in the heart of the hood.

"Quick stop to tie up one last loose end," he replied. Edwin froze in fear when he reached into his inside pocket. He just knew he was going for a gun to kill him, but instead he produced a sizeable bankroll that he tossed into his lap as he pulled to the curb.

"What's this for?" Edwin asked as Cash lowered the window. He missed the answer because Kenyatta rushed from the shadows and fired a bullet into his temple. He then snatched the cash from the dead man's lap and disappeared back into the shadows.

"Payment for your murder!" Cash laughed. Once he stopped laughing he called the cops to report the robbery and murder. The location was picked because the grainy surveillance camera would be able to capture the shooting but not identify the shooter.

Once again he felt like he was unstoppable. On top of the world. The baddest nigga on the block. But as the bible says pride comes before the fall.

Chapter 50

"Pastor, your one and two o'clock appointments are here and...yeah," Tammy said shaking her head at the two troubled teens in front of her. The girl wore a mid-thigh tube skirt with a halter top and she had a face full of make-up and a headful of weave. The boy had on a pair of skinny jeans, a tight skinny shirt, and watermelon lip gloss.

"Send...her in first," he replied as if he had to think about it. He'd been waiting all week to get lil' mama alone. It paid off immediately with those big thighs she had on display.

"I'on even know why I'm here! My daddy be trippin'! If I wanna turn up, I'ma turn up!" Shante fussed sounding like a ghetto girl even though she'd never set foot in one. Her problems came straight from the radio and videos. "I smoke, I drank, I twerk!"

"Are you having sex yet?" Cash asked softly.

"Hell yeah! I fuck, I suck! I twerk!" she laughed and stood up and began twerking. She'd hoped to embarrass him like she did her father but she had no idea who she was fucking with.

"Well turn up then!" he said and hit the radio, loud enough for her to dance to but not loud enough to be heard through the door. Once he was nice and hard the nasty pastor made his move. "Come on around here!"

"What's up?" Shante dared as she came around his desk. He replied by sitting her on the desk and snatching her legs wide open. He then pulled her panties to the side and stuck his tongue in her tight teen pussy.

Once he sucked a nut out of the girl he stood and out came the dick. He shoved his tongue in her mouth to muffle the sounds of the fucking that followed. Shante scrunched her face up and clenched her fist tight as he rearranged her insides. He gave her vagina an open floor concept by blowing its walls out and raising its ceiling. He knew better then to cum in the young girl, but did it away.

"Whew!" Cash sighed once he'd recovered. "Now check this out. You're to come once a week and I'm going to give you this and this."

"Okay," Shante agreed to getting both the dick and the hundred dollar bill he extended.

"Oh and listen to your mama. And wear more clothes too. Ain't nothing wrong with being a hoe, just don't dress like one. Now send your brother in."

"Okay," she sang again and rushed out of the office.

Kenny came in next and got the same thing his sister had gotten. The reverend pulled his panties to the side and fucked him too. He also left with a hundred bucks and a promise to do better at home.

****

"I don't know why my wife thinks I don't love her. Or why she thinks that I don't like having sex with her," Mr. Hudson said as he and Reverend Cash conducted a counseling session via telephone. His busy work schedule prevented him from coming to see him in person. "Work is not more important to me than my family, but we have bills!"

"Go on," the preacher urged since he was recording the session. Little did he know so was Mr. Hudson because he was fastidious like that. He expected good useful advice so he recorded it to playback and apply.

Reverend Cash was glad he had a couple of hours before Mrs. Hudson was due to arrive since he had work to do. Once he finished drawing all he could out of the man he let him get back to work and did the same. It came out better than expected so he made a change of plans.

"Oh Pastor! I'm just leaving out to come down now," Mrs. Hudson said as she took his call.

"I'm not in my office at the moment. One of our family members had a crisis so I had to rush over to them. Actually I'm not far from you guys. You know the Inn on Steve Lawrence Blvd?"

"Oh yeah, it's up the street. So you wanna just come here?"

"It would probably be more convenient if you came here," he replied without saying why.

"Um...okay," she agreed. "I'm on my way."

Reverend Cash wisely met her in the lobby so she wouldn't feel uncomfortable. He was right because she felt a little apprehensive about meeting a man in a hotel. It was only because he was her pastor that she agreed.

"Mrs. Hudson," Reverend Cash stood and greeted with a handshake.

"Pastor," she replied and sat across from him. "I must tell you I've seen remarkable changes in the kids since they've been coming to see you! I only pray that you can do the same for my husband and me."

"I plan to do the exact same for you, but your husband...I'm not so sure if I can reach him," he said play acting. "Anyway, I want to put Kenny on my Junior Pastor Team. I was in one when I was his age, and it changed my life."

"Okay, but what about my husband?" Mrs. Hudson wanted to know.

"I...um...well. I guess I better let you hear our session. I can't play it here so meet me at my office next we-"

"No! Just come over to our house, it's only a mile or so away," she urged.

"Actually I do have a room here. Come on, we'll do it there," he said getting up and leading the way before she had time to think about it. Once they got into the room he sat her at the table and played the edited recording.

"I don't love my wife. I don't like having sex with her. Work is more important"

"Oh!" Mrs. Hudson reeled and clutched her chest upon hearing the heartbreaking statements. She had no idea it was this bad but that was definitely her husband's voice on the recording. Tears dumped from her eyes and mixed in with the sad sobs coming from her mouth.

"It's not your fault. You didn't do anything wrong," he assured her as he came around and wrapped her in his arms. He pulled her close and held her. He rocked her gently and let her get it all out. Then, he got hard.

"Pastor Cash!" she reeled when she felt the erection grow and throb against her. She tried to push him off of her but he held onto her. He then walked them a few feet and fell on the bed. "What are you doing?"

"Don't worry, Pastor gon' make it all better," he said as he pulled her dress up. He snatched her panties off and felt the wetness beneath. That was all he needed to know, with that he pulled out his rock hard dick and shoved it inside of her.

Mrs. Hudson was in total shock as her pastor pumped in and out of her. She never said no or stop. She never screamed or clawed at him trying to get him to stop, but it was still rape. He didn't choke or beat her. He didn't have a gun nor a knife, but it was still rape.

"See that, see how wet that lonely pussy got for Pastor," he cooed into her ear. The end was near and he went deeper and ground against her cervix and came. He rested in her vagina until he got soft then he pulled his bloody dick out. "Why you ain't say you had your period? I brought my Crisco."

****

"Honey? Janice?" Ralph Hudson called as he entered their bedroom. It was well after midnight, the same as it was most nights, when he got in but tonight he had flowers and candy. He knew that sex was out of the question since she was on her cycle but that cleared the way for conversation and a foot massage. The bed was empty so he followed his ears into the bathroom. The first thing he noticed was several empty douche boxes, then he noticed his wife rolled up into a ball inside their walk-in shower.

"Baby, what's wrong?" he asked as he climbed under the scalding hot water with her. She was beet red from the abuse of the water and crying hysterically.

"He-he-he said you said that you don't love me anymore!" she wailed since him not loving her was priority. It was more painful to her that he didn't love her than it was to have been raped or to feel the near boiling water raining down on her naked skin.

"Who? Who said what?' he demanded as he turned off the water. Looking down he noticed that the shower floor was covered with empty douche bottles.

"Pastor did. Reverend Cash. And don't lie because I heard the tape!" she shouted.

"Tape? What tape? What are you talking about?" he insisted. She had calmed down just enough for him to guide her out of the shower. He wrapped one of their thick bath sheets around her and took her back into their room.

"He taped your session. I heard what you said," she said accepting it.

"Well, I taped our session too, and here is what I said..." he said and played the recording. Janice burst into a huge smile upon hearing her husband proclaim his love for her. According to what he'd confessed he loved her more than he loved himself. He loved God, her, and the children, in that order. She then burst back into more sobs just as quickly.

"What?" he pleaded, hoping she wasn't having a mental breakdown. She wasn't, but he was about to.

"He raped me! He held me down and forced himself on me," she said shaking her head in disbelief. Her husband looked at her then to the empty douche boxes and cried with her. This was all his fault and he knew what he had to do.

Chapter 51

"Blessed are the peacemakers..." Reverend Cash recited as service began. As usual thousands of smiling people hung on his every word. Kenyatta trailed him as he roamed the stage co-signing everything he said.

Earl fronted the choir like an orchestra conductor as they 'oohed and ahh' along with Pastor. Only one face wasn't smiling. Instead it had an ice grill and murderous glint in its eye.

Ralph Hudson's family was safe and sound at home while he'd come to straighten his face. It almost ended before it started when his pistol set off a metal detector when he entered. The security guard had seen him so many times that he just waved him in without patting him down. Had he done his job he would've discovered the brand new thirty-eight revolver in his suit coat. He'd never fired a gun before but he planned to today.

Actually the metal detectors were in place not to protect the pastor but to prevent anyone from bringing coins in. Reverend Cash was still Dollar Bill and that's all he wanted in the collection plates. He'd also installed ATM machines and had plans to open a bank branch in the lobby. Dollar Bill, indeed.

Ralph didn't hear a word of what the preacher preached, but he didn't miss anything since it was all bullshit anyway. It was all smoke and mirrors designed to separate man from his money. Once he wrapped up people filed out so the next service could be held. Ralph lagged behind so that he could catch the good Reverend alone. With death on his trail he retreated to his office to sip a little cognac, smoke a little weed, and snort a few lines.

"One second!" Reverend Cash shouted when he saw his office door easing open. He threw a magazine on top of his pile of coke but the room still reeked of marijuana.

"Oh, don't mind me," Ralph growled. He stepped fully inside and closed and locked the door behind himself.

"How can I help you?" the preacher asked hoping to dismiss him quickly before his next show.

"By dying quickly, you bastard!" he replied and pulled his gun. He raised it eye level, like the YouTube tutorial had shown, but didn't shoot.

"What's the matter? Don't tell me you scared to shoot!" Cash dared and stood.

"You raped my wife!" Ralph shouted instead of shooting. His watch rattled loudly as his hand shook wildly.

"Is that what she told you?" Cash asked as he inched forward. "Let's talk about it. Be easy, okay?"

"No, it's not okay!" Ralph screamed still shaking. He'd fucked around and let the thug get too close and it was all she wrote.

"Nigga!" Cash shouted as he knocked the gun away with one hand and slapped a spark out of him with the other. He then spun the smaller man around and scooped him under his arms then locked his hands behind his neck in a full Nelson.

"Let me go! Put me down!" Ralph insisted when his feet left the ground. Cash let him thrash around for a second until he realized he couldn't get loose unless he let him loose.

"Yeah, I fucked yo' wife. I fucked her so hard that her period came down. But not as hard as I fucked that daughter of yours. But you know what, yo' son got the best pussy in the whole family," he cracked.

"You're the devil!" Ralph shouted back. "Let me down!"

"Nah, maybe I'll fuck you too," Cash said grinding his crotch against the man's backside. Ralph really kicked when he felt the erection on his ass. Cash gave him a few humps and cracked up some more. "Now, I'ma let you down. You gon' home and relax. I want to see the whole family in my office next week."

****

Ralph considered killing himself as he drove home. He contemplated running into the median or going to buy another gun and shooting himself in the head with it. The next thing he knew he was in a bar nursing a beer.

"Penny for your thoughts," the bartender said seeing that the man was clearly in distress.

"You wouldn't believe me if I told you," he chuckled. He had a hard time believing it himself.

"I've heard it all, try me," the bartender dared. Ralph took him up on the dare and proved him wrong. He had never heard anything like this in all of his thirty years behind a bar. "Damn!"

"Damn is right. Now ain't a damn thing I can do about it," he moaned.

"Sure it is! Go to 1-800-Killa," the bartender suggested like it was just that easy.

"1-800..." Ralph asked in confusion.

"It's a website. You go on and log a complaint and that dude's ass is grass," he said like a true Killa fan.

"Oh, I don't know. I better go home and try to put my family back together," Ralph said. He dug into his pocket to pay the tab but the bartender smacked it away and declined his money.

"This one is on me!"

****

"This is silly," Ralph fussed to himself as he pulled up the 1-800-Killa website. He let out a deep sigh and began to type...

I need some help. My entire family has been destroyed by our Pastor. He's fucked my whole family. My wife, my daughter, and even my son. He got the little fellow floating around here humming show tunes and gospel songs. The preacher...

He wasn't the only one making appeals to the hitman for hire via the website. There were several other members of the congregation who were also voicing their complaints about the perfidious pastor on the site as well. There were so many complaints that they couldn't be ignored.

"Damn!" Killa concluded after reading the many post. "I just may have to pay this Reverend Cash a visit."

Chapter 52

So many people attended Greater First Baptist Church that no one even noticed the new face amongst them. Well, actually a couple single sisters smiled and batted their lashes at the handsome newcomer, but he didn't see them. He was on a mission and therefore he had his eyes locked firmly on his target.

Killa was a wise man and as such he was well versed in all of God's books. He knew The Gospel, The Torah, and the Qur'an better than some of the so-called best learned men. He knew more than enough to know dude at the pulpit was making shit up.

Reverend Cash knew the bible backwards and frontwards so it was easy to twist it to fit his desires. Just like the devil he would tell one truth and then add ninety-nine lies to it. The human soul accepts the truth but it also takes in the lies that accompany it.

"This dude is high," Killa mumbled to himself. He knew the difference between the Holy Ghost and good coke. He was already here to kill the man but grew to hate him more and more with every syllable that came out of his mouth. This was going to be ugly.

Reverend Cash wrapped up his second performance with the announcement that the church would begin charging admission as well as parking fees. He figured why not since he'd heard that they were doing it at Al Green's church in Memphis. Good thing that this was his farewell sermon, because he wouldn't be back next week.

****

Reverend Cash rolled around town in his Bentley with death following close on his tail. It was there when he pulled into the trap to cop more weed and coke for a night on the town. Had the opportunity arose it would've gotten him as he sat at a stop light. However, the calm killer was patient and decided to wait for the right moment. A quick head shot seemed too quick and too easy. The man who'd caused so much pain, suffering, and destruction deserved to die a slow and painful death.

"Bad timing, sucks to be you," Killa said aloud when Cash swung by a mid-town condo and picked up Kenyatta. A wise man once said, "You are like your friends," so for Kenyatta to be with Cash he had to be just as bad, and by the end of the night he would be just as dead.

Killa followed the dead men to a downtown strip club. Once he watched the valet take the Bentley away he found a spot to park and joined the two inside. He found a table and paid for a couple of table dances that he paid no attention to. His focus was on the men in VIP popping bottles.

"I'ma make an extra forty or fifty grand charging admission and parking fees!" Cash laughed to his partner.

"You a fucking genius!" Kenyatta cheered like a good hype-man does. They clinked their champagne flutes together in a celebratory toast.

Two strippers came over and began dancing for the men. Cash played in one's box until his fingers were wet and slippery. It came as no surprise when he stood up and took her into one of the private rooms. He paid the admission and paid the dancer.

"You gotta use a condom!" the girl protested as he tried to enter her raw. Not out of fear of disease or pregnancy, but because she didn't want cum running out of her while she was dancing. It wasn't good for business.

"I got another hundred that says I don't," he said holding the colorful new bill in the air.

"Okay!" she agreed and snatched it from his hand. She bent over the table and moaned as he pushed inside of her.

"Grrr," the preacher growled as he pounded the girl's hot box. Men tended to abuse rental pussy just like they did rental cars. The girl winced in pain as he savagely slammed in and out of her. He was numb from the cognac and coke so he felt nothing as he punished her young ass. Staying in school would have been a lot easier and less painful than this.

It came as an uncomfortable relief when she finally felt him begin to skeet inside of her. He pushed in to the hilt one last time and pumped her full of semen. She'd still be up ninety-nine dollars even after she purchased a dollar store douche so she stayed still.

"I may have to go again," Cash stated as he caught his breath.

"I cain't, I gotta...um...we..." the stripper stumble for excuses. The vile man had the ability to make even a hoe feel low.

"You lucky I got a meeting in the morning. Otherwise I'd spend the night in that pussy!" he warned. "I'll see you next weekend."

"I won't be here. I'm going back to school!"

****

"Whew! I'm fucking wasted," Reverend Cash announced as he drove.

"Shit, just head home. I'll crash in one of the guest rooms," Kenyatta offered to save him the extra trip of dropping him off. Cash agreed by hitting his blinker and switching lanes. He jumped on the highway with death right on his ass.

Killa still hadn't decided on a manner of death by the time he'd reached Cash's house. However, he had a bag of tricks in the trunk that would make Felix the Cat jealous. He cut his lights and pulled into the driveway behind his prey. Once they were both out of the car Killa hopped out with a cannon.

"Evening gentlemen," Killa greeted from behind a huge desert eagle. The triangular shaped barrel looked like it was throwing up the Roc sign while the huge black hole it formed looked like the Holland Tunnel.

"You know who the fuck I am?" Cash asked hoping to intimidate the stranger. But it was he who had no idea who he was fucking with.

"Of course, you're Reverend Cash. Your congregation sent me," Killa replied. "Now, pop the trunk and you, get in."

"Who?" Kenyatta asked when Killa pointed to him. "I ain't getting in no damn trunk. Fuck that! Shoot me, nigga!"

Killa shrugged like okay and shot him. His head exploded like a water balloon filled with blood and brain matter. Reverend Cash was instantly sober and ready to comply with any demands made.

"Now, put that mess in the trunk!" Killa demanded. Cash quickly complied while Killa grabbed a duffle bag out of his own trunk. "Let's go down to the basement. To the stripper pole."

"You been in my house?" Cash asked since he knew the layout.

"Yeah, a couple of times," Killa shrugged and followed his prey downstairs. Once they arrived he pulled out some leg irons and made Cash cuff his ankle to the pole. He then took his keys and two cell phones.

"I ain't with no freaky shit!" the pastor protested and cracked Killa up. Tears streamed down the killer's face as he rolled on the floor laughing out loud. It took at least five minutes for him to regain his composure.

"Okay, look. I need to know if you have any children," Killa said.

"Not a one!" Cash replied lifting his chin proudly. It wasn't true but it technically wasn't a lie either since he didn't know that he did. By the time a woman found out that she was pregnant she'd already seen how foul he was and never bothered telling him.

"That's good because I would have had to kill them too, and I don't usually kill kids. Whatever you got could be hereditary though and I can't take any chances that your kids might end up around mine."

"So what, you here to kill me? Somebody paid you to kill me? I got a quarter mil in the safe upstairs and another quarter mil in jewelry. Plus I got a Bentley, a Range, a Benz, and a Porsche. You can have it all. Take all that shit and let me go," Cash offered.

"Dude, they haven't printed enough money to save you! You're dying. The only issue is how."

"Do what you do then. Shit, I'll take one to the dome like you did my partna," Reverend Cash said triumphantly. "I had a good run."

"Yeah, so I've heard. That's why you ain't getting off that easy! Your death is going to be slow, painful, and ugly," Killa smirked.

"What's in the bag?" Cash's nosey ass asked of the black duffle bag.

"Oh this?" Killa asked giddily like a child opening a toy box. "I got all kinds of shit in here. Guns, knives, brass knuckles..."

"What the hell is that?" Cash asked as Killa emptied the bag. The shiny hoop device always got a lot of attention.

"This...oh, it's the DC 2000. You put it over the head and..." Killa finished by hitting the switch.

"Damn!" Cash replied rubbing his neck.

"Too quick for you. This however might work," he said pulling out a small twenty-two caliber pistol. "Let's see how many shots you can take before you die. I'll start at yo' feet and work my way up. Yolo, my baby mama, has the record with eighty-seven."

Killa's phone vibrated and he held up a finger as if to say one second and took the call. He started off eagerly but it was clear that he'd received disappointing news.

"Okay, keep me informed," he said with a frustrated sigh. He saw Cash looking curiously at him and explained, "My kids are missing."

"Good! I hope you never find them!" the preacher cackled. Killa laughed too because he didn't buy it.

"Dude, you're not getting a quick death. You deserve to die every day!"

"So, how about a last meal? Ain't I 'posed to get a last meal?"

"That's it!" Killa exclaimed snapping his fingers as he figured out a fitting death. "Sure you do. What would you like?"

"Well, since it's my last I may as well do it up! Steak, lobster, scrimp, a bake potato..."

"Un uh. Okay, okay," Killa said jotting down the laundry list of food. "I'll be back."

****

"Told you I was coming back," Killa laughed upon seeing Cash's bloody ankle. He'd been pulling and kicking to get free since Killa had left.

"Whatever, just give me my food," he spat in defeat. "Probably put poison in it."

"Nope, too easy," he reminded as he handed the food over. He sat back on the plush leather sofa and watched the man eat his last meal. A small jar of white cream caught Killa's attention so he picked it up. He opened the lid and sniffed to examine its contents. "Crisco?"

"Mm hm," Reverend Cash mumbled around a mouthful of surf and turf. Killa sat back again and lit a blunt of Pastor's weed as he scarfed down his food. Once he was done he asked," Now what?"

"Now you die. Slow. That was your last meal."

****

It took several days for it to set in that Killa intended to starve him to death. To add insult to injury Killa would pop in daily to eat in front of the man.

Every day the killer received the same disappointing news about his missing children.

Every day the preacher lost a few more pounds from his once solid frame. Soon he was nothing more than a pile of skin and bones that couldn't shit, pee, or even sweat because there was nothing left in his frail body to expel. To the arrogant man's credit he never once bitched up or begged for his life. He just slowly died a little more each day. Oddly the man who lived in ignominy died with dignity.

"Damn, you still hanging around, huh?" Killa asked when he entered the house on the thirtieth day. The preacher was too weak to speak or even blink and his vital organs had started to shut down. It would only be a matter of time before the preacher passed on. The only signs of life in him were the slight up and down movements of his frail chest. Killa let out a sigh when his phone rang.

"Here we go again," he muttered as he took the call. "Yo."

"Daddy?" a little girl asked eagerly. He could hear her brother demanding, "Let me talk!"

"Shyne?" Killa asked in disbelief, but got no reply since his twins were wrestling over the phone.

"Hello!" Christi yelled happily as she got on the phone. "They're home! They're home! Sun and Shyne are home!"

"I'm on my way!" the relieved father shouted back happily and clicked off.

Reverend Cash released his last breath with a soft rattle indicating that his rotten soul had left his body.

The End

Epilogue

A Memphis grandmother sat sipping her tea while watching the national news. Donald Trump had just converted to Islam and closed down all of his casinos. That was astonishing news but the next story topped it.

"We have a bizarre story from an Atlanta suburb. The body of missing preacher Reverend William Cash suddenly turned up at his former church today. The preacher's emaciated body was found earlier today behind the wheel of his 2015 Bentley parked in the spot reserved for the pastor of Greater First Baptist Church. Hundreds of thousands of dollars in both cash and jewelry were found along with the body inside the car.

"Oh my!" AnJanay shouted and spilled her tea at the story. Her son Carl heard her distress and came rushing into the family room to check on her. The familiar face on the screen froze him in his tracks. The face was so familiar because it looked just like his.

It was abundantly clear from the shriveled state of his body that the preacher did not drive himself to the location. The coroner placed the approximate time of death at about twelve hours prior to the body's discovery.

To add to this bizarre and disturbing story, another corpse was found inside of the trunk. Police have identified the decomposing body as that belonging to one Reverend Kenyatta...

"Mama, who was that man?" Carl demanded of his mother.

"Nobody," she spat since she had long lied to her son about his father being dead. "Good for him, with his nasty ass!"

Did you enjoy the story of Reverend Cash? Please leave a review and spread the word.